The Girl
with the
Irish Secret

BOOKS BY SUSANNE O'LEARY

MAGNOLIA MANOR SERIES
The Keeper of the Irish Secret
The Granddaughter's Irish Secret

The Road Trip
A Holiday to Remember

SANDY COVE SERIES
Secrets of Willow House
Sisters of Willow House
Dreams of Willow House
Daughters of Wild Rose Bay
Memories of Wild Rose Bay
Miracles in Wild Rose Bay

STARLIGHT COTTAGES SERIES
The Lost Girls of Ireland
The Lost Secret of Ireland
The Lost Promise of Ireland
The Lost House of Ireland
The Lost Letters of Ireland
The Lost Mother of Ireland

Susanne O'Leary

The Girl
with the
Irish Secret

bookouture

Published by Bookouture in 2024

An imprint of Storyfire Ltd.
Carmelite House
50 Victoria Embankment
London EC4Y 0DZ

www.bookouture.com

Storyfire Ltd's authorised representative in the EEA is Hachette Ireland
8 Castlecourt Centre
Castleknock Road
Castleknock
Dublin 15 D15 YF6A
Ireland

ISBN: 978-1-83618-029-6
eBook ISBN: 978-1-83618-026-5

1

The waiting room was, as always, chilly. Vi wrapped her legs around each other and zipped up her short down jacket as she sat on the hard chair. She looked at the receptionist, trying to gauge how long she would have to sit there before she was asked to go in to the office. The woman was dressed in what looked like several layers of cashmere. She was busy peering at the screen of her computer and kept typing, not seeming to notice Vi's discomfort. Well, all those sweaters had to keep her warm, Vi mused as she tried to think of something cheery while she waited. But all she could do was to go through all the frustrations of the past few months.

Her acting career, which had seemed so promising, had stalled. She was beginning to wonder if she shouldn't consider giving up altogether. But she had worked so hard to get even where she was today: a working actress in Ireland, the kind who was cast in small productions and local plays, but who was always the second lead, the heroine's best friend or sister. Then there were the historical dramas where she played the serving wench in medieval costume with a dirty face and blackened teeth. It felt like being always the bridesmaid, never the bride, and she was sick of it. She was about to turn thirty and felt that she had somehow missed that breakthrough that was supposed to happen just out of drama school.

Her agent, in whose office she was waiting, kept saying she would soon get that big part, but nothing much had happened yet and now Vi was quite sure it never would. The acting world was fickle; what if she was seen as too old soon? Vi wondered if it wouldn't be better to give up acting altogether if she kept getting mediocre parts. It was tempting as it sometimes felt as if she was running up a very steep hill never to reach the top. She decided to tell Hugh what was going through her mind when he was finally free to see her. She was wondering what was keeping him. He was usually so punctual and correct.

The secretary was still busy at her computer and Vi considered leaving when the phone on the desk rang. After a brief conversation, the woman looked at Vi as if she had just noticed her.

'Violet Fleury?' she asked.

Vi shot up from her chair. 'Yes, that's me. Can I go in?'

The woman nodded. 'Yes. Hugh will see you now. He's just been on the phone to LA. Long conversation,' she added. 'But he says he wants to talk to you.' She smiled apologetically. 'Sorry, I haven't been here long so I don't know all of Hugh's clients yet. My name is Fiona, by the way.'

'Hi, Fiona,' Vi said as she walked to the door into the main office. 'I hope you'll like your new job.'

'I will if they fix the heating in this building,' Fiona replied. 'But these old Victorian piles are often freezing anyway. I seem to be wearing all the woollies I own today.'

'I know how you feel,' Vi said. 'I should have put on my thermals instead of these leggings.'

'You're right. Oh, I wish I could go to LA to work instead of sitting here in dreary London,' Fiona said with a sigh. 'The weather has to be better in California.'

'Yes, it is. But I prefer being over here. I've heard LA isn't what it's cracked up to be.' Vi opened the door to the main office. 'See you later.'

'Good luck,' Fiona said before she turned back to her screen.

Vi walked into the large office which was a lot warmer than the reception area. The thick carpet muffled her footsteps and the man at the big mahogany desk was busy looking at his phone and didn't see her until the door closed behind her. Then he looked up and smiled.

'Vi. Hello. Come in and sit down. Sorry to have kept you waiting, but I wanted to get all the details before I spoke to you.'

'What kind of details?' Vi asked, sinking down into a leather armchair opposite Hugh. He was in his early sixties with balding fair hair and kind eyes behind horn-rimmed glasses. Vi had known him since she had graduated from acting school nearly ten years ago when he had landed her a part in a romantic comedy shot in Scotland. She had stayed with his agency because he always got her parts, even if they were often small. She'd heard a lot of bad stories about agencies dropping their clients, but Hugh was loyal to her. He was her friend.

'I'll get to that in a moment.' Hugh looked at Vi and smiled. 'I have bad news and good news.'

'Let me have the bad news first.'

'Okay.' Hugh looked serious again. 'You didn't get the movie you went for, sorry. But that was a good thing, actually.'

'Why?'

'Because I was just on the phone with Liz Wall of Wall & Montgomery Pictures.'

'WMP?' Vi asked.

Hugh nodded. 'That's the outfit, yes.'

'What did she say?' Vi's heart skipped a beat at the mention of this well-known movie company. 'What details were you discussing with her?'

'The setting and the costumes and the budget for a start,' Hugh said.

'For what? An audition?' Vi began to feel excited. Hugh was looking as if he was about to break some amazing news.

'No audition,' Hugh started, his eyes sparkling. 'No need as you're the best of the bunch they've been considering. Violet, I think you have finally got *that* part. The part that will be your major breakthrough.'

'What?' Vi stared at him, her head buzzing with anticipation. Here it was, the moment she had been waiting for all these years. 'You mean a main part?' she asked. 'I'm to play the heroine at last? In what kind of movie?'

'A biopic,' he said.

'Oh.' Vi sat back. 'Of whom?'

'Someone you must know very well,' Hugh replied. 'When I heard they were going to make this thing, I just knew you were the only choice. You're the spitting image of her.'

'Spitting image of whom?' Vi asked, confused.

'Kathleen O'Sullivan. Remember her?'

'Of course I do,' Vi replied, feeling excited at the thought. Kathleen O'Sullivan had been a huge star in the 1940s and 50s. With her blazing red hair and green eyes, she had had great success in Hollywood as the epitome of the Irish colleen and played against a number of big male stars such as Clark Gable, Cary Grant and Tyrone Power and many more. She had also been one of the actresses who stood their ground and fought hard to improve pay for women in the business. 'She is the unofficial patron saint of all actresses. We all admire what she did for us. Amazing woman.'

'A legend,' Hugh agreed. 'And the casting director has been on the lookout for someone lesser known. Someone Irish, with Kathleen's look.'

Vi put her fingers through her red mane and laughed. 'I never thought the colour of my hair would be what got me the big break. I have always had to dye it some other colour to fit whatever movie I was cast in.'

'I know,' Hugh said. 'Isn't it a stroke of luck that they're looking for someone like you? And here's another thing that will swing it for you: the movie will be shot in your very own county. Kathleen O'Sullivan came from Kerry, as you might know. Your own back yard. Amazing, don't you think? The Wild Atlantic Way and all that.'

'But she was from a village near Castleisland, not Dingle,' Vi corrected. 'Which is inland, you know. Not near the coast at all.'

'Yes, whatever.' Hugh made a dismissive gesture. 'But who cares? Nobody outside Ireland would have a clue. They want to film it by the sea and along the Wild Atlantic Way. They have already decided on the area and the location for a lot of the scenes. It's going to be in some manor house down there. A big house near Dingle town. It has a great garden. Fabulous for this kind of thing. Can't remember the name of it but it was something to do with flowers... Rhododendron House, or...'

'Magnolia Manor?' Vi asked, sitting up straighter, her heart beating.

'That's it,' Hugh exclaimed. 'You know the place?'

'Very well.' She couldn't believe it. If they were going to use Magnolia Manor as a set, she would be going back home. The big house overlooking Dingle Bay, surrounded by lush gardens, had always been a haven where she could rest and recover from the turmoil of life and strenuous work. Except she hadn't been there for a whole year. Not since the angry words she'd exchanged with her sisters. They hadn't been in touch since then, despite Vi's efforts to make peace.

'You've been there?' Hugh asked.

'I grew up there,' Vi said, smiling. 'My family own it. It's being turned into apartments for seniors, and parts of it are used for weddings and other big events, so we don't technically live there any more, but it's where I spent most of my childhood.' She looked at Hugh, feeling puzzled. 'I don't see how that can be authentic, though. How does Magnolia Manor fit in with Kathleen's life?'

'What's wrong with a little poetic licence?' Hugh asked with a wink. 'What Hollywood wants Hollywood gets. In any case, Kathleen and her last husband lived in a big house somewhere on the west coast. So the house would kind of fit. The producer went to look at it and loved it. The owner, some old gal with attitude, drove a hard bargain, but they were able to stay within budget in the end. She was like a bulldog, while managing to look like a real lady, they said.'

Vi burst out laughing. 'Oh yeah, she would. That's my grandmother.'

Hugh blinked and stared at Vi. 'Your grandmother? Are you pulling my leg?'

'No, I'm not. She really is my grandmother,' Vi assured him.

'That's some coincidence,' Hugh said, shaking his head.

'Isn't it?' Vi grinned. 'I can imagine her arguing with the movie company.'

'Tough as an old boot, they said,' Hugh remarked. 'But that place is supposed to be amazing. The researchers for the film company said it would look fabulous in the movie. I pushed hard to get you the part, you know. Said you even speak with a Kerry accent.'

'Well, that part is true, even if you have tried to beat it out of me,' Vi remarked.

'That's true. But now you'll be able to talk away like the real Kerry girl you are.' Hugh picked up a sheet of paper from the desk. 'So, it's nearly all fixed. You are only up against one other actress. But if you do well at the audition, you should have it in the bag.'

'Audition?' Vi asked. 'But you said the part was mine.'

'This is not really an audition, it's just a little chat with the producer and director and maybe the male lead. Nothing too difficult. They just want to have a look at you and take a few shots to see how you'd look on the screen.'

'Who's the male lead?' Vi asked.

'Jack Montgomery.'

'Really? Wow.' Vi stared at Hugh, feeling excited. Jack Montgomery was a well-known actor. He was British and good-looking in a rough, romantic way and Vi remembered that she'd seem him featured in a magazine recently. This wasn't his first lead part. He had starred in *Letters from Amsterdam* and *The Wilderness Year*, both popular movies that had done very well at the box office. 'He's quite famous now, isn't he?'

'Yup,' Hugh said. 'And he's in the production team of this movie. He needs to see you in person so he can decide if the two of you click. Chemistry is very important in this case. So that's why he has a say in who they hire to play Kathleen.'

'When's the interview?' Vi asked.

'Three o'clock.'

'Today?' Vi asked, beginning to panic. She glanced at her watch. 'It's twenty to three already and I haven't done my makeup or fixed my hair or anything. Where is this interview anyway?'

'At the movie company's London office,' Hugh replied. 'It's five minutes' walk from here.' He handed her a card. 'Here's the address. You'd better get your skates on. Don't worry about hair or makeup. They want you to look natural. A blank canvas. Remember how Kathleen would always look so wholesome?'

'Yes, but...' Vi got up from the chair. 'I need to look my best, don't I?' She looked down at her navy down jacket that had seen better days and the black leggings and scuffed trainers. 'I didn't think I'd need to dress up to see you. I came straight here from the gym and I have to be on the set of *The Dockland Mysteries*, the TV series I'm in, at five.'

'How's that going?' Hugh asked. 'I know it wasn't the best part for you but...'

'Any part is better than nothing,' Vi said. 'But it's been a bit of a struggle. They're going to kill me off soon, as you know, so then I'll be off the hook and ready for anything new.'

'Like this amazing role,' Hugh cut in. He looked at his watch. 'It's a little tight time-wise but you'll make it if you hurry.'

'Did you spring this on me on purpose?' Vi asked suspiciously. 'So that I'd look "natural" for this interview?'

'Would I?' Hugh asked, grinning. 'But whatever. Go on now and do your best.'

'I'll have to sprint if I'm to be there in time,' Vi remarked, moving to the door. 'I thought we were just going to chat about my future plans. But now you've sprung this on me and I'm a mess too.'

Hugh leaned forward and smiled at her. 'You always look great, sweetheart. Just be yourself and smile.'

'Easy for you to say,' Vi replied. 'Okay, I'll go there and try my best to be myself. Smiling might be a little difficult, though.'

'Break a leg,' Hugh said. 'I know they'll love you. But please try to be polite whatever they say.'

'I will,' Vi said with a wry smile. Hugh knew she could be a little hot-headed; it had affected her earlier auditions, when casting directors had been dismissive of her she'd found it hard to stay quiet. 'Or I'll try my best. Thanks for this chance, though, Hugh. You're a brick.' She blew him a kiss at the door and then walked out of the room, practically running to the ladies' toilet. 'Got to go and freshen up,' she said to Fiona, who was still typing away at her laptop. 'Important interview in a minute.'

'Break a leg,' Fiona shouted after her.

'That's what Hugh just said,' Vi remarked with a nervous laugh. 'I hope that won't jinx it.'

'If it's meant to be, it'll happen, my granny used to say,' Fiona called after Vi as she raced to the ladies'.

'I hope it is,' Vi shouted back.

Once inside, Vi walked to the mirror and stared at herself. 'Jack Montgomery,' she said. 'I'm going to work with Jack Montgomery. If I get the part. How am I going to get him to like me?' She pinched her cheeks and tried a smile, tossing back her red hair that hung like a heavy curtain to the middle of her back. 'Be myself,' she said to her image. 'That's harder than being Lady Macbeth.' Her huge green eyes stared back at her with defiance and also a touch of fear. *If I don't get this part, I'm giving up acting*, she promised herself as she touched up her lips with bright red lipstick which accentuated her fair complexion and made her freckles stand out. Then she took a step back and nodded to herself. 'There. Very nineteen fifties. The typical girl from the Emerald Isle, that's me. Who could do that better? Nobody, that's who.'

Feeling a lot more positive, Vi walked down the stairs and out of the building, marching up the street with a mixture of determination and fear.

As the traffic rumbled up the street, Vi tried her best to boost her confidence. She desperately wanted this part, but the fact that it was going to be filmed at Magnolia Manor was making her feel nervous. Her sisters, Lily and Rose, might not like to see Vi arrive at the house with a film crew. Not after the bitter row last year.

Why did it have to happen? Vi thought. *We were so close – until that awful row which wasn't really my fault. We must try to make peace with each other. Maybe this is a chance for us to be sisters again like we used to.* She longed to have that close connection with them again, which had felt like a solid wall of support, just like in boarding school when her older sisters had defended her if anyone tried to bully her. But now that wall had crumbled and she didn't know how to build it up again.

Vi couldn't help but think about all the things she had sacrificed for her career. Her love life, her friendships, a steady income... and recently her family. The long nights and unreliable schedules had got in the way of most of her relationships. And other actors didn't tend to warm to her.

But she forced herself to shake off her concerns as she arrived at the building where the London office of the film company was housed. This was her last chance. And perhaps it was an opportunity to mend things with her sisters and show them it was all worth it: she was getting somewhere. She pressed the button beside the intercom and said her name when prompted. Then she pushed open the heavy door and entered the building, mentally steeling herself for the ordeal that was to come: facing a bunch of film people and trying to act natural. Especially to Jack Montgomery.

2

Getting out of the lift on the eighth floor of the building, Vi looked around a deserted lobby and then spotted a door with a sign that said, CONFERENCE ROOM. She knocked on the door and as there was no reply, opened it slowly to find a large room that smelled faintly of paint. The white walls were covered in posters advertising movies the company had produced and Vi saw a huge photo of Kathleen O'Sullivan on the far wall. Five people – three men and two women – sat behind a long table chatting and drinking coffee. Then there was silence as they noticed Vi. She shot them a nervous smile.

'Hello,' she said. 'I'm Violet Fleury.'

'Hi, Violet,' one of the women said. 'Please sit down.' She had short dark hair and pale blue eyes behind black-rimmed glasses. 'I'm Laura, the casting director.'

'Hi, Laura,' Vi said, relieved to sit down as her knees wobbled. She looked at the people behind the table and noticed a man studying her. It was Jack Montgomery, who with his tall, lean frame, shaggy brown hair and brown velvet eyes was even more handsome in the flesh than on the screen.

He studied her for a moment. 'Thanks for coming in at such short notice.'

'You're welcome,' Vi mumbled, twisting her hands in her lap under his critical gaze.

'This is Dave, the director,' Jack Montgomery said, gesturing at the man beside him. 'And then we have Liz Wall, the producer and finally Leo, our stylist, who will be doing hair and makeup.'

'Hi, everyone,' Vi said and waved. She felt all eyes on her as she sat there and tried her best to look unperturbed.

'She *is* quite like Kathleen, even more so in the flesh,' Liz the producer said to Jack. She had long blonde hair and brown eyes below thick black eyebrows which made her look faintly sinister.

'She will be the spit of her when I've finished,' Leo the makeup artist said. He had sandy hair, very blue eyes and was dressed in a navy sweatshirt. He looked at Vi with a friendly smile. 'How do you feel about perming your hair and maybe putting on a little weight? Would you be prepared to do that?'

'I've done worse things for a role,' Vi replied, smiling. 'Like dyeing my hair all kinds of weird colours, cutting it all off, blackening my teeth and other things that made me look terrible. A perm is a minor detail compared to all of that. Not sure I can put on weight, though. I eat like a horse but I've never managed to gain much weight.'

'Ugh, a naturally skinny girl,' Liz said. 'I already hate you. But you're perfect in every other way. Isn't she, Laura?'

The casting director nodded. 'Oh yeah, I couldn't agree more. The hair, the eyes, that voice... We can certainly turn her into Kathleen.'

Liz smiled. 'That's what I thought.' She looked at Vi. 'So you're familiar with Kathleen O'Sullivan?'

'Of course,' Vi said. 'She's my role model in many ways.'

'Why?' Liz asked.

'I mean the way she stood up to the movie moguls of the day and got them to pay her a decent wage,' Vi replied. 'And how she managed to change some of the scripts that were derogatory to women, making them into little housewives with no brains. She wanted to portray independent women with a will of their own and she managed to do that.' Vi drew breath, wondering if that was the right answer.

'Well, yeah, but sometimes that was not great for her career,' Liz remarked, staring at Vi. 'This is going to be a movie with a romantic theme. The love story between her and Don Williams, who she married after a lot of drama.'

'I don't remember the drama,' Vi started. She wondered if this was what Kathleen would want her story to be about. 'I'm sure you'd agree that it's important to portray Kathleen the way she truly was. It would be awful if what she did was not recognised or skimmed over by some romantic story.'

Liz glanced at Jack. Vi wondered if it would have been better to keep quiet, knowing she risked losing the part if she spoke her mind. This had happened twice before when she argued with casting directors. Hugh had been very annoyed and told Vi she had to be more flexible. But she couldn't be dishonest, it wasn't in her nature.

'If I'm to play Kathleen O'Sullivan, then I'd want to show who she truly was,' Vi went on.

'I see,' Liz said. 'Interesting.' She shot another conspiratorial look at Jack Montgomery. 'So... what do you say to that, Jack?'

'Well...' Jack, who had not yet voiced an opinion, looked at Vi for a moment while she squirmed on her seat, feeling she had blown it. 'You have an interesting attitude.' She sat awkwardly waiting for the verdict when he suddenly smiled. 'Well, you got the part.'

'Really?' Vi exclaimed, breathless with excitement. 'Are you sure?'

He nodded. 'Yes, if you agree to the terms of the contract.

We'll send it over to Hugh and he can go through it. We start shooting in early March next year.' He paused, looking amused. 'I assume you're free then?'

'Oh yes,' Vi replied, forgetting all about being aloof and standing her ground. 'Very free. I'm about to be killed off in *The Dockland Mysteries*, the TV series I'm in at the moment, and there was nothing else on the horizon, so that's absolutely terrific. I'm ready and willing to play the part of one of our biggest stars. So proud to be Irish right now – and from Kerry, especially.' She knew she was gushing but she couldn't stop herself. It was as if all her dreams had come true at last and she couldn't hide her delight.

Jack lifted one eyebrow when she had finished. 'Great delivery. Are you going to sing as well?'

Vi felt her cheeks go red. 'No. Sorry. Didn't mean to blather. It was just that I'm so excited to get the part.'

'I see.' Jack's smile broadened. 'That's terrific. Welcome aboard, Violet.'

'Thank you, Mr Montgomery,' Vi whispered. 'It'll be an honour to work with you.'

'It'll be a blast to shoot this thing in Ireland,' Liz declared, her eyebrows dancing. 'Won't it, Dave?' she said to the director, who until now had just sat there looking at Vi without uttering a word.

David, a tall man with receding blond hair and gold-rimmed glasses, kept looking at Vi. 'As long as she knows how to take direction, we'll get on fine. At least she has a bit of acting experience, unlike some of the other candidates.' He shot Vi a polite smile. 'You come highly recommended. I hope you'll live up to it.'

'I'll do my best,' Vi said demurely.

'Of course you will.' Liz looked suddenly more friendly. 'Hey,' she said. 'Let's all go to the pub next door and celebrate.'

'Great idea,' Leo said and got up. 'We'll have a chance to get to know Violet and start making plans.'

'The shooting doesn't start for another few months,' Jack said. 'So there's plenty of time to make plans.'

'And to do research,' Liz filled in. 'We do know a lot about Kathleen already but we don't have all the facts about her early life, before she came to Hollywood. So...' she paused and looked at Vi, 'as you're from Kerry, would it be possible for you to go there and do some research? Get under Kathleen's skin, so to speak. As you're playing Kathleen, you need to *be* her in this movie. And you can only do that if you know as much about her early life as possible.'

'Yes, I could do that,' Vi agreed. 'And I do actually have a connection to the manor you're intending to film at. Magnolia Manor is, or was, my ancestral home. It's my grandmother Sylvia you will have been negotiating with.'

'Oh, that's incredible,' Liz said, looking amazed at this revelation. 'I had no idea. So the old bird we were dealing with is your grandma?'

'Yes,' Vi said, not sure if she liked her grandmother described that way. 'I'm very fond of her. She's not as hardnosed as you might think. She's just a very shrewd businesswoman.'

'And a very successful one,' Leo soothed. 'Liz didn't mean any disrespect.'

'Of course not,' Liz said, looking contrite. 'I actually liked her. A very classy woman. I'm sure you're very proud of her.'

'Yes, I am,' Vi said. 'Very proud.' She conjured up the image of her grandmother in her mind and wondered if she was proud of Vi. But they had parted on bad terms and now Vi didn't know how she could go back to Magnolia Manor before she had yet again apologised for what had happened the last time she had been there. *Oh my darling granny*, she thought, *how can I make you understand that I'm truly sorry? And how can I get close to my sisters again after what I said to them? I don't blame them for being upset. But I was in a bad place then and felt so lost...*

'So, we're all agreed?' Jack Montgomery asked and gathered up his notes. 'And we're all going to the pub, then?'

'I can't,' Vi said and got up. 'Sorry, but I have to get to the set. So nice to meet you all. I'm really looking forward to working with you.'

'You sure you can't join us?' Leo asked.

'Not possible, I'm afraid,' Vi replied. 'We're shooting a scene in the Docklands area this evening.' She checked her watch. 'I'm already running a little late.'

'We'll see you soon, though,' Jack cut in. 'We'll meet sometime in the near future to discuss the schedules and so on. We need to take some publicity shots too. We'll be in touch with your agent to set it up.'

Vi nodded. 'That'll be great.'

'Let us know when you'll be in Ireland,' Leo said. 'I'm going there myself for Christmas. I have family in Cork. Not a million miles from Kerry.'

'That's true. It would be nice to meet up somewhere halfway between Cork and Kerry.' Vi smiled and prepared to leave. 'Well, goodbye for now. See you all soon.'

'Lovely to meet you,' Laura the casting director said. 'I'm really happy we found you. Nobody could be more perfect for the role than you.'

'Thank you,' Vi said with a happy smile. 'I'm thrilled to play Kathleen.' Then she walked out of the room while the others gathered up their bags and coats and prepared to go to the pub.

Vi was sorry she couldn't join them but perhaps it was a good thing in a way. She needed to digest what had just happened. It seemed as if all her wishes had come true at once: playing the main character in a Hollywood produced movie and acting with Jack Montgomery, the man who had appeared in her dreams many times. The perfect man, handsome, suave, clever and chivalrous.

If only the setting was different, everything would be perfect. That was the one thing she found hard to deal with. Going back to Magnolia Manor and facing her family.

3

Jack Montgomery caught up with Vi as she was in the downstairs lobby about to leave the building.

'Hey,' he said, tapping her on the shoulder. 'We should get to know each other as I'm to play your husband. How about a drink sometime?'

Vi's heart beat faster as she looked up at his handsome face, his brown eyes looking into hers. He was dressed in a navy blazer with a discreet crest and a light blue shirt under a Burberry raincoat which was flung across his shoulders. She noticed his long eyelashes and his slightly tanned complexion, breathed in his expensive aftershave and kept staring at him, wondering if this was really happening. Jack Montgomery was asking her to have a drink? It seemed like a dream and she felt like pinching herself yet again. 'Er, yeah,' she said. 'That would be grand.'

'I'm going back to LA in a little over a week, so it would be good to meet up before then. Just to talk, you know?'

'That would be lovely,' Vi said and picked up her phone. 'What's your number?'

He beamed a thousand-watt smile at her. 'Let's decide on

the date, time and place right now. Then we don't need phone numbers.'

'Oh, of course,' Vi said, feeling stupid. She should have known he wouldn't want to give his phone number to someone he didn't know well. 'Sorry,' she said, putting away her phone. 'When and where, then?'

'How about that Irish pub near Piccadilly? It's called Paddy's. Looks nice and easy to find for both of us. Thursday next week at five p.m.? Call the office and leave a message if you can't make it. I'll get them to call you if I have a problem, okay?'

'Great,' Vi said, now completely overwhelmed. She was having a drink with one of the biggest stars of both film and TV. Was this really happening?

'See you then.' Jack walked to the door and held it open for her. 'Looking forward to our chat,' he said as she stepped out.

'Me too.' She breathed in his expensive aftershave as he walked past her towards a waiting car that took off down the street as soon as Jack had got in.

Vi stood there, staring at the taillights, thinking that this was the most exciting day of her life.

'Feeling a little starstruck?' a voice said beside her.

Startled, Vi whipped around to discover Leo the make-up artist standing behind her. She laughed. 'Yeah, a little. But who wouldn't be? He's so...'

'Charismatic?' he asked, smiling, his blue eyes amused as he looked at her.

'Something like that,' Vi confessed.

'And a little more,' Leo suggested. 'But be careful. He's a great slayer of women and has left a trail of broken hearts behind him.'

'I know. I've seen what's posted about him online,' Vi said. 'Don't worry, I might be starstruck but my heart won't break.'

'I bet,' Leo said. 'But now I'd better get to the pub with the others.' He paused, looking a little shy. 'You did well in there.

You made sure they knew where you stood. Not easy under the circumstances.'

'Gosh,' Vi said. 'I thought I'd blown it. But I'm such a blabbermouth and can't help saying exactly what I think. No filter, that's me.'

'Well, it was a good thing. Got you the part and all. Hey,' he continued, 'would you think it forward of me if I asked for your phone number? I thought it might be nice to meet up when I'm in Ireland during the holidays.'

'Why are you going to Ireland for Christmas?' Vi asked. Then she remembered what he had said earlier. 'Oh yes, you have family there, right?'

'Yes, I do. My last name is Shanaghan, by the way. Can't get more Irish than that. So can we get together when I'm there?'

'That would be great,' Vi said. She picked up her phone again. 'Give me your number and then I'll send you a text and then you can put it into WhatsApp.'

'Perfect,' he said and read out his number. 'I'll be in touch when I get to Ireland.'

'Where will you be?' Vi asked as she put away her phone.

'Bantry,' he replied. 'Only a few hours' drive from Dingle. Never been there, though, so I'll need a guide.'

'That'll be fun. I know all the great places,' Vi said, feeling as if she knew him already. He seemed such a nice, easy-going man and she was sure he'd be a great ally during filming. 'I hope you like storms and rain. That's what it's like in late December in Kerry.'

'I've never been there at Christmastime,' Leo said. 'How do you cope with the bad weather?'

'Oh, I love it,' Vi laughed. 'We were always told that there is no such thing as bad weather, only bad clothing.'

'Sounds like the kind of thing a father might say,' Leo remarked.

'I didn't really have a father,' Vi said. 'So I wouldn't know.'

'Oh, I'm sorry,' Leo said.

'He died when I was only two, but I had my mother and grandmother,' Vi said. 'They brought us up during various stages in our lives.'

'Us?' Leo asked. Then he laughed. 'Sorry, I didn't mean to pry.'

'I don't mind,' Vi said, smiling. 'I don't think having two sisters is a personal detail I need to hide.'

'Great. Maybe I'll meet them during filming? But now I'd better catch up with the others. See you in Kerry soon.'

Vi smiled and said goodbye, happy to have met someone who could be a friend. Especially during the making of a movie, which could be a very long process. Playing the main character and trying to get close to a woman who had been dead for a long time would be a challenge. She'd better get hold of the old movies from the 1940s and 50s and study Kathleen O'Sullivan's voice, movements and facial expressions. And then she had to find out as much about this woman as possible: her childhood and youth, her love life and relationships. It seemed like a huge task but she was determined to do it. One of her teachers at drama school had told her to use her body as a tool when playing a character. 'Body language is a great way to relay emotions and feelings,' he had said. In this case, it would come in very handy and she was committed to following that advice. By the time filming started, Vi would truly *be* Kathleen, just as Liz the producer had suggested.

Vi knew she had to get to Kerry as soon as possible to start her research. She had told Leo she would be there for Christmas, as if her relationship with her family was normal without any problems or bad feelings. But that was far from the truth. Her sisters were still not talking to Vi after that falling-out the year before, and her grandmother had not got over her disappointment in Vi, even though she was still affectionate whenever they spoke.

Unconditional love, Vi thought, knowing Granny would always love her no matter what, which made her feel even more guilty. All this made it very difficult to plan a visit to her childhood home. She would have to negotiate carefully with her grandmother in order to stay at Magnolia Manor for Christmas and beyond, and then do her best to mend fences with Lily and Rose, who both lived nearby with their families. It seemed like a very high mountain to climb.

Lily was married to Dominic, an engineer and local contractor, and lived in a gorgeous house overlooking Ventry beach with their two small children. Rose and her husband, Noel, and eighteen-month-old daughter had recently moved out of the gatehouse of Magnolia Manor into a newly built bungalow on the hill above Dingle town. They both seemed to have perfect lives, happy marriages and lovely children. Despite what Vi had said to them during that horrible argument, she often felt envious of her sisters. She sometimes thought she would never have what they had, and when her career seemed stuck, it felt even worse, having nothing to be proud of.

But now she could at least go back home with something to show for all her hard work. Perhaps they might finally be proud of her?

Vi knew she had to go to Kerry soon in order to find out everything she could about Kathleen O'Sullivan. She felt apprehensive about calling her grandmother but she couldn't put it off much longer. As she went into the Tube station, she promised herself she would call that evening and be completely honest. It would be hard, but it was the first step to a reconciliation that simply had to happen very soon. Otherwise, how could she work on a film that was set in her own back yard?

Vi didn't have to call, however, as her grandmother beat her to it. The phone rang that evening just as Vi had opened the door to her tiny studio apartment in Croydon. She fished the phone out of her bag, stepped over the debris of books and scripts on the floor and sat down on the easy chair in front of the window, without checking the caller ID.

'Hello,' she said, 'this is Violet Fleury.'

'Of course it is,' her grandmother's voice said in her ear. 'And this is Sylvia Fleury, your grandmother.'

Vi shot up from the chair. 'Granny! I was just going to call you.'

'Of course you were,' Sylvia said, her voice light. 'How could you not when you're going to star in a film that's going to be shot at our manor? I just heard the news from that producer woman. Liz – something. Quite a character, I have to say. Smokes cigarettes with a holder and argues like a man. But she had the decency to go outside when she wanted a puff, so I can't complain. In any case, we had a good old discussion before she backed down. Pity, I was just getting into the swing of it.' Sylvia drew breath.

Vi laughed. 'Oh, Granny, I can imagine. You always enjoyed a good argument.'

'A good one, yes,' Sylvia said drily, 'not like the one you had with your sisters just before you left in a huff. They're still in a snit over it. How are you going to cope with them when you come here as the big star, I wonder?'

'I don't know,' Vi said miserably. 'I'll have to wear a big hair-shirt and crawl to the cross.'

'You might indeed,' Sylvia remarked. 'Although that sounds a little uncomfortable.' She paused. 'So when are you coming over? I believe the filming starts in April.'

'I have to go to Kerry way before that,' Vi replied. 'I need to do some research on Kathleen O'Sullivan and that will take some time. I was hoping...' Vi stopped.

'Hoping what?' Sylvia asked.

'That I might come next week and stay until Christmas. I

know it will be difficult and Lily and Rose won't want me there but I'm hoping I can patch things up, or keep out of their hair. Whatever is best.'

'Hmm,' Sylvia said. 'It could be difficult. But we have to try. Life is too short to carry a grudge. Family is all we have in the end, isn't it?'

'I know that now,' Vi said.

'Good.' Sylvia took a deep breath. 'All right, Violet, do come whenever you want. I'll talk to your sisters.'

'Thank you,' Vi whispered. She wondered if Sylvia was proud of her. 'Are you excited about the movie? It's a dream come true for me.'

'What dreams are they exactly?' Sylvia asked.

'I'm to star in a movie with Jack Montgomery,' Vi said, surprised that her grandmother didn't realise the significance of the part. 'It's the first time I've had a lead role. And with a very successful actor. Isn't that so incredible?'

'Oh,' Sylvia said. 'I would be careful if I were you. Reality never turns out like your dreams. Life is too complicated for that. You don't know what hardship is around the corner.'

'Oh, please,' Vi begged, knowing her grandmother was, as always, just trying to stop her building castles in the air. 'Don't do the gloom and doom now. Let me be happy for a while. I know what you're saying and I'm sure I'll land back on earth with a thump. But right now, I'm floating on a cloud and loving it.'

'I see. Enjoy this happy moment, then. If you're aware that it's just for a while, you'll be fine,' Sylvia said. 'But I think you should come here as soon as possible. You can have the gate-house as Rose and Noel have moved into their new house. If you don't mind being on your own.'

'I'm on my own now,' Vi said, looking around the dreary little flat. 'I'll be less alone in the gatehouse than here, I think. I can catch up with my old pals in Dingle anyway. I don't have many friends here in London because I'm away so much on location. This is just a base, not a home, and never will be.'

'That sounds a little sad,' Sylvia said, her voice soft. 'Maybe it's time you faced up to that.'

'Oh, I know,' Vi said, remembering the old saying. 'It's something I've been thinking about a lot. Family and friends are like the stars,' she said to Sylvia. 'You can't always see them but you know they're there.'

'Exactly,' Sylvia said, sounding satisfied. 'And you know what? Even if your sisters are still angry, I'm not. I'd love to have you here with me. Goodness knows I could do with some company right now.'

'What about Arnaud?' Vi asked, surprised by the hint of sadness in Sylvia's voice. She was also surprised that Sylvia had forgiven her so quickly, but then the row had not been about her but with Lily and Rose. Sylvia always tried not to interfere in their arguments, preferring to stay neutral in order to mediate between them.

'Arnaud? Oh, he's in the South of France during the winter,' Sylvia said. 'He thought I might like to spend the cold months there with him. But I missed Kerry too much. The wind and rain don't worry me. They pass very quickly and then we have the sunshine back and the glorious views of the ocean. There's nothing like it in the whole world. Today was one of those days.'

'No, there isn't,' Vi agreed, imagining how lovely Kerry would be right now, the water of Dingle Bay glittering in the sunshine and the ocean beyond stretching out to the horizon where sea met sky and the sun would sink behind the islands in a riot of pink, red and orange. She could nearly smell the salty air and taste the newly caught fish cooked in batter and served with chips and mushy peas in one of the restaurants on the quays. 'I'll come home as soon as I can,' she promised. 'I want to start looking into Kathleen O'Sullivan's life from the very start.'

'That might come with a few surprises,' Sylvia remarked. 'Not always good ones.'

'What do you mean?' Vi asked. 'What do you know about her?'

'Not much, but what I've heard is not all so lovely,' Sylvia said cryptically. 'But I have to go. Nora is expecting me for dinner. Let me know when you'll be arriving and we'll have the gatehouse all warm and cosy for you.'

'Thank you, Granny,' Vi said. 'But what was that about Kathleen O'—?'

'Bye for now,' Sylvia said, and hung up.

Vi sat there with the phone in her hand, wondering what Sylvia had meant. Did her grandmother know something about Kathleen O'Sullivan? Something that went against the sweet, wholesome image she had presented to the world? Vi realised that her grandmother was of the same generation and that they had both grown up in Kerry around the same time. Maybe Vi's research would start much closer to home that she had imagined.

4

A week later, Vi found herself having a drink in an Irish pub with Jack Montgomery. Feeling as if she was dreaming, or in some kind of parallel universe, she wandered into the dim, crowded pub dressed in a navy suit with a short skirt, high heels and her hair in a messy bun with tendrils around her face. It looked natural, but the style and the 'natural' makeup had taken her over an hour to achieve. She scanned the room, but didn't see Jack, so she sat down at a small round table in an alcove to wait for him. A waiter appeared asking what she wanted, but she told him she was waiting for someone, so he nodded and disappeared. Then after a few tense moments, when she thought he wouldn't show up, there was a sudden murmur through the pub and there he was, pushing through the crowd, looking unperturbed by the eyes on him.

He looked around for a moment and when he spotted Vi, walked swiftly to her table and sat down. 'Hey,' he said, smiling. 'You chose the best spot in the place. Clever of you. Nice to see you again... eh... Vera?'

'Violet,' she corrected.

'Oh, of course. I knew that. Hi there, Violet.'

'Hi, Jack,' she said. 'How are you?'

'Great.' He looked at her for a moment. 'You look cute. What did you do to your hair?'

Vi touched the back of her head. 'Oh, I just put it up out of the way.'

He nodded. 'Nice. What do you want to drink?'

'I'd love a pint of Guinness,' she said without thinking.

'A whole pint?' He raised one eyebrow, his mouth quivering. 'You're that thirsty?'

Vi shrugged. 'Sure. Why not? This is an Irish pub, after all. Nothing like draught Guinness on a Friday night.' She suddenly felt reckless and wanted to show him she didn't care what he thought. Did he think she was going to sit here and be prim and proper and mind her ps and qs just to impress him? *Be yourself*, she said to herself. *Don't try to be something you're not.*

'It's Thursday,' he said.

'I know, but I've just finished filming. It feels like Friday night to me.'

'Oh, I see.' He waved at a waiter. 'A pint of Guinness for the lady and a Jameson's for me. Best whiskey in the world,' he said to Vi when the waiter had left. 'You Irish do make the best drinks.'

'We do,' Vi agreed. 'Except for wine. The French do that better than us.'

'Yes, of course. If you're into wine.' He smiled. 'So you just finished filming?'

Vi nodded. 'Yes, my character, Jane, has just been killed in an accident under suspicious circumstances. Such a relief. Didn't really enjoy the part I was playing. The dialogue was terrible and the whole plot was deadly.' She giggled. 'Well, it would be, being a murder mystery.'

He smiled. 'I'm sure you let them know how deadly it was.'

Vi nodded. 'Yeah, I'm afraid I did, so they killed me off. It wasn't really in the script but they changed it when I started to complain. So glad to have finished that one. And now I can prepare for my role as Kathleen.'

'You'll be perfect,' he said, looking at her with amused eyes. 'It'll be interesting to see what you do with the role.'

'I'm going to try to get to know her properly. You'll be terrific playing her husband,' Vi said.

'I'll do my best.'

'I can't believe I'm going to work with you,' she continued, feeling her cheeks turn pink. 'I've seen a lot of your movies and always thought you were one of the best actors ever.'

'Thank you,' he said with an odd little smile. 'That's very flattering. I think we'll have a great time working together.'

'I'm looking forward to it,' Vi said. 'As far as I know, Kathleen was engaged twice but Don, the man she finally married, was the love of her life, even though they had quite a stormy relationship.'

'She was no pushover,' Jack remarked. 'But a very skilled actress.'

Vi nodded. 'I think she was. I've only seen two of her movies, but I've downloaded all the other ones and I'll be watching them when I get to Kerry. Haven't had a chance to do that yet, but now that I have some time off, I'll get started.'

'Good idea. That'll help you study her voice and body language. But it won't tell you much about her private life or her relationship with Don. She was a little wild before she met him but he calmed her down and made her happy at last.'

Vi smiled, trying not to be affected by the flirty look in his brown eyes, or the lock of dark hair falling across his forehead. 'You were going to say he tamed her, weren't you? But that would have sounded too domineering. Or even abusive.'

'These days, yes,' he said, sitting up. 'But we're going back to the nineteen fifties. Things were different then.'

'Hmm, yes, they were. Is that going to be a problem?' Vi

asked. 'I mean, audiences will be looking at it from the point of view of today.'

'Not a problem if it's done with subtlety. I think it will be. I haven't read the screenplay yet. Have you?'

'Not yet. Hugh is sending over the script before I go to Ireland,' Vi replied. 'But it will just be a first draft. I'm supposed to do some research on Kathleen and then the script will be adjusted if we find anything interesting to add to her story.'

'Well, there isn't much in her official bio,' Jack remarked. 'Born in that little place in Kerry in 1929, went to the local school and so on, and then she went to study drama and dance in Dublin and was spotted by a talent scout from Hollywood when she was only nineteen. Then a list of all her movies, which are all well known. Her personal life doesn't feature much and all we know is that she was engaged twice, both times briefly before she met the man she married.'

'I'm sure I can find out more than that,' Vi said.

Their drinks arrived and Vi took a swig of her pint before she continued. 'So what do you know about Don Williams? He was American, wasn't he? From Texas, I think. Can you do the accent?'

Jack nodded and cleared his throat. 'Sure, darlin'. I'll be so in character you'll wonder where I parked my horse,' he said in a nearly perfect Texas accent.

'I think you need to dial that down a bit,' Vi said, laughing. 'You wouldn't want to turn into some kind of caricature.'

'Of course.' Jack sipped from his glass. 'I was just doing it to make you laugh. I've listened to a clip on YouTube with the two of them talking to a journalist. Don Williams was educated at Harvard, so his accent was barely noticeable. Not easy to imitate, I have to say. But I'm working on it with a voice coach.' He smiled. 'You won't have any problems, though. Your accent is spot on. You just have to lower your voice a little. Kathleen had quite a throaty thing going. Very sexy, I have to say. She could buy a pint of milk and make it sound suggestive.'

'I never noticed that,' Vi said, wondering if he was joking. 'Her voice was rich and deep, yes, but...'

'Oh, never mind,' he said, laughing. 'I didn't mean to make you uncomfortable. Kathleen's voice was lovely. Yours isn't bad, but you'll need to work on the intonation and the timbre.'

'Ah, well, I'll have to watch her movies and listen carefully,' Vi replied. 'We did impersonations in drama school, so I'm sure I'll manage.'

He nodded and took another sip of whiskey. Then he leaned forward again, gently touching her hand. 'You'll be fine. And I think we'll be good together. We just have to get used to each other. Get the chemistry going and all that.'

'I know,' Vi said. The slight touch of his fingers and his eyes on her made her feel a little dizzy. He was so attractive, but that wasn't what made her feel drawn to him. His eyes were kind and his voice gentle as he spoke to her, as if he was trying to put her at ease. She knew there would be no problem 'getting the chemistry going', as he had put it.

'So you're going to Kerry soon?' he asked.

'Yes. In about a week. I'm going to spend the rest of the year at Magnolia Manor. That's the place where the movie is going to be shot.'

'Tell me about the family there.'

'Oh, nothing much to tell,' she said casually. 'My grandmother lives at Magnolia Manor with her fiancé. But he spends the winters in the South of France. Can't stand the wind and rain, apparently.'

Jack nodded. 'Understandable. Who else lives there?'

'No family. Most of the manor has been turned into apartments for seniors, except for some of the rooms downstairs. But I have two sisters who live nearby. Lily and her husband have

two children and Rose and Noel had their first baby a little over
a year ago.'

'Lily, Rose and Violet,' Jack said. 'That's quite a bouquet.
Are they like you, with red hair and green eyes?'

'Oh no,' Vi said, smiling. 'Lily has dark hair and eyes like my
grandmother and Rose is blonde with blue eyes.'

'Interesting.' Jack looked at her while he drained his glass.
'I'm looking forward to meeting them.'

'I'm sure they'll be excited to meet you, too,' Vi said.

'I suppose you're very close?'

Vi's spirits sank at the thought of her sisters. 'No, not really.
Not any more. We had a... disagreement a while back, I'm
afraid.'

'Oh? That's a pity. But maybe you can sort it out between
you?'

Vi sighed, the memory of her rift with her sisters taking the
gloss off the moment with the man of her dreams. 'It doesn't
look possible right now, I'm afraid. But maybe the movie and all
the excitement around it will cheer them up.'

'Could be. We could give them small parts in the movie,' he
suggested.

Vi laughed. 'Yeah, that might be fun for them.'

'I'm looking forward to my trip to Ireland,' he said. 'Especially Kerry. Never been there before.'

'Then you're in for a treat. It's a wonderful county. Especially around Dingle,' Vi told him, her heart beating faster at the
thought of going back to her hometown. 'It's incredibly beautiful. Wild and dramatic, with mountains and beaches and views
of the ocean to die for. Dingle town is the cutest little town, too,
with houses in all kinds of colours and quaint little shops and
pubs where they play trad music and...' She stopped and
laughed. 'Sorry to be blathering on about it.'

He looked at her with a glint of warmth in his eyes. 'No
need to apologise. I'm looking forward to it even more now.'

'You'll love it.' She finished her pint in one go, dabbing her mouth with a paper napkin to remove any foam.

'Would you like another pint?' Jack asked.

Vi shook her head. 'No thanks. I'm not *that* thirsty.'

'Well, I have to leave in a minute anyway,' he said. 'A car is picking me up to take me to my hotel and then I'm leaving early tomorrow. Would you like a lift anywhere?'

'I don't want to take you out of your way. I live in Croydon, so that would really be a big detour.'

'Oh.' He looked suddenly a little awkward. 'That is rather a hack.'

'I'll just take the Tube and then the train,' Vi said. 'It's okay, really. I'm used to the "hack".'

'Well, if you're sure,' Jack said, looking as if going to Croydon would be like a trip to the Outer Hebrides.

'Oh yes, absolutely.' She smiled reassuringly. 'You might get stuck in traffic anyway and then you'd never get to your hotel.'

'You're probably right, even if I feel bad about it.'

'Oh, please don't,' Vi said and got to her feet at the same time as Jack. 'I'd feel doubly bad about making you go all the way out there.'

'That's very nice of you,' Jack said. He hesitated for a moment, looking at Vi with a warm smile. 'Well, it was great to have that chat. I know we'll work well together. See you in Kerry in a few months. I'll be there a few weeks before shooting. Just to get the local colour and all that.'

Vi nodded. 'Good idea. Give me a shout when you get there.'

'Of course. I'll get your number from Liz.' He paused. Then he leaned forward and kissed her lightly on the cheek. 'Bye for now, Violet.'

'Bye, Jack,' Vi managed before he turned and swept through the crowd, ignoring the attention from everyone in the place.

Vi stood there for a moment, the kiss burning her cheek,

feeling as if she had been hit by a hurricane. *He was just being polite*, she thought. *I hope he couldn't hear my heart beating like a drum or notice the effect he had on me. How am I going to cope when we're working together, playing husband and wife? Looking lovingly into those brown eyes won't be a problem when we're acting, but off camera, I'll have to learn to switch off the adoration.*

But then, as she travelled home, she felt a tiny dart of disappointment that Jack had not insisted on driving her. Yes, Croydon was a long way to go, but he had a car and driver to take him there and back. He probably thought Vi wasn't worth the effort. Well, she would be less enthusiastic the next time they met. That would put all her acting skills to the test.

5

Vi spent the trip on the Tube thinking about Dingle and how wonderful it would be to go home for a while. She had meant what she'd said to Jack and telling him about it had awoken all the good memories. She pushed the thoughts of her sisters to the back of her mind and simply reminded herself of the delights of Kerry and how good she always felt when she came home. It was the soft air, the friendliness of the people who were always happy to have a chat about anything under the sun, the ever-changing skies, the endless ocean, the cries of seagulls and the green hills above the town. She had longed to see the world, to go to exciting places and have a career as an actress. Now that she had succeeded, it would be good to come back to show everyone. She might not stay in Kerry for good, but this time she wouldn't feel like running away. For a while, anyway.

Just before Vi left for Kerry, her agent called her saying the film team wanted to take a few publicity shots of her for the press release. 'Looking as close to Kathleen as possible,' he added.

'Gosh, I'm not sure how to do that, but I'll have a go,' Vi said.

'Their makeup artist is going to be there and do everything. Hair, face, the lot,' Hugh said. 'He needs to practise on you, they said. After all, he is going to have to do it every day during filming.'

Then Leo called her to confirm he was doing her makeup for the photo shoot. 'I'll make you so like Kathleen they'll think she's back from the dead,' he said which made Vi laugh.

It was a fun shoot, with the photographer and Leo doing their best to get Vi to resemble Kathleen O'Sullivan. They had blown up several photos of Kathleen and pinned them to a board next to a mirror in front of which Vi sat down. She looked at the face of the woman she was going to portray and marvelled at how Kathleen came alive in the various shots. She was posing with a little poodle in her arms, her flaming red hair blowing in the wind in one of them, and sitting demurely, dressed in period costume in another. Her amazing green eyes under thick dark brows stood out, along with her freckles and full mouth. Vi glanced at herself in the mirror and felt like a pale copy of the vivacious film star. She was quite a blank canvas, apart from the basic features.

'I don't know how you're going to make me look even faintly like Kathleen,' Vi remarked.

Standing behind her, Leo put a black cape around Vi's shoulders and told her to close her eyes and relax. 'Don't worry. I've got this. All you have to do is think happy thoughts and not move or open your eyes until I tell you.'

'Okay.' Vi did as she was told and slowly relaxed as she felt Leo's gentle touch on her face, applying foundation, eye shadow, mascara, blusher and finally, a dusting of powder. Then he started on her hair with gentle brush strokes.

'I'm going to put your hair in a low bun, like Kathleen used to wear it in the early nineteen fifties,' he said. 'And curl some of it around your face.'

'Can't wait to see it,' Vi said, fighting to keep her eyes closed while she slowly relaxed.

'So you're going to Kerry soon?' Leo said in her ear. 'I bet you can't wait.'

'It'll be nice to be back,' Vi replied.

'What family do you have there?' Leo asked, as he pinned her hair back.

'My grandmother and my two sisters,' Vi replied.

'You must be looking forward to seeing them,' he said.

'My granny, yes,' Vi said. 'I'm a bit nervous about seeing my sisters.'

'You fell out?'

'Yeah, something like that.'

'Sibling rivalry?' he suggested.

'Partly, yes. But...' She stopped. 'Oh, it's so complicated. It's about an interview I did with a Kerry newspaper about a year ago,' she continued, as Leo kept brushing her hair. It felt so good and he sounded so interested, as if he cared about her and wanted to help her through the trauma of what had happened. Even though he was complete stranger, she felt she could trust him. 'It happened when the interview was over,' she said in a low voice. 'Or so I thought. She asked me about my family and I talked about my sisters, telling her that we weren't always getting on. My sisters took it to mean that I felt that they were jealous of me because of their dreary lives. I didn't put it quite like that and what I actually said was supposed to be off the record, but they used it anyway. It was on the front page of the local newspaper the following week. I had no idea they were going to include all that in the article.'

'Not your fault, then,' Leo said. 'Except you should have been aware that you were talking to a journalist. They are always after a good story.'

'She seemed so nice and understanding,' Vi said. 'She had these kind eyes and warm voice. I wanted to tell her the story of my life.'

'Must have been good at her job, I'd say.'

'Yes. She knew how to get me to spill the beans using fake kindness and understanding,' Vi said with a touch of bitterness. 'I didn't mean to put it like that, and it sounded as if I was sneering at Lily and Rose. I wasn't, it's just that I've never understood why they returned to Dingle. I thought they wanted more out of life. They were very upset about it. And then we had a row and we all said things we didn't really mean. They cut me off and have refused to speak to me since. They thought I was using them to get publicity.'

'How awful for you.' Leo pulled a few strands of Vi's hair around her face and curled them around a curling iron. Then he stepped back. 'There. You can open your eyes.'

Vi looked at the mirror and gasped as Kathleen's face came into view. Only it was Vi, looking like a cloned version of the film star. 'Oh holy mother,' she exclaimed. 'It's scary. I look like... *her*, I really do. Except for the nose, but that doesn't seem to matter.' She leaned forward and studied her image. 'I feel as if I've been shot back in time. To the nineteen fifties. It's incredible.'

'Fantastic,' the photographer said. 'Leo, you're a genius.'

'I had good material,' Leo said. 'There's only the nose that we have to remodel with special clay. But we'll do that during the filming. Must say that Vi is a perfect choice for the part.'

'True,' the photographer said. 'Okay, Vi, sit on the stool in front of the white backdrop and we'll take a few shots. Just act natural, smile and pretend you're Kathleen.'

Vi sat on the stool and did as she was told. But she found it hard to relax and smile the way Kathleen had in the old photos she had just been looking at. It took over an hour and a lot of different positions before the photographer and Leo were happy. But then, when she saw the final results, she was amazed at how like the old photos they were.

'You're going to be amazing as Kathleen O'Sullivan,' the photographer said as they looked at the proofs together. 'I'll send these over to the team, Leo. Thanks for coming here so late. You did a fabulous job.'

'Vi was a trooper,' Leo said. 'Come back to the mirror and I'll help you remove all the makeup and brush out your hair.'

'Thanks,' Vi said, feeling exhausted. 'I'd do it myself but I'm tired after all that.'

'Of course you are.' Leo put the cape back on Vi and proceeded to remove the makeup with a special lotion that left her skin feeling smooth and refreshed. Then he brushed out her hair and she slowly watched the Kathleen-look disappear to be replaced by her own persona.

'There,' Leo said. 'You're you again.'

'Strange,' Vi said as their eyes met in the mirror. 'Really eerie, actually. Being her, and then me again. I don't know how I'll feel when the filming starts. It's going to take some adjustment. Maybe I'll need therapy when it's all over?' She laughed.

Leo nodded as he sorted his paraphernalia of makeup and brushes into different pouches and boxes and put it all into a big bag. 'It might be hard at first. But you'll get used to it.'

'I hope so.' Vi's thoughts drifted to Jack Montgomery and their conversation in the pub. 'It's just that I want to be as close to Kathleen as possible and that might carry with it certain risks. I mean, in the relationships with my co-stars.'

Leo looked thoughtfully at Vi. 'I know who you mean and also what you're worried about. But you'll be okay if you give yourself a reality check now and then. I'll help you if you like. I'll be with you doing you up every day, after all.'

'That's very comforting,' Vi said, feeling relieved at the

thought. It would be nice to have someone on her side all the time. Someone who might be there for her if things got difficult emotionally.

They said goodbye and Leo promised to call Vi when he came to Ireland. She left the studio feeling she had so much to look forward to. If only she didn't have to face her sisters.

6

The trip to Magnolia Manor was tiring and stressful. Heathrow was very busy and getting through security a huge hassle. Then the flight to Dublin was delayed and Vi had to sit at the gate for over two hours before boarding. She found herself in a middle seat, squashed between two rugby players on their way back after a match. Both of them fell asleep as soon as the plane took off and snored loudly all through the trip. When she finally arrived and had got her luggage, she just missed the bus that would take her to the train station and had to wait half an hour for the next one. She should have bought a flight to Cork instead but they were all booked out so she had been forced to fly to Dublin.

While she waited for the bus, her thoughts went back to her family. She smiled as she thought of the film company negotiating with her grandmother, Sylvia Fleury, who, despite her eighty-five years was still as fresh as a daisy in both body and mind. Vi had always thought of her grandmother as a steel rod, strong and unbendable even in the worst storms. And there had been storms all through her life, especially when both her husband and son, Vi's grandfather and father, were killed in a boating accident off the Kerry coast. Vi had only been two years old at the time and couldn't remember either her father or grandfather. But the tragedy had affected her life nevertheless.

Vi's older sisters, Lily and Rose, had been devastated and the trauma of that awful day would always stay with them. Vi had always been envious of her sisters because they had memories of their father that Vi could never share, which felt like a loss all on its own.

By the time Vi got on the train at around six o'clock in the evening, it was already dark. She normally enjoyed the journey through the charming landscape of rolling green hills but she was exhausted and fell asleep, not waking up until she arrived in Mallow, where she changed for the train to Tralee. It didn't arrive there until after ten o'clock and, as she hadn't wanted to ask her grandmother to meet her, she would have to take a taxi, which would not be cheap. But she had no choice and she realised that there was nobody to call for help.

She walked into the old building that she had always found so interesting with its façade built of granite and the original sash windows. It had been built in 1859 when Kerry became a popular area for holiday makers. Vi had always loved the old interior with its wooden benches where she imagined people sitting waiting for trains all through the years. But now the waiting rooms were cold and deserted and she walked out, feeling lost and lonely. She had been away too long and Kerry suddenly felt more alien than London.

Vi was standing on the platform considering her options when she heard someone calling her name. She looked around and saw a figure waving further down the platform. Then she realised who it was. Nora, who used to work as housekeeper at Magnolia Manor and was now her grandmother's friend and confidant.

'Nora,' Vi called, running towards the woman while she pulled her suitcase behind her. 'Hi. What are you doing here?'

'We came to meet you and take you home,' Nora replied as Vi arrived by her side. 'Sylvia said you'd be coming today and we figured you'd be on the late train. Martin is parking the car and sent me to look for you.'

Vi stared at Nora as tears welled up. 'Oh, how lovely,' she said and fell into Nora's arms. 'I'm so glad to see you. I thought nobody would come and meet me.'

'Oh, my dear girl,' Nora said, giving Vi a tight hug. 'Of course we'd come. Aren't you one of our Fleury girls that we're so very fond of?'

'I just wasn't sure,' Vi said. She didn't want to admit that she thought Nora might have heard what she'd said about her sisters. 'We had that disagreement last year, so...'

'Your sisters will come around eventually, I'm sure,' Nora soothed, as if reading her mind.

'Eventually,' Vi said bitterly. 'Like when hell freezes over?' She looked at Nora and noticed only a few small changes in her appearance. In her mid-sixties, Nora had greying short hair and lovely blue eyes around which there were only a few wrinkles. 'You look good,' she said to Nora. 'Fit and bright and youthful.'

Nora laughed. 'Well, thanks. Coming from a young thing like yourself, that's a big compliment.' She took Vi's suitcase and started to roll it towards the exit. 'Now come on. Martin will wonder what happened. It'll take just under an hour to get home. Sylvia is waiting up with supper and then you can settle into the gatehouse. We turned on the heating and made up the bed for you. You'll be as snug as a bug in a rug.'

'Oh, that sounds so great,' Vi said as she hitched her tote bag onto her shoulder and followed Nora, all the tensions about meeting her sisters nearly forgotten. 'Can't wait to see Granny.'

'She'll be happy to see you too.' Nora turned around and peered at Vi. 'There was something in the newspaper about you making a film about Kathleen O'Sullivan – with a photo of you looking the spit of her.'

'Oh, was there?' Vi realised that the press release was out there already. 'Yes, as you know they'll shoot some of it at Magnolia. I'm sure Granny told you.'

'She did. Good news. It'll bring in some money and publicity for the manor and Lily's café and garden centre. It's getting hard to make ends meet in the wintertime.'

'I can imagine,' Vi said as they exited the station. She scanned the street for Martin and spotted him a little further away, getting out of a Toyota SUV. 'There's Martin,' she said, quickening her step. 'And you have a new car.'

'We do,' Nora said. 'A bit big but Martin loves it. It's a hybrid so we're doing our bit for the environment.'

'That's great,' Vi said and hurried to greet Martin with a hug. 'Hi, Martin. So good to see you. How are you?'

Martin hugged Vi back. 'I'm grand, girl. And you're all grown up and a famous actress and all over the papers for the film they're going to shoot here. How about that for excitement, eh?' He drew breath and beamed at her.

Vi laughed, feeling sheer joy at seeing Martin after such a long time. He was a little stooped and his hair white but he was still the father figure from her childhood, the one who had been there for the little girls after the tragedy, even though Vi had been just a toddler then and not known what had happened until she was older. Martin and Nora had been such a support to Sylvia all through the years and still were, even though they were now both retired. But Sylvia knew she could count on them whenever she needed support or a helping hand. Vi had always found it comforting to know her grandmother had people around her who were loyal and dependable. But now that two of her granddaughters lived locally, Sylvia had even more support and would never have to worry if something should happen.

'Please get in, ladies,' Martin said when he had put Vi's

luggage in the boot. 'It's going to be wet and windy tonight so we need to have Vi all tucked up before we go home.'

They laughed and piled into the car, and Martin took off at speed down the empty street. Vi looked out the window at the little houses lining the road, their windows lit up and smoke coming out of the chimneys. The old-fashioned street lights shone on tiny front gardens with neatly clipped hedges and camellia bushes that would be flowering in early spring, which didn't seem too far away in this mild climate. Even now, in late November there were roses still in bloom. She could smell turf smoke and slowly began to feel that she was coming home.

Her thoughts drifted to the press release that had been in the local papers and she wondered how Lily and Rose had taken the news. Maybe they thought history would repeat itself and Vi would yet again talk about them in a derogatory way. But it had been completely accidental and her words had been twisted to make her sound as if she was belittling Lily and Rose and felt somehow superior. This was far from the truth and she wished with all her heart that she had kept her mouth shut and not talked to the journalist when she had thought she was off the record. In any case, the article had not been helpful to her career in any way. Of course it was yesterday's news, or even last year's, but still fresh to Lily and Rose, who could not forget or forgive Vi for letting them down in this way. And now she was coming home and they would be giving Vi the cold shoulder for all to see. Dingle was a small town and everyone knew everyone's business, so Vi knew she would be looked at askance by all the people she knew, even old friends. It was not a good feeling.

'Here we are,' Martin said what seemed like a short while later, as they made their way up the drive towards Magnolia Manor. It was a cold night with clear skies after the heavy showers, and

Vi could see the manor gleaming in the moonlight at the end of the avenue. Soft lamplight shone in some of the windows of the big house and she figured that these were the senior apartments now all occupied. It looked so nice to see the lights instead of the huge empty house with dark windows that she remembered. How lovely that the house was now full of people who were probably happy to live in such a beautiful place.

Martin drove around the corner and pulled up in the courtyard where a light shone over a green door. 'Your granny is waiting with supper,' he said. 'We'll go back to the gatehouse with your luggage and then pick you up after you have eaten.'

'That's okay,' Vi said. 'I'd love to walk back to the gatehouse in the moonlight. I've been sitting all day and the fresh air will be good. You go on home.'

'Are you sure?' Nora asked, looking doubtful.

'Absolutely,' Vi insisted. 'You were brilliant to meet me and drive me home. But now I want to manage on my own. I know the gardens like the back of my hand, you know. I could walk down the path with my eyes closed and still find the gatehouse.'

Nora nodded. 'Okay, Vi. I see what you mean. But we're so happy to see you back, aren't we, Martin?'

'We are,' Martin agreed. He got out of the car and held the door open for Vi. 'You go inside now. Your granny is waiting.'

Vi jumped out of the car and reached up and touched his cheek. 'Thank you for everything, Martin. You and Nora saved my life tonight.'

'Oh, you'd have been all right,' Nora said, sticking her head out the window. 'But I'm glad we could help out. Don't worry about that old story. The girls will come around. Silly of them to carry a grudge. Tell them I said that.'

'Thank you, Nora,' Vi said, opening the passenger door to give Nora a hug. 'Goodnight. See you tomorrow, I hope.'

'Goodnight, pet,' Nora said and patted Vi's arm. 'Sleep tight when you get to bed. I'll turn on the electric blanket for you.'

'Wonderful. Goodnight, darlings,' Vi said and blew them both a kiss before she went to the green door and pressed the button beside it. She shivered slightly as Martin's car drove off, feeling a dart of dread at facing her grandmother.

But then the door flew open and Sylvia stood in the doorway beaming, her arms open. 'Violet,' she said. 'How wonderful that you're here.'

Vi stifled a sob and fell into her grandmother's arms, breathing in that special scent of expensive perfume mingled with newly baked bread. 'Granny,' she mumbled and hugged the old woman tight. 'I'm here at last.'

'So you are,' Sylvia said, stroking Vi's hair. 'Welcome home, Violetta.'

Vi smiled as she heard the old nickname. 'Thank you, Granny. I'm so happy to be here.' She sniffed the air. 'Is that freshly baked soda bread I can smell? And Irish stew?'

'It is indeed,' Sylvia said and pulled Vi into a small cosy hall. 'Hang up your jacket and come into the kitchen and I'll feed you. I want to put some flesh onto those bones.'

Vi laughed and hung up her jacket on a peg among a lot of other jackets and coats. 'I do need to put on weight for this role.'

Sylvia smiled and led the way into a cosy kitchen where the smells of fresh bread and Irish stew were even stronger. She pulled out a chair at the round table in the large alcove. 'There was an item in *The Irish Times* about it today with a photo of you looking the spit of Kathleen. Quite eerie, I have to tell you.'

'I know. The makeup artist did a great job. I was quite amazed myself.' Vi sat down at the table while Sylvia went to the cooker to ladle stew onto a plate. Then she sat down while Vi dug in to the food.

'So how was it?' Sylvia asked. 'Finding out you got the part, I mean.'

'I was quite shocked actually.' Vi put down her fork. 'I didn't expect to get it. Not even when they were saying I was the image of Kathleen. I'm still trying to get used to the idea. Me playing a major part in a movie? Unbelievable.' She shook her head and started eating again. 'This is delicious. Just like you always used to make it.'

'Why would I change it?' Sylvia asked. 'It's the one dish I do well. The rest I leave up to Arnaud when he's here and Nora when he's not.'

'But now he's not? And you would normally be in France,' Vi said, looking at her grandmother with concern.

'I know,' Sylvia said with a shrug. 'France was nice and warm and sunny. Quite lovely this time of year. But I just didn't fit in. There wasn't much to do there on the Riviera in the winter. It was full of old people sitting around playing cards and boules and generally shuffling around trying to pass the time. Quite pleasant but I got bored. Arnaud was running his business from his villa and was busy a lot of the time. I missed home too much. Here I have things to do and friends I have known all my life. And then there are my committees and charity work and my granddaughters and great-grandchildren. The tenants of the apartments are all very nice people too and I'm getting to know them.'

'I can't hear any noise,' Vi remarked. 'You wouldn't know that there was anyone upstairs.'

'That's because they go to bed around ten o'clock,' Sylvia said. 'I love knowing they're there and that the house is giving such comfort and companionship to older people. This is my home and I love it. Too much to miss for a bit of sunshine, food and wine.'

'And the company of a handsome man,' Vi cut in.

'I know,' Sylvia said with a wistful smile. 'I do miss him, that's the worst part. But he'll be here for Christmas and then in the spring, summer and early autumn.'

'I'm so glad you're not in France,' Vi said. 'I couldn't bear it if you were away now that I'm going to spend some time here.'

'That's good. But what are you going to do while you wait for the filming to start?' Sylvia asked. 'It's not until March according to the producer. That's four months away.'

'I want to find out everything I can about Kathleen O'Sullivan,' Vi replied. 'Get under her skin, so to speak. I want... Oh, Granny, this has to be a huge success or I'm finished. I need to be as good as Meryl Streep playing Margaret Thatcher.'

'A very tall order. She was outstanding in that movie.' Sylvia held out her hand for Vi's plate. 'Some more stew?'

'No thanks, Granny. It was yummy, but I'm stuffed.' Vi pushed her plate away.

'How about a slice of Nora's apple pie?' Sylvia asked with an amused smile. 'With whipped cream. That might help pile on the pounds. You look like you need some flesh on those bones.'

'I think I could fit that in,' Vi said, laughing. 'You know that's one of the things I can't resist.'

'I thought you might make room for that.' Sylvia went to the oven and took out a dish with half a pie. 'I heated it for you. And I whipped some cream too.'

'Oh, lovely.' Vi tucked into the large slice with whipped cream heaped on top. 'Funny how sweet things are easier to eat than anything savoury.' She swallowed her mouthful and looked at Sylvia. 'I was thinking, Granny, that you might know some things about Kathleen's early life here in Kerry. I mean, you're the same generation, aren't you?'

'Well,' Sylvia said, 'I suppose we were in a way. But Kathleen was born in nineteen twenty-nine, eleven years before I arrived. That's quite an age difference.'

'I know but...' Vi paused while she finished her apple pie. 'You must have known something about her, or known people who knew her. She grew up not a million miles from here, after all.'

'Very different places,' Sylvia said, her mouth in a thin line.

'And her family was... Well, not of the same social class, if that doesn't sound too snobby.'

'It does,' Vi remarked. 'But I know what you mean.' She looked at her grandmother for a moment. 'Can you tell me anything about her that might help me get to know her better?'

'Oh, much to tell,' Sylvia mumbled. 'But nothing I can talk about.'

'Why not?' Vi asked.

'Well, *de mortuis nil nisi bonum* and all that.' Sylvia got up and took Vi's plate. 'Maybe it's time to go to bed now anyway. It's nearly midnight.'

Vi nodded, knowing there was no use pushing her grand-mother. It was late and Vi was tired after a long day's travelling. The questions would have to be put more diplomatically at the right moment. 'You're right. It's been quite a long day,' she said, getting up. 'Dinner was lovely and the apple pie fantastic. Thanks for waiting up, Granny. It's so great to see you.'

'Of course I'd wait up for you, my darling Violetta.' Sylvia put the plate in the sink. Then she turned and took Vi's hands in a tight grip, her eyes full of love. 'I'm so glad you're here.'

'That's good to know,' Vi said. 'Because I'm happy to be home despite what everyone might think.'

'Don't worry about what everyone else thinks,' Sylvia said. 'You were such a gift and you always will be to me. You were our bright spark when you were a little girl. The only one who wasn't touched by the tragedy. You were only a toddler but every time you came into a room you were like a ray of sunshine, smiling, laughing, playing games, bringing me a bunch of dandelions you had picked especially for me. You looked at me with your huge green eyes and your smile was like a balm to my soul. You had no idea what had happened and didn't understand our tears. It helped us all through the worst of it.'

'Oh,' Vi said, touched by the emotion in those words.

'That's such a lovely thought. I always felt that I missed something because I don't remember Granddad or my father. I don't really remember anything about that sad time either. I understood it better when I grew up. It must have been a terrible time for you all.'

'It was unbearable.' Sylvia squeezed Vi's hands and then let them go. 'But here we are, years and years later and you're a young woman on the cusp of a great career as an actress.'

'Oh, well. That's not exactly set in stone,' Vi said, feeling the old insecurity set in. 'The movie might flop.'

'Or it might not,' Sylvia retorted. 'All I know is that it being shot here is like a little miracle. We need the money and the publicity. Things aren't really working out as we hoped, you see. Your sisters are both going through a tough period in their lives. Maybe you can be that bright spark to them again.'

'If they'll let me in,' Vi mumbled, feeling worried to hear Rose and Lily were struggling. What could be wrong? With beautiful families and perfect husbands, surely they didn't have anything to complain about.

'They will in time,' Sylvia promised. She stifled a yawn. 'But now, little Violetta, I need my beauty sleep. And so do you. Are you strong enough to walk down to the gatehouse on your own?'

'Of course,' Vi said. 'I want to walk down the path and smell the sea and listen to the owl, if he's still around.'

'He is,' Sylvia said, smiling. 'Or maybe it's a she? I think the bed is made down there in the house and Nora said she'd turn on the heating and leave lights on. You should be fine there.'

'As snug as a bug in a rug,' Vi said with a fond smile. She leaned forward and kissed her grandmother's soft cheek. 'Night, night, Granny. See you in the morning.'

Sylvia patted Vi's cheek. 'Sleep tight. We can have a lazy morning tomorrow. And then we could have lunch somewhere nice when you've settled in. How about that?'

'Sounds perfect,' Vi said, smiling. 'Looking forward to it already. See you soon.'

She left her grandmother and stepped out of the house and into the dark courtyard. She turned the corner to walk down the moonlit path, the gravel crunching under her feet. She breathed in the smell of turf smoke and sea, and heard the owl hoot above her as its dark shadow swept across the lawn. It was both eerie and beautiful and it brought Vi back to her childhood. She thought of her grandmother's words about how Vi had been their ray of sunshine during those dark days long ago. That thought made her feel more hopeful and she wished her sisters might remember her like that; the bright spark that helped them feel a little better.

Then her thoughts drifted to Kathleen O'Sullivan and what her grandmother had said. *De mortuis nil nisi bonum... Don't speak ill of the dead,* she thought, *but what did Granny mean by that?* It made her suspect that Kathleen's youth might not have been as sunny as everyone thought.

Maybe there were things behind the glossy Hollywood image that nobody knew about.

7

It only took Vi a week to settle in to the gatehouse. It was a much bigger space than she was used to; her accommodations in London had always been tiny bedsits and studio flats, for which she often had to pay astronomical rents. But here she had a whole house, with three bedrooms and a bathroom upstairs and a living room and small but cosy kitchen downstairs. The house had been renovated a few years ago, when Rose and Lily lived here, one after the other.

The living room was especially cosy, with a sofa piled with cushions in front of the fireplace and a bookcase crammed with books waiting to be read. There was a tiny patio outside where Vi imagined it would be lovely to sit once spring arrived. The largest bedroom had been cleaned and aired and the bed made up the first evening she was there. It was as if little elves had been around the house, lighting the fire, stocking the fridge and turning on the lamps, but she knew it was Nora and Martin. She had gone to bed feeling not the slightest bit lonely, knowing there were people nearby who cared about her. If only she could make peace with her sisters, life would be perfect. But real life wasn't like that, so she would have to be patient and

wait for the right moment to take the first step towards a reconciliation. She wanted to keep in touch with her little nieces and
nephew, which had been difficult because of the rift. But now, if
only her sisters could put the past behind them, she would at
last be able to get to know the children as they were growing up.
She wanted to be a real auntie who they knew they could have
fun with.

Vi decided to forget about her sisters for a while and
concentrate on her research into Kathleen's early life. But first
she had to watch the movies she had downloaded and do her
best to learn how Kathleen used to speak and move and pick up
any other mannerisms that were typical of her persona. She had
found a voice coach who was willing to teach online through
Zoom, which suited Vi perfectly. They would have daily
sessions until Vi had perfected Kathleen's voice and manner of
speaking as much as she could. It was a daunting task, but one
that Vi found very challenging and fascinating. The old movie
star's way of walking and moving she would have to study
herself but she felt that would be less of a problem than the
voice.

Vi became hooked on watching the movies. Kathleen was so
graceful – nearly like a dancer – and when Vi found a more
detailed biography online, she discovered that Kathleen had
indeed studied classical ballet at a dance studio in Dublin. She
had been the only daughter of the local teacher in a village near
Castleisland, a small town not far from Tralee. She had gone to
Dublin when she was seventeen to study drama and dance in
order to become an actress on the stage. Then she had been
spotted by a talent scout from Hollywood when she was in her
final year and been cast in a few minor movies until her big
breakthrough, starring against Henry Fonda in a blockbuster
film set in Texas.

Vi wondered if the dance studio was still there and tried to
find it by googling. She saw, to her delight, that it was still in

business and that it was now also a gym and yoga studio combined which offered courses in all kinds of dance techniques, including Irish, flamenco and ballroom dancing. She decided to call them, just to see if they had any records of Kathleen O'Sullivan's attendance. But it was over seventy years ago so it was a real long shot. They might not even know who Kathleen was.

She waited with bated breath while the phone rang and rang. Then, finally, someone replied.

'On Your Toes dance studio, Finbarr speaking,' a pleasant male voice said.

'Hi,' Vi replied. 'I wonder if you could help me. My name is Violet Fleury and I'm doing some research into the life of Kathleen O'Sullivan. She was a movie star in the nineteen fifties, so maybe you don't know who I'm talking about, but she was a student at your dance school in her youth.'

'Of course I know who she was,' Finbarr said. 'She's a legend here at our school. We have her framed photo on the wall in the reception area. She was spotted by a talent scout from Hollywood right here in the dance studio in nineteen forty-eight. And the rest, as you know, is history.'

'Wow, that's amazing,' Vi exclaimed. She did the maths in her head. 'She must have been only nineteen then.'

'Something like that,' Finbarr agreed. 'Long time ago. She's our most famous student. Not sure how I can help you, though, as that's all I know. Apart from her movies, of course. I've seen one or two on TV years ago. Great looking woman.'

'She was indeed.' Vi paused. 'I don't suppose you know anyone who might remember her? I know it's a long shot, but I thought I'd have a go all the same.'

'I'm sorry,' Finbarr said. 'It was so long ago. I don't think...' He stopped. 'Well, maybe... Hang on sec. There might be someone. A very old lady who trained with her. I mean, she's old now, but she was only a teenager then. She used to come in here to watch the lessons. Must be around ninety now, if she's still alive. I have to ask if anyone knows where she is. Can I call you back?'

'Yes,' Vi said and gave him her number.

'Great,' Finbarr said. 'I'll get back to you as soon as I get the information.'

'That's very kind of you,' Vi said.

'No problem,' Finbarr replied. 'I've been a fan of Kathleen O'Sullivan for a long time. Are you writing a book about her or something?'

'No, it's for a movie based on her life.'

'Oh yeah,' Finbarr said. 'I saw the press release in *The Irish Times*. The actress playing her is so like her it's spooky. Can't remember her name.'

'I know,' Vi said with a laugh. 'Great resemblance. Quite scary.'

'Exactly. Hey, I'll be in touch in an hour or so. Talk to you then.' Finbarr hung up.

Vi sat on the sofa in the living room, wondering if Finbarr would find the old lady he had mentioned. And if he did, would Vi be able to contact her? Or was she too old to remember anything about Kathleen?

While she waited, Vi started to tidy up the breakfast dishes, keeping her phone on the table. Then it rang, making her jump. But it was not the man from the dance studio, but Nora asking if she was all right and if she needed anything from the shop. 'As you don't have a car, I'll pick anything up for you,' Nora offered. 'Or you might come with me into town, if you like.'

'Oh eh,' Vi said, feeling she wanted to stay where she was in case Finbarr called. It would be awkward to take that call when she was out and about. 'I'll leave it for now and go later. Granny said she'd call in. I could do my shopping with her. Thanks for offering, though, and for making the house so nice for me when I arrived. I've only been here a week but I feel at home already.'

'You're very welcome,' Nora said. 'I'm glad you're spending time with your granny. She needs a little care and attention right now.'

'I have a feeling you're right,' Vi said, remembering the sad look in her grandmother's eyes just before they'd said goodnight that first evening. 'Is it Arnaud? Is she sad that he's not willing to spend the winter with her in Ireland?'

'Partly,' Nora said. 'But also the girls. They're both a little frazzled right now. They need cheering up, I think. But don't tell them I said that.'

'I won't,' Vi promised. 'Not that I'll meet them any time soon. I'm sure seeing me would not make them feel any better.'

'Oh, that old stuff.' Nora sounded annoyed. 'I wish they'd come off their high horses. I'd bang their heads together and get them to behave if I could.'

Vi laughed. 'I don't think that would improve their humour. But I'm glad you're on my side.'

'I wish there was no side,' Nora said. 'I love all you girls as much.' She sighed. 'Well, I'd better get going. Have fun with your granny and I'll see you soon.'

'Thanks, Nora,' Vi said. 'Bye for now.'

'Bye, sweet pea,' Nora said and hung up.

The phone rang again as soon as Nora had signed off. Vi picked up and saw that it was a Dublin number. It had to be Finbarr calling her back.

'Hello?' she said. 'Is that Finbarr?'

'Yeah,' he replied, sounding amused. 'It's me. Hey, I got the name of the old lady I was talking about. Her name is Fidelma Sheridan. She is ninety-four, she told me, and she is as sharp in her mind as a tack. Told me all about her dancing days all those years ago. And she just read about the movie in *The Irish Times*, she said. It appears she knew Kathleen well in the old days. She was only fifteen when she met Kathleen but they became friends during that time. I asked her if she would mind talking to you and she said she'd be delighted. So I'll text you her number and you can call her yourself. She's great gas, actually.'

'Oh, that's incredible,' Vi said, nearly breathless with excitement. 'You've been hugely helpful. I'll call Fidelma as soon as I can. I'm really looking forward to hearing what she has to say about Kathleen.'

'I'd call her after two o'clock in the afternoon,' Finbarr said. 'She says she has a snooze after lunch and then she's in good form. She's looking forward to talking to you.'

'I can't wait to talk to her,' Vi said. 'I don't know how to thank you for all your help.'

'Ah sure, it was nothing,' Finbarr said modestly. 'Us Kathleen fans have to stick together. But if you're ever in Dublin, call in and say hi.'

'Of course I will,' Vi promised.

'Great. Nice to chat to you, Violet. I'll text you Fidelma's details as soon as we've hung up.'

'Brilliant.'

They said goodbye and Finbarr sent a text with the old lady's number nearly straight away.

Vi looked at the name and number, thinking what a stroke of luck it had been to call the dance studio. It was amazing to have got so much information straight away. She couldn't wait to hear about Fidelma's memories of Kathleen O'Sullivan's early days as an actress. She might remember what Kathleen was like in those days. What had been her hopes and dreams? How had she reacted to the talent scout's invitation to go to Hollywood? Vi hadn't explained to Finbarr that she was the actress who was going to play Kathleen because then the spotlight would be on her. Better to be a little bit anonymous, at least for the time being.

8

Vi's thoughts were still so full of what she had learned that she was only listening with half an ear to what her grandmother was talking about during their drive into Dingle for lunch a few days later. She had tried to contact both Lily and Rose but only got their voicemails, so she had left a short message to each of them, saying she would be at the gatehouse and would love to see them. There had been no response from either of them, but Vi knew they were busy and maybe also wary about meeting her, so she decided to try to forget about the rift and enjoy spending time with her grandmother. Mending all the fences would be a long process in any case, and she wanted to be patient with her sisters. Especially if it was true that they were both a little stressed.

The view out of the window of the car was an added distraction, as it was a glorious winter's day with cold winds but bright sunshine from a clear blue sky. The spray of the green-blue waves lashed the shores and the seagulls squawked above them as they got out of the car that Sylvia had parked near the harbour.

'Oh,' Vi said as the wind whipped her hair around her face.

'I'd forgotten how the air feels here when it's windy. Cold but still soft, salty and sweet at the same time. I love it.'

'Yes, it's very special,' Sylvia agreed as she locked the car. 'A lot of people don't understand why I love stormy weather so much. But I know you share that strange feeling. We're winter girls, aren't we?'

'We are,' Vi said, smiling at her grandmother, who was looking fit and energetic today, her cheeks rosy and her brown eyes sparkling. Her grey hair, cut in a chin-length bob, blew around her face and then settled again into the same perfect shape. She was dressed in a white polo neck under a bright red down jacket and blue trousers, which made her look both chic and warm. 'And you look like the perfectly dressed Kerry woman, ready for any kind of weather.'

'That's nice to hear,' Sylvia said. 'But let's go and get lunch before we blow away. I've booked a table in Fins. It's a new fish restaurant just up the street from here. Lovely views of the bay, if you manage to get a table by the window.'

'Which you did, no doubt,' Vi remarked, winking.

'Of course,' Sylvia said, zipping up her jacket. 'Come on,' she said and led the way up the street and into a charming little restaurant with floaters and fishnets in the ceiling and blue and white tiles on the floor. There was a lovely smell of woodsmoke from the fireplace where logs blazed, making the room warm and comforting after the cold winds outside. They were greeted by a cheerful waiter who showed them to a table by the window and handed them two menus.

'The special today is chowder with freshly baked brown bread,' he announced. 'Mrs Fleury, would you like the usual with that?'

'Yes, please,' Sylvia said. 'And my granddaughter will have the same.'

'Grand,' the waiter said and smiled at Vi. 'Lovely to meet you, Miss Fleury. And congratulations on landing the part of

Kathleen O'Sullivan. We're all very excited to see the movie shot here in Dingle.'

'Thank you,' Vi said and looked at her grandmother. 'What's the usual?'

'A small glass of Chardonnay,' Sylvia said. 'But don't worry, it'll be a while before we drive home.'

'If that's all you'll be drinking, I'm not worried,' Vi replied. She looked at the waiter. 'Yes, please. The same for me, then.'

'Perfect.' The waiter hesitated. 'Would you mind if I asked you for your autograph? Better to get it before the stampede, so to speak. Everyone will want one very soon.'

'Gosh!' Vi blushed. 'That's... Of course. No problem,' she ended.

'Great. I'll get a piece of paper and a pen when I bring you your drinks.' The waiter smiled and walked off.

Vi stared at Sylvia in shock. 'Goodness. That's never happened to me before.'

'You've never been the star of the show before,' Sylvia said. 'And of course, the town is buzzing with the news right now after that piece in the paper. It'll die down soon, though, so enjoy it while you can.'

'Enjoy it?' Vi said, horrified. 'I don't think I want all the attention on me right now. I'm trying to get used to playing this part and getting to know Kathleen and find out what her early life was like. I thought I'd get some peace and quiet here.'

'Peace and quiet?' Sylvia said with an amused smile. 'After that bombshell in the press? Local girl hits the big time with a starring part in a movie that will be shot in a place everyone knows and loves. How could you expect them not to be excited?'

'I didn't realise,' Vi said. 'Never thought it would be such a big deal.' She shook her head and laughed. 'But when Jack Montgomery rides into town, they'll forget all about me.'

'Probably,' Sylvia agreed. 'But until then you'll be in the spotlight.'

'What do Lily and Rose think about all this?' Vi asked.

'I haven't seen them since the news broke. I spoke to Rose, who thought the actual filming will be good publicity for the gardens and the café. Everyone will want to see where the movie was shot. It'll be like when *Ryan's Daughter* was filmed in Kerry. Long time ago but people still want to see the locations.'

'I know. Well, that sounds positive, anyway.'

Their drinks arrived and shortly afterwards the waiter brought two steaming bowls of chowder. 'There you go,' he said as he carefully placed a bowl in front of each of them. He slipped a piece of paper towards Vi. 'Could you sign this, please?' he asked, handing her a pen.

'Of course.' Vi quickly scribbled her name on the piece of paper.

'Thanks a million,' the waiter said.

He was about to walk away but Vi stopped him with a hand on his arm. 'Hang on,' she said. 'I think I saw chocolate cake on the menu.'

He grinned. 'Yes, indeed. It comes with whipped cream. You want that after the chowder?'

'Yes, please,' Vi replied. 'A large dollop of whipped cream, please.'

'No problem,' he said and walked off.

Vi met her grandmother's puzzled look. 'I told you I have to put on weight for my role. They said I'm too skinny and Kathleen was quite curvaceous. Like a lot of women in those days.'

Sylvia laughed. 'Oh, yes, I remember. Well, isn't that a nice challenge for you? I'm looking forward to seeing you fill out a bit.'

'I'm going to do my best,' Vi said and picked up her spoon.

'But it'll be a bit of a struggle. I eat like a horse as it is and never put on weight.'

'Just like your father,' Sylvia said. 'He was skin and bone like you despite his huge appetite.'

'I didn't know that,' Vi said and put down her spoon. 'I barely know how to picture him.'

'Well,' Sylvia said between mouthfuls, 'he was tall and skinny and had reddish hair and green eyes. Just like you really.'

'Oh, I know all that,' Vi said impatiently. 'But what was he like? I don't know much about his personality.'

'He was a very cheerful lad,' Sylvia said. 'Always looking on the bright side. Loved fooling around, telling jokes and playing tricks on people. In a nice way, of course. He made people laugh but he didn't suffer fools gladly either. He was a great judge of character and had everyone taped immediately.' She paused as her eyes gleamed with unshed tears. 'I miss him so,' she whispered.

Vi put her hand on her grandmother's arm. 'Of course you do. I'm sorry. Shouldn't have asked.' Vi had always been reticent to ask too much about her father, but she'd thought it was finally the right time. Perhaps she was wrong.

'You have the right to know as much about him as you can,' Sylvia said. Vi looked across the table at her with a smile, feeling relieved. 'And I will tell you more soon. We can look at the photos in my albums together.'

'I'd love that,' Vi said as her chocolate cake arrived.

'And now you must eat up,' Sylvia urged. 'To be a little sturdier, just like Kathleen O'Sullivan.'

'I know.' Vi picked up her spoon. 'What was that you said about her that night I arrived? I have feeling you know stuff you won't tell me. Something bad.'

Sylvia shrugged. 'It's just gossip and talk that I picked up when I was young. I don't like to repeat it. You know yourself how things get twisted and changed as people talk about celebrities. No idea how true it was. No smoke without a fire, though, I suppose,' she ended cryptically.

'I'd still love to know,' Vi said, taking a bite of cake and waiting to see if Sylvia would respond. As she didn't, Vi went on. 'But if it's not true, I suppose it wouldn't be fair. In any case, I've found someone who knew Kathleen in the early days.'

'That someone must be very old by now,' Sylvia remarked drily.

'A little over ninety but as sharp as a tack, I've heard. She's an old lady who went to the same dance school as Kathleen. I'm going to call her in about an hour. She has a nap after lunch and then she is as bright as a button, apparently.'

'I can believe it,' Sylvia said, smiling. 'I quite like a nap myself from time to time. It's very refreshing. So who is this person?'

'Her name is Fidelma Sheridan,' Vi said. 'She lives in Dublin. That's all I know.'

'Interesting,' Sylvia said. 'Let me know what she says.'

'I will,' Vi promised and went back to her cake. 'This is very good. You want to taste it?'

'No thanks,' Sylvia replied, pushing her bowl away. 'I, unlike you, have to watch my waistline. So I'll just have a coffee and then we should go. All that talk of naps has made me sleepy, so I think I'll have a little lie down when I get home.'

'Okay, Granny,' Vi said, scraping her plate. 'Gosh, this putting on weight is quite nice, actually. I hope it works.'

'It should, the way you laid into that cake.' Sylvia waved at the waiter. 'Hello, could you bring us two coffees and the bill please?' she called.

When they had paid the bill and drunk their coffee, they left the restaurant and walked along the quay for a while 'to blow the cobwebs away', as Sylvia put it. Then they got back in the car and drove the short distance to Magnolia Manor, Sylvia stopping to let Vi out at the gatehouse.

'Thanks for lunch, Granny,' Vi said as she got out. 'Give me a shout when you want company and we'll look through the family albums together.'

'That'll be lovely,' Sylvia said.

Vi went inside and instead tried to think about what she was going to say to the old lady who had known Kathleen O'Sullivan. It might be tricky to get any information out of her, especially if her memory was failing. But she'd have a go all the same. Every lead had to be followed in order to learn as much as possible about the woman whose life must have had many ups and downs through the years. Vi was determined to find out everything she could in order to be as close to the original as she could. She couldn't wait to talk to this Fidelma Sheridan.

9

A little after two o'clock, Vi sat down in the living room and dialled the number Finbarr had given her. It rang several times and Vi was about to hang up when she heard a click and a soft voice said: 'Hello?'

'Is that Fidelma Sheridan?' Vi asked.

'Speaking,' the woman said.

'Oh, hello,' Vi said. 'My name is Violet Fleury and I'm—'

'You're going to play Kathleen O'Sullivan in the movie about her life,' Fidelma interrupted.

'How did you know?' Vi asked.

'I read the article in *The Irish Times*,' Fidelma explained. 'You look so very like her, you know.'

'Oh, thanks,' Vi said. 'I'm glad you think so.'

'That Finbarr didn't have a clue who you were,' Fidelma scoffed. 'He said you were some kind of journalist doing research. You'd think he'd pay attention. But young people are so into their own world and don't know how to read properly. Always on those dratted phones, whatever it is they do on them. It's a curse of the times we live in.' She paused. 'So... where were we? Oh yes, Kathleen O'Sullivan. You're going to play her, so you need to know all about her, is that right?'

'Yes,' Vi said. 'I just felt I should have all the background information in order to be as close to her character as possible. There isn't much in any biography that I can find, just the bare bones of her life. Birth, youth, marriage, movies and so on. But not anything that will tell me who she really was.' Vi thought fleetingly about the production company and how they seemed not to have been in touch with people Kathleen might have known. But perhaps the dance studio was too much of a long shot for them.

'I see,' Fidelma said. 'Well, I can only tell you what I remember of the early days. She was at the dance school at the same time as she went to drama school. She wanted to learn to dance in order to move gracefully on the screen. I thought it was a very good thing for her to do. She was quite a big girl and a little awkward when she first started dancing. But then she improved, all thanks to Maximilian. He was a Russian teacher of modern dance. He inspired her. In fact he inspired us all, I have to say. Marvellous man.'

'Tell me more,' Vi urged, intrigued. 'It's great to talk to someone who knew Kathleen.'

'Oh, I knew her better than a lot of people,' Fidelma said. 'I was young, only fifteen, and very shy when I started taking lessons at the studio. Kathleen encouraged me and gave me confidence. Taught me how to stand up for myself. She had been up against some difficult times early in her life and that had hardened her. She was quite feisty and some would say mean, but she was like a big sister to me.' Fidelma drew breath.

'That's very interesting,' Vi said. 'I didn't know Kathleen had had a difficult childhood.'

'I think we all did to some degree,' Fidelma said. 'People were generally poor in those days. The war years were not easy, even though Ireland was not involved.'

'I can imagine,' Vi said. 'Especially in Kerry. So Kathleen would have felt that growing up here.'

'Oh, yes, she would,' Fidelma said with feeling. 'Her parents didn't approve at all. She ran away from home and hid in some kind of hostel while she worked as a cleaner while she went to drama school. Then she got small parts in plays and managed to live on the meagre wages from that.'

'I had no idea,' Vi said, taken aback. 'There's nothing about that in her biography.'

'I think she wanted to keep that quiet,' Fidelma said. 'It wasn't the kind of thing she wanted people to know.'

'I see.' Vi felt a dart of pity mingled with admiration for Kathleen. It must have been difficult to make ends meet and to go against the wishes of her parents. She seemed to have fought hard to realise her dreams. 'I suppose cinema was really what she wanted to do,' she suggested.

'I think so. Do you dance yourself?' Fidelma asked.

'No,' Vi replied, startled by the sudden change of subject. 'I did a bit of Irish dancing when I was younger, but that's all.'

'Maybe you should have lessons,' Fidelma suggested. 'If you want to move as gracefully as Kathleen. I think body language and way of moving are important in this case.'

'That's a good idea,' Vi said. 'I think there is a school of dance in Dingle. Only for children but I could ask if I could have private lessons perhaps.'

'Excellent,' Fidelma said.

'So could you tell me a bit more about Kathleen?' Vi asked. 'I'd love to know as much as I can about her.'

'Not much more to tell,' Fidelma said. 'She left the school as soon as she got that offer from Hollywood. So I only knew her for a little over a year.'

'Oh,' Vi said, disappointed. 'I was hoping...'

'But,' Fidelma interrupted, 'we formed a close friendship

during that year. I think she saw me as a younger sister to whom she could tell things nobody else knew.'

'Oh,' Vi said. 'Like what?'

'It's a little complicated to talk about it over the phone. But I have letters you might be interested in. We wrote to each other, you see. And sent cards at Christmas. She told me all about what she was doing and who she met and so on. Fascinating for me who had just done a bit of dancing for fun and then went on to get married and raise a family. Those letters were the high point of Christmas for me. A little hard to read as Kathleen's handwriting was not the best. Not exactly calligraphy, if you know what I mean,' she added, laughing.

'Gosh,' Vi said, her heart beating faster at the thought of reading those letters. 'I would love to read them. Would it be possible for you to send copies to me?'

'I suppose,' Fidelma said, sounding doubtful. 'You can see the originals, if you like. If I can find them. My house is not very tidy these days. I still live in the same house my husband and I bought over sixty years ago. He passed away three years ago and now I'm on my own. My children keep telling me to move to somewhere smaller, but who is going to sort out the house and put it up for sale and all that, I wonder? They're all too busy to help.'

'I can imagine,' Vi said, feeling sorry for the old lady. It must be hard to sit in a big old house full of things from the past. 'Moving house is always difficult.'

'It'll be like moving a mountain,' Fidelma said with a sigh. 'I'm lucky I can still manage on my own, or it would be the old folks' home for me. I'm dreading the day that will happen.'

'It might not,' Vi soothed. 'You seem very fit and healthy to me.'

'But I'm old,' Fidelma said. 'Sorry to be so gloomy. You didn't call me to hear me complain. In any case, whenever I have to move to that home, my children will have to come and sort out the house without me. Then they'll be sorry they didn't do it sooner.'

'I'm sure,' Vi said, not quite knowing what else to say. She was dying to see those letters but it didn't look as if Fidelma could even find them if she still had them. This whole conversation was turning into a wild goose chase. The only thing she had learned was that Kathleen had had a difficult childhood and that she was good at dancing. Not much to go on.

'I will look for those letters,' Fidelma promised. 'I have a feeling you should see them. Much to learn about Kathleen and some of it might surprise you. I'll contact Finbarr as soon as I've found the box and have him send it to you. That's all I can do.'

'That's very kind,' Vi said, touched by the old woman's willingness to help. 'I have a feeling it will help me be more like her.'

'Oh, you wouldn't want to be like her in real life,' Fidelma said. 'Only in the movie, I mean. She wasn't quite what she pretended... Well, you'll find out in time. It was good to talk to you, Violet. Goodbye.' Fidelma hung up without waiting for an answer.

After that abrupt end to the conversation, Vi sat there for a while, thinking about what Fidelma had said. There was something that felt ominous, as if Kathleen had had some kind of trauma in her life that had changed her. Vi wondered if she really wanted to play Kathleen after all. She knew the director wanted to tell Kathleen's story, mostly her romance, but it sounded like there was much more to Kathleen than that, much more that they hadn't even bothered to find out. *Why not?* she wondered. *And if I find something shocking in Kathleen's past, will I still want to play her when I know the truth?*

Vi was startled out of her reverie by the doorbell. Who could be at the front door? Most people in Kerry would call at the back door of a house so this felt unusual. Was it the post-man? No, he had been earlier that day. The bell rang again. Puzzled, Vi opened the door and stared in shock at the person on the doorstep.

10

'Leo!' she exclaimed. 'What are you doing here?'

Leo grinned. 'I had a gap between jobs so then I decided to come to Ireland for a break. It's my aunt's sixtieth birthday on Sunday as well and they're throwing one of those great Irish parties. Thought I'd come and look you up as I was in the neighbourhood, so now I'm here.' He drew breath. Dressed in a leather bomber jacket and jeans, he looked quite different to the shy young man she had met in London. His blue eyes sparkled and his cheeks were rosy from the wind.

'Cork is not the neighbourhood,' Vi said, laughing. 'Or anywhere near it.' She glanced behind him and spotted a motorbike on the gravel. 'I like your mode of travel, though.'

'Yeah, it's great,' Leo agreed. 'My cousin was kind enough to lend it to me for the day.'

Vi opened the door wider. 'Come in,' she said. 'Sorry to have you standing there without inviting you in. It was just that I was so startled to see you.'

'I should have called you,' Leo said, looking contrite as he hovered on the doorstep. 'I'm sure you're busy with your family.'

'Not at all,' Vi assured him. 'I had lunch with my granny earlier and I've just had a long conversation with an old lady who knew Kathleen O'Sullivan when she was young. How about a cup of coffee?' she asked over her shoulder as she walked inside with Leo following behind her. 'Or tea or water? I'm afraid I have no beer or anything stronger.'

'I don't need anything stronger,' Leo said. 'I have to drive that thing back later. I only have it for the day. My cousin wants it back tonight. It's his most precious possession.'

'How kind of him to let you borrow it,' Vi remarked as they walked into the living room.

'Well...' Leo paused, looking a little guilty. 'I didn't actually ask. It was there in the driveway with the key in it. So I thought I'd go for a bit of a spin. I love motorbikes, you see.'

Vi stared at Leo. 'What? You just took it? Won't he be furious when he finds out?'

'Maybe. But he'll be so happy to see it back in one piece he'll accept my apologies and understand the reason.'

'What reason was that?' Vi asked.

'That I needed to go and see a woman I'll be working with I a few months,' Leo replied. 'You, I mean. Anyway, he's a good sport and won't make too much of a fuss once I take him out for a beer. We're very close, actually.'

'You'd want to be,' Vi remarked. 'Sit down and I'll get some coffee. Or do you prefer tea?'

'Coffee would be great,' Leo said. 'I had a burger and chips in town so don't bother making me anything to eat.'

'I wasn't going to,' Vi said, laughing. 'But I could open a packet of ginger snaps if you like.'

'Amazing,' Leo said with a glint of laughter in his eyes. 'I'm touched that you'd do that for me.'

'Relax there on the sofa while get the coffee and stuff,' Vi said and went into the kitchen. She was delighted to see Leo again. She had liked him from the start and had been touched by his kindness during the photo shoot. He was the only one of the film crew she felt comfortable with – except for Jack Montgomery, but that felt more like a flirtation she didn't quite know how to handle. With Jack, she had been excited and slightly nervous, but Leo made her feel completely at ease.

Leo was wandering around the room when she came back with the coffee and biscuits, and turned from the bookcase as she put the tray on the little coffee table. 'Some great books here,' he said. 'I haven't seen such an eclectic library in a while. Poetry, detective stories, nature books, romance and history. Have you read them all?'

'No,' Vi said as she settled on the sofa and pulled her legs up under her. 'Those are books my sisters left when they moved out. Lily likes detective stories and romance, Rose read a lot of poetry at some stage and Noel, her husband, is the nature and history buff.'

'And what are you interested in?' Leo asked as he joined her on the sofa.

'I read everything,' Vi said. 'But I do love a good romantic comedy, I have to confess. And a cosy detective story is great too.'

He nodded. 'I like that kind of book from time to time too.'

'I also like a good horror story,' Vi said. 'Stephen King and so on. But never before going to sleep.'

'I know what you mean,' Leo replied. He leaned forward and studied Vi for a moment. 'How about doing a horror film? Would you like that?'

Vi giggled. 'Oh yes, I would. That would be such great craic. How about you? Do you like doing makeup for that kind of movie?'

'Love it,' Leo said. 'Then I can really lay it on. I could make you up like a zombie. Black-rimmed eyes, dark lips and with your pale skin you'd be perfect. I'd paint a drop of blood beside your mouth too.'

'That would make me look like a vampire,' Vi said, laughing again. 'But hey, why not? That'd be a hoot.'

'Pity Kathleen didn't do any of those movies,' Leo remarked and picked up his mug of coffee. 'She was mostly in romantic stories.'

Vi nibbled on a ginger snap. 'Hmm, yes, but she was also in some historical dramas like *Jane Eyre* and *A Tale of Two Cities* by Dickens. I thought she was terrific in those. I hope I get to wear some of those costumes in the biopic.'

'You might,' Leo said. 'That was around the time she met Don.'

Vi nodded. She drank her coffee and looked at Leo. 'If you could go back in time to any period, what would it be?'

'Oh,' Leo said, looking thoughtful. 'Paris in the nineteen twenties, perhaps. Have you seen the Woody Allen movie *Midnight in Paris*? The guy in that story went back in time and met all those authors and painters. Wouldn't that be something?'

'Nah,' Vi said. 'I don't think so. I'd go to London in the sixties. That was a fun period. The music, the clothes – what an amazing time it must have been. Some of those film stars and the musicians, wow.'

'Mick Jagger, Paul McCartney,' Leo said. 'Of course, they're still alive.'

'In those days they would have been real rebels, I bet,' Vi remarked.

'Maybe we're better off now, though,' Leo suggested. 'The past looks great in movies but I'm sure real life was full of negatives, just like it is for us.'

'Yeah, I suppose.' Vi took another ginger snap. 'But it would be cool to go back and meet Kathleen, I have to say. I'd be able to ask her a few questions and then get back in the time machine and know exactly how to play her.'

'Now all you have are the old movies.' Leo put his mug on the table.

'I have to watch more of them to get a real feel for her. But there is one thing I will find very difficult,' Vi said, changing the subject.

'What's that?' Leo leaned back on the sofa, looking at Vi with interest.

'The smoking. In all those movies, everyone smokes, including Kathleen. It's as if lighting a woman's cigarette was a flirty moment.'

Leo grinned. 'Oh yeah, I bet it was. You get in very close, light the cig and then gaze into her eyes with a smouldering look that says more than a million words. Then she gives a sultry look back and blows out the smoke through those red lips. Very suggestive.'

'Yeah, but do I have to start smoking now?' Vi asked miserably.

'No, they always use prop cigarettes when filming now. It should be in your contract that you agreed to smoking on set, even if it's only herbal cigarettes or vapes,' Leo explained.

'Oh, I see.' Vi brightened. She normally paid so much attention to what she signed, but she'd been so excited when she'd eventually got the papers, desperate to get to Ireland. 'I think I saw that when we went through the contract. To be honest, I was so delighted to do this part that I'd have signed anything. But now I feel better about that, so thanks.'

'You're welcome. I'm sure you can't wait to get started.'

'Of course.' Vi nodded. 'But I have to do a lot of work beforehand.'

'Including having a drink with Jack Montgomery?' Leo asked. 'How did that go?'

'Oh, it was great,' Vi replied dreamily. 'He was very charming and fun. We got on really well.'

'Good, but don't be too starstruck around him. He has quite a big head as it is.'

'Of course he does,' Vi exclaimed. 'He's a talented actor. Why wouldn't he be proud of that?'

'Yeah, I suppose he's earned it.'

'I'd say he has,' Vi said. 'But I feel there's a nice man behind all the glamour. Right now he's in his prime, I think.'

'At his age, he should be.'

'Thirty-six must be a good age for a man,' Vi remarked. 'It's different for a woman. I'm already quite old for some parts.'

Leo looked surprised. 'But you're only in your twenties. I was just thinking about how I'm going to age you for the movie.'

'I'm about to turn thirty,' Vi said glumly.

'Welcome to the club.' Leo smiled at her. 'I turned thirty last year. It doesn't hurt at all.'

'You're a man and you're not an actor,' Vi retorted. 'For me, the party's over.'

'Of course not,' Leo protested. 'The best is yet to come, you know. Life is not about age, it's about your attitude to it.'

'That makes me feel marginally better.'

'That's good to hear.' Leo got up. 'But now I have to get back or my cousin will call the Guards on me.'

Vi scrambled to her feet. 'Okay. But it was great to see you.'

'I'll be back around Christmas,' Leo said.

'Give me a shout then and come over and meet my granny,' Vi suggested.

'If I can steal the bike again, I'll come over,' Leo promised.

'Sure, there are buses and trains, too, you know,' Vi retorted, smiling.

'Of course. But the bike is more fun.' Leo walked out to the hall and through the open front door. He zipped up his jacket and put on the helmet he had left hanging on the motorbike. 'Good luck with the research,' he said, his voice muffled by the visor of the helmet. 'I'm sure next time we meet, you'll be so like Kathleen we'll think she's back from the dead.'

'Oh, go on out of that,' Vi said, laughing. 'I won't go that far.'

'Get some fake cigarettes and practise the smoking,' Leo said before he kickstarted the bike. 'Thanks for the coffee and chat,' he shouted before he took off through the gates.

Vi shook her head and laughed as she watched the taillight disappear. What a fun guy Leo was. She knew she'd enjoy working with him. But while they chatted, she had felt a little shiver of fear at the pressure she was under. Everyone had such high expectations. If she failed to represent Kathleen accurately, she'd be out of a job. In the heat of their argument Rose had said Vi put her career before her family, and that one day she'd realise it wasn't worth it. If she failed to play Kathleen to perfection, her sisters would be proven right.

11

Sitting in the orangery with a cup of coffee, Vi read through the script very quickly. It was a good place to sit on a winter's day, with the mellow winter sun streaming in through the tall windows, illuminating everything outside in a golden hue. She stared at the walled garden with its neat flowerbeds and clipped hedges, thinking what a wonderful job Lily had done with the space. It truly had an old-world atmosphere and anyone walking around would feel themselves transported to the early 1800s when vegetables and fruit for the household were grown here. The orangery itself consisted of one big room with the stonework exposed. The restored tiled floor now had underfloor heating to make it more comfortable on cooler days. The café was closed but Sylvia was at the counter helping with accounts and inventory, so she had said to Vi she could sit here today if she wanted a change of scene. 'I'll put the heating on for you and leave you alone,' Sylvia promised. Vi had been grateful to get out of the house on this cold, windy day despite the sunshine. Sitting in the garden was not an option today.

Vi turned back to the script, and tried to assess what she thought of it. The dialogue was good and the scene settings excellent and it gave her a good idea of the feel of the movie. But there were a few things missing, such as Kathleen's fiery temper and the stormy relationship between her and Don that weren't touched on in much detail. But Vi couldn't make notes of how that could be changed as she didn't have enough information. She made another attempt to speak to Fidelma Sheridan the following day, but there was no answer. She tried again just after six o'clock with the same result. The old lady might have gone away for some reason, or be spending time with her children and grandchildren. Vi decided to keep trying, just to get some more information about Kathleen O'Sullivan and what she had been like in private. Anything at all, some small detail would bring her closer to the woman she was about to portray. It probably wouldn't be as bad as she imagined.

Vi thought about the conversation with Fidelma and her suggestions that Vi should study ballet. She decided to contact the school of dance in Dingle to see if she could have private lessons. A sweet woman's voice answered the phone and when Vi explained who she was and why she was calling, there was huge excitement.

'Oh wow, I read about that movie in *The Irish Times*,' she said. 'My name is Claire Ryan, by the way. I'd be happy to give you a few lessons. Have you ever done classical ballet before?'

'No,' Vi replied. 'Just a bit of Irish dancing. But I do yoga whenever I can, so I'm quite flexible.'

'That sounds like a good start,' Claire said. 'We could begin with basic barre exercises to get you going and then a little floor work to get that softness that Kathleen had in her movements. I saw some of her movies on TV a long time ago and as a dancer I noticed how graceful she was. Oh gosh, I can't believe I'll be working with a real live film star!'

'Well, I wouldn't go that far,' Vi said, laughing. 'I'm just a jobbing actress.'

'Now, yes,' Claire said. 'But gee, when that movie comes out you'll be so famous. And you'll be acting with Jack Montgomery as well. Your sisters must be so excited.'

'I don't know,' Vi said drily. 'So far there hasn't been much excitement from them.'

'But your niece Naomi comes to classes here.' Claire sounded confused. 'She said her auntie was going to be in a movie.'

'I didn't know Naomi did ballet,' Vi said.

'Oh yes, she does,' Claire said. 'She's only five but she's really good. Very sweet girl.'

'I know,' Vi said, not wanting to reveal the fact that she hadn't seen Naomi since last Christmas. Just before that horrible row. 'She's a gorgeous kid.'

'Loves her auntie, she said. I'm sure she's excited that you're here now. Will you be around long?'

'Yes, I plan to stay until we start shooting. I have to do a lot of research and preparations,' Vi explained.

'Brilliant. Then you'll have plenty of time to practise dance and movement,' Claire said. 'And to come and see Naomi in our Christmas show. She's going to be one of the little fairies. So when would you like to start? I'm free most mornings. Afternoons are very busy.'

'As soon as possible,' Vi said.

'Great. How about tomorrow morning?' Claire suggested.

'That would be perfect. I could come at ten o'clock,' Vi said.

'Grand. My studio is at the top of Goat Street. Number twenty-five. There's a red car in front of it.'

'I'll find it. See you then,' Vi said.

'Looking forward to it. Bye for now.'

Vi said goodbye, happy to have made the appointment. Then, on an impulse she looked up Lily's number in her contact list and called it. Better get it over with, and even if Lily refused to see her, the ball would be in her court.

It rang a few times and then a little voice said: 'Lily Doyle's phone, Naomi speaking. Mum is busy right now because Liam had pulled down all the dishes from the table and there's an awful mess and Mum is really cross with him.' She drew breath. 'Who's this on the phone?' she asked.

'It's your auntie Violet,' Vi said, smiling at the long diatribe from her little niece.

'Wow,' Naomi said. 'My famous auntie?' Then there was a noise as if she had dropped the phone and Vi could hear Naomi shout: 'Mum, it's Auntie Vi on the phone. Come quick before she goes away!'

Then Lily seemed to have picked up the phone. 'Hello,' she said. 'Is that you, Vi? What do you want? I'm really busy. Can't talk, the kids are acting up and I have to clear some broken china before there's a nasty accident. I was putting all my cups and saucers on the table for my Christmas café event in a few weeks to see what I needed. My au pair has just left and I have nobody to help.'

'I could come over,' Vi offered, noticing the panic in her sister's voice. This would be a great opportunity to earn some brownie points and make Lily feel more positive about Vi.

'What?' Lily asked. 'You'd come over here? I got your message on my voicemail, so I knew you were here. I wasn't really in the mood to call you back, to be honest. Well, you're not exactly my favourite person after all the stuff you said. But oh, right now I'd be happy for any help I can get from anyone. Even from you. When can you come?'

'Right now,' Vi said, jumping at the chance. 'I'll borrow Granny's car. I can be with you in ten minutes.'

'Okay,' Lily said and hung up.

Vi quickly called her grandmother and asked if she could borrow her car, explaining where she was going, to which Sylvia heaved a sigh of relief and said, 'Finally. Maybe this will be the best moment to make peace. I'd go myself but the accountant is coming to do the figures for the past year. Has to be done before Christmas. Of course you can have the car.'

'Okay, thanks. I'll be up at the house in a few minutes.' Vi hung up and grabbed her bag and her jacket.

It didn't take her long to run up the path to the manor and as Sylvia was at the door with the car key, she could jump in and start the car at once.

'This is a golden opportunity for you to make up,' Sylvia said before she closed the door. 'Eat as much humble pie as you can, it won't hurt a bit.'

'I will,' Vi promised and took off, happy the car was an automatic and easy to drive.

The trip to Ventry didn't take more than fifteen minutes and she parked the car just above the beautiful bay, where the blue-green water lapped the white sands of the beach. She fleetingly thought of the many outings and picnics to this lovely spot when she was a child, before she started down the narrow lane to Lily and Dominic's house.

The green door flew open before Vi had a chance to knock and Lily, with a little boy balanced on her hip, pulled her sister inside and slammed the door shut behind her. She handed Vi the boy. 'Here, take him for a moment, willya? I have to sweep up the broken china before Naomi cuts her feet to ribbons. That's Liam, by the way.'

'Of course it is,' Vi said and smiled at the little boy, who looked at her with huge brown eyes. His dark hair was ruffled and the front of his T-shirt was covered in mashed banana. 'Hi, Liam, we met last year and then you were just a baby. But now, look at you. Such a big boy.'

'Big boy,' Liam said and stuck his thumb in his mouth.

'Auntie Vi!' a voice shouted as Vi walked into the large bright living room. A little girl with brown hair and her father's dark green eyes rushed forward and threw her arms around Vi's legs.

'Hi, Naomi,' Vi said and crouched down, still holding little Liam. 'You have grown so big since the last time I saw you.'

Naomi nodded. 'Yes, cos I eat my dinner all up and go to sleep and practise my dancing. And I go to school now and learn my letters.' She drew breath and looked at Vi. 'Mum said you have a nerve to come back here. What's a nerve and where do you have it?'

'Oh eh... I'll explain later,' Vi said, shooting a look at Lily. Then she noticed the mess of broken crockery all over the polished floorboards. 'Maybe we should help Mum to clear this up? Looks like a huge explosion happened here.'

Naomi giggled. 'No, it was Liam. He pulled down the table-cloth but I don't think it was on purpose. It was an accident. Mum had put all that stuff on the table because she needs cups and plates and things for the Christmas coffee party at the café.'

'Stupid of me,' Lily said behind them as she started to clean up the mess with a sweeping brush. 'I should have known some-thing would happen with a two-year-old toddling around, pulling at everything. I usually have help with the kids, but the au pair just left to go home to Germany for Christmas.'

'Her name is Gretel,' Naomi piped up. 'But she has no brother called Hansel. I asked and she said no. And she has never been lost in the forest and met the witch. That's just a story, you know.'

'Yes, I thought it might not be true,' Vi said as she sat down on the blue sofa that faced the picture window with spectacular views of the sea. She bounced Liam on her knee which made him chuckle. 'Again,' he shouted when she stopped, so she bounced him again and he laughed and laughed.

'Could you bring him upstairs to the nursery and change his T-shirt?' Lily asked.

'Okay.' Vi got up and holding Liam at arm's length away

from her beige cashmere sweater, she carried him across the floor to the hall and up the stairs. Naomi trailed behind them, chatting away, filling Vi in on her life's ups and downs.

'My teacher says I'm getting *very* good at reading,' she said. 'But my best friend Nuala is even better. I think her mum helps her a lot but my mum can't because she's too busy with Liam and the café and helping Daddy with his accounts and sometimes even going to Uncle Noel's office to do some work there when Vicky is off sick. That's Uncle Noel's secretary.'

'I know,' Vi said as she entered a bright room with pictures of Winnie the Pooh and Paddington Bear and other nursery characters on the walls. There was a bed beside a chest of drawers against the far wall and the green carpet was strewn with toys. The curtains had a pattern of tiny flowers and leaves and little Bambi figures here and there. It was a charming child's room and Vi stood for a moment looking around, then gazed out the window at the view of the mountains. 'Lovely room,' she said, putting Liam on the bed.

'My room is even nicer,' Naomi stated. 'Liam's room is a mess.'

'Just a few toys,' Vi said absentmindedly while she pulled out a drawer looking for a clean T-shirt. 'We can tidy it up very quickly. I'll just change Liam's shirt and then we'll go and look at your room.'

'Okay,' Naomi said.

Vi found a T-shirt with Mickey Mouse on the front and managed to change Liam into it, despite his wriggling and trying to get away. Once he had it on, she took him by the hand and they all walked into Naomi's room that was very similar to Liam's except for the Barbie bedspread and a blue carpet. 'Very nice,' Vi said, smiling at Naomi.

Naomi sat on the bed and pulled a large storybook from under the pillow. 'Read us a story,' she ordered. 'I love the one about Rapunzel. Read us that one.'

'Only if you ask nicely,' Vi said, settling on the bed with a now sleepy-looking Liam on her lap.

'*Puleese*, darling Auntie Vi, read us a story,' Naomi pleaded as she handed Vi the book. 'Rapunzel is on page twenty-five,' she said.

Vi couldn't help laughing. She took the book and started reading while Liam leaned his head against her chest and Naomi listened intently, filling in when Vi paused for breath. When Vi had finished reading, she found that Liam had fallen asleep. 'Will I wake him up?' she asked Naomi.

'No, put him in his bed and let him sleep for a while,' Naomi instructed. 'That way we'll get some peace for a bit. That's what Gretel says anyway. And don't forget to close the gate at the top of the stairs when we go down.'

'Okay.' Vi laid Liam on the bed and covered him with a blanket. Then they tiptoed out of the room and went downstairs, not forgetting the gate.

'Where's Liam?' Lily asked when they came into the now cleaned-up living room.

'Asleep on Naomi's bed,' Vi replied.

'Oh no,' Lily moaned. 'I should have told you not to let him go to sleep. Now it'll be all hours before we get him down tonight.'

'Sorry,' Vi said. 'I had no idea. He was so sleepy, I didn't have the heart to wake him.'

'I told Auntie Vi to do it,' Naomi piped up. 'I wanted some peace and quiet so we could read the story.'

'I bet you did,' Lily said drily. 'Well, whatever. You can watch *Dora* while Vi and I have a cup of tea.'

'Okay,' Naomi said and sat down on a cushion in front of the flatscreen TV on the far wall. She picked up the remote and expertly turned the TV to her favourite channel.

'Let's have tea in the kitchen,' Lily suggested. 'Sit down at the breakfast bar and we'll talk. I think we need to sort some things out.'

The breakfast bar divided the kitchen area from the living room and the window on the gable end provided a view of both the mountains and the sea. Vi sat down on a high stool and watched Lily turn on the kettle and take two mugs out of a cupboard. 'No cups left, after Liam's little shenanigans,' Lily remarked.

'What are you going to do about crockery for the café Christmas thing?' Vi asked.

'I'll get some stuff from the ballroom. There's china there for events such as weddings and other kinds of parties. I should have asked to use that instead of my own, but my stuff is much nicer. Silly of me. And the crockery in the café is okay, only it's all white. It'll be fine. But I'm a little sad about what was broken here, though.'

'I'm so sorry,' Vi said sympathetically. 'It must be tough to mind two children and have all these things to do as well.'

'It's my own fault,' Lily said, putting tea bags into the mugs. 'I take on too much, Dominic says. And I do. I must learn to say no. I should maybe take a year off and get someone else to run the café.' She sighed, looking sad. 'But that's the one thing I love the most. Running the café and the garden centre. Getting my hands dirty with plants and flowers. Seeing people sitting in the orangery and in the garden having coffee and enjoying the beautiful scenery. I just love that so much. It's a great break from the kids and the housework.'

'Then you shouldn't give it up,' Vi said. 'But maybe you could cut down on the other stuff? Naomi said you do Dom's accounts and chip in at Noel's office when his secretary is off sick. Would it not be better if you weren't available to everyone all the time, like everyone's big sister?'

Lily let out a laugh. 'Yeah, I know what you mean. But how can I do that? They're all so used to having me as a backup.'

'You just have to put your foot down,' Vi remarked.

'Easy for you to say,' Lily retorted, her eyes turning cold as she looked at Vi. 'But right now, we need to talk about that enormous elephant in the room. What you said in that interview was horrible. How could you betray your own family like that?'

Shocked by the venom in Lily's voice, Vi didn't know how to reply. But then, feeling suddenly fed up with being the culprit for so long, she decided to attack rather than defend. She found she didn't care any more what her sister thought of her. The truth had to come out and then, even if Lily didn't see her side of the story, she'd walk away and never look back. Vi took a deep breath and tried yet again to explain what had happened.

12

Vi began to speak. 'Look, Lily, I have tried and tried to make you all understand what happened. That journalist twisted my words and made it look completely different to what I actually said. She didn't mention the part where I said that I sometimes felt I could change places with *you*. That I often just want to come home, find a nice man and have a family, just like you. But she didn't include that part of the conversation.' Vi drew breath. 'That's the truth. I wish you could believe me and try to understand. Mum, Granny and Nora believe me, but you won't.'

Lily stared back at Vi without speaking. While they looked at each other, time seemed to roll back to the days when Vi had been a little girl, lost in a world of grieving adults. Lily had been the one to help then, to tuck Vi into bed at night, read her stories and stay with her until she went to sleep. Lily had been Vi's rock for a long time and she had always turned to Lily first when she needed help and support. How she longed to have her big sister back like in the old days.

'Can I just tell you that I'm a little scared?' Vi said in a low voice. 'This is my big break, but what if I fail? I feel so alone sometimes. We've been distant for so long but now I want my big sister back.'

Lily still didn't respond.

Giving up the battle, Vi got up. 'I'll leave now. Maybe you need to think about all this.'

'Wait.' Lily suddenly grabbed Vi's arm. 'Don't go. I'm beginning to see your side of it. Not that I don't think it was really stupid of you to trust a journalist, especially one who writes for one of those local rags, but...' She paused. 'I can see how it happened.'

Vi sat down again. 'Good. I'm so relieved you're finally beginning to see it from my point of view. Yes, you're right, it was stupid of me. To be honest, though, I never really understood why you and Rose were so angry.'

'Probably because it was true,' Lily said in a flat tone. 'We *were* jealous of you at that time. We were both coping with babies and nappies and broken sleep. Rose had put on a lot of weight before she had her baby and she was exhausted after the birth. Neither of us looked our best, and there you were, looking glamorous and young, probably flying off to LA and all kinds of fabulous places to shoot movies. Who wouldn't be pea-green with envy about that? Especially on a Monday in January when the washing machine breaks down, the rain is lashing down outside, the kids are crying and...'

'Oh,' Vi said, taken aback. 'I didn't realise. Possibly because my life is a lot less glamorous than you think. I don't get to fly first class, you know. Or stay in five-star hotels. I haven't been playing any main characters at all until right now, when I got this break. It's been quite a slog, to be honest. That trip to LA last January was for an audition that resulted in nothing. Then I had this small part in a terrible drama series that just ended. I was about to give up acting and look for some kind of job, any job, when my agent told me about this biopic and that they had chosen me for the part.' She picked up her mug and took a sip of tea, her throat suddenly dry. 'So that's the reality of my so-called glamorous life.'

'I suppose an actor's life is different to what we imagine,' Lily remarked.

'And I suppose a mother's is too.'

'That's for sure.' Lily drained her mug and put it down. 'Okay, now that we've cleared the air, so to speak, and I have said sorry for all the...' She stopped. 'I didn't, did I?' She paused and cleared her throat. 'Vi, I'm really sorry I got so angry,' she continued. 'Now that you have explained, I understand what happened and that you didn't mean what we thought you meant. Maybe it was partly your fault but let's move on.'

Vi heaved a sigh of relief. 'Oh, yes, please. Can we put it all behind us and not talk about it any more?' She looked at Lily, not wanting to reveal what she really thought; that Lily had somehow taken a step down, leaving a brilliant career and a glamorous lifestyle to live here, in the country where nothing much happened in the wintertime. It was a beautiful place to visit and when the weather was nice, there was nowhere in the world lovelier to spend a holiday. But to live here permanently didn't seem like a good choice.

'Of course,' Lily replied with a bright smile. 'It was getting a little boring.' They both laughed and Lily held out her arms. 'Come here and give me a big hug.'

Close to tears, Vi fell into Lily's arms and hugged her tight. 'Oh, this feels so good,' she mumbled. 'Thank you for listening and forgiving me.'

'I'm happy to have it all behind us,' Lily declared, pulling away. 'But now I want to hear all about the movie and Jack Montgomery.'

'Oh, well,' Vi started as she sat up, 'it's a bit—' She was interrupted by a wailing from upstairs.

'Liam,' Lily said. 'Hang on, I'll get him. He'll be all grizzly and grumpy for a while after that sleep.'

'Mum, I'm hungry,' Naomi called from in front of the TV. 'Can I have a bikkie?'

'Not this close to dinner,' Lily replied. 'But Auntie Vi will get you a carrot stick to chew on and then we'll have fish fingers with chips.' Lily looked at Vi. 'Can you stay and help me for a bit longer?'

'Of course,' Vi said. 'Fish fingers are my favourite.'

The evening turned out to be very pleasant, if a little stressful as Vi tried her best to help with the children while Lily cooked dinner and talked to Dominic, who had just arrived home. With him was Larry, a large white fluffy dog of uncertain pedigree who romped around with the children causing even more chaos than before.

When Vi was finally saying goodbye, both children were tucked up in bed fast asleep, the kitchen tidy and Lily and Dominic were settled in front of the TV to watch the late-evening news, Larry at their feet.

When Vi got up to leave, Lily hugged her goodbye. 'Thank you so much for coming,' she said. 'I'm so glad we had that talk.'

'Me too,' Vi said. 'I'm so happy to have my sister back.'

'One of them, anyway,' Lily said. 'You still have to tackle Rose.'

'I know, but I'll leave her alone for now.'

'Good idea. She's a tougher nut than me to crack. You know how she can stay mad for a long time.'

'Yeah, I remember how she let Henri stew for ages before she forgave him.'

'And now they're the best of friends and work so well together managing the senior apartment business,' Lily said. 'Anyway, you were great with the kids. You managed to calm them down and me too.'

'I enjoyed it. They're adorable. Let me know if you need help. I'm relatively free right now, so don't be afraid to ask,' Vi offered. 'I mean it.'

'I hope you won't regret that,' Lily said, smiling. 'Because I do need help and a lot of it. I'll call you tomorrow and we can work out some kind of plan.'

'Grand,' Vi said. 'I'll do my best to help you whenever I can.'

'And then I'll also want a full report on Jack Montgomery,' Lily added as they walked to the door.

'Not much to report,' Vi said. 'I had a drink with him before I left London, that's all.'

'That's all?' Lily rolled her eyes. 'You had a drink with Jack Montgomery in London? There you go again, making me jealous,' she teased.

Vi laughed.

Lily pushed Vi out the door. 'Now go home and get some rest. And tell Granny we're friends again. And Mum if you talk to her. I know she's busy with all that probate stuff in Donegal, but if you're in touch with her, let her know what happened.'

'I will,' Vi promised. Then Lily closed the door and Vi walked away, feeling happier than she had been for a very long time. She and Lily were close again and even though she still had to tackle Rose, it felt good to have had that talk and to have helped out when Lily needed her. She had meant what she said, the children were truly adorable, even if they were hard work at times. She was looking forward to coming back and playing with her little niece and nephew. It would be a break from preparing for her role and all the work associated with it.

Vi's phone rang just as she had pulled up in front of the gatehouse. She turned off the engine and checked the number. It was a UK mobile phone number she didn't recognise. She hesitated for a moment and then decided to answer.

'Violet Fleury,' she said.

'Hi, Violet.'

The deep voice made her heart flutter. Could it be...? 'Hello?' she said. 'Who is this?'

'Jack Montgomery here,' he continued.

'Oh yes, of course. Hi,' she croaked.

'Forgive me for cold calling like this,' he continued, his voice full of laughter. 'I can tell it made you nervous. I hope I'm not disturbing you.'

'Not at all,' she said, finding her normal voice. 'Hi, Jack. How are you? How are things in LA?'

'I'm not in LA,' he said. 'I left as soon as the shooting was over. I'm on my way to Scotland for the next part of this movie I'm in. I had a few days off so I thought I'd come and see you.'

'What?' Vi said, her heart racing. 'You're coming to see me? When?'

'Well,' he drawled. 'Actually right now. I'm just outside Dingle, staying in this quaint little boutique hotel.'

'You mean The Dolphin?' Vi asked. It was a brand-new hotel in a restored Georgian house and it had just opened. 'You must be one of the first guests.'

'I think I must be,' Jack replied. 'It's very quiet but the room is great and room service excellent.'

'Oh good. They must have been so excited to have you stay there.'

'They don't know it's me,' Jack said mysteriously. 'I know how to be incognito. I think you'd laugh if you saw me when I arrived. Blond wig, steel-rimmed glasses, baggy sweatpants and a green anorak. Not fashionable but a great disguise. I called myself Bill Higgins from Birmingham, just so you know. I'm here to market a new line of waterproof hiking gear. Officially.'

Vi giggled. 'I love it.' She couldn't believe he was here just to see her and she assumed there had to be more to his story.

'I'm going to turn in now. I'm a little jetlagged after the trip from LA. But would it be possible to see you tomorrow?' Jack asked. 'I need someone to show me around the area.'

'Oh.' Vi tried to gather her thoughts. She didn't want to appear too eager even if she was dying to see him. 'Well, I'm busy tomorrow morning until lunchtime.'

'So lunch then?' he asked. 'And maybe a bit of a tour around the place afterwards?'

'I don't think lunch in Dingle is a good idea,' she said. 'I mean, I'm not in disguise and everyone knows me here. They know I'm playing Kathleen and you're playing Don. They're obsessed with Kathleen... *The Irish Times* article has spread the news. If I was to have lunch with... Bill Higgins, everyone in town would know about it within half an hour and start guessing and insinuating. I think your cover would be blown very quickly. They'd guess what was going on fairly soon.'

'Are you saying you won't see me?' he asked incredulously.

Vi realised no woman had ever hesitated like this when Jack Montgomery asked them out. 'I'm not saying that exactly. I've just had an idea. I'm guessing you rented a car?'

'Yes, I did. So?' he asked, now sounding slightly irritated.

'If you pick me up at my house, we could go over the mountain pass and have lunch in one of the villages on Tralee Bay. Like Cloghane, for example. A bit out of the way but it would be safer. That's if you want to stay incognito.'

'Sounds very quaint. Well, you're the local here and you know where to go. And yes, let's not attract too much attention to ourselves right now. Could be a bit stressful for you. When we start shooting the movie, it'll be a different story. But let's take it easy for now and just get to know each other. So yes, that's a good plan.'

'Wonderful,' Vi said, feeling breathless with excitement. 'Could you pick me up at the gatehouse of Magnolia Manor around twelve?'

'That sounds really romantic,' Jack remarked. 'And Magnolia Manor is where we'll be filming for a few weeks, I believe. Maybe we could take a peep at that too?'

'Of course we can,' Vi replied. She wondered, if there was a time, the café would be nice and quiet. 'Not much to see in the winter and all the upper floors are now apartments. But I can show you the ballroom and the library, if you like.'

'That would be interesting. So then I'll see you tomorrow at twelve.'

'That's absolutely perfect,' Vi said. 'I'm really looking forward to seeing you.'

'Splendid,' Jack said. 'Goodbye, Violet.'

'Sweet dreams,' Vi said without thinking. Then she hung up and sat in the darkness mentally kicking herself for gushing at him like that. *Why didn't I stay cool and calm?* she asked herself angrily. *And what was that I said? Sweet dreams? How utterly stupid. Now he'll think I'm a total eejit with a big schoolgirl crush on him. And what will I wear for this outing?*

Oh come on, get a grip, she told herself after a while. This was not a problem but an opportunity to get to know a man who had been her idol for a long time. Maybe the man behind the glamorous façade was completely different. Now she had a chance to find out. Not something anyone would actually complain about...

Laughing at herself, Vi got out of the car and went inside, trying to ger her heart and breathing to return to normal. But she couldn't stop herself being nervous. Jack was a big star with all that came of being very famous. He was spoilt and used to women fawning over him. But what was he like deep down? Maybe he would reveal his true self during the outing tomorrow. It would be fascinating to find out what he was like out of the limelight.

13

Vi's first private ballet lesson turned out more exhausting than she had imagined. Claire, the tall, lithe, dark-haired teacher, who looked to be about the same age as Vi, was a strict task master. Dressed in a black leotard, she put Vi through her paces, getting her to use muscles she didn't know she had. Claire showed her how to do pliés in all positions, except fifth, 'which is very hard for a beginner and it might result in you walking like a duck,' Claire explained. 'Not what we are after here, I think.'

It was hard to keep her back straight, shoulders down, head up and the arms lifted. Even though the movements were slow, Vi's body felt as if it had been through some kind of torture. Dripping with sweat, her face shiny, she finally came to a stop after a gruelling forty-five minutes. Her T-shirt stuck to her back and her hair was plastered to her head,

'Well done,' Claire said and handed Vi a towel and a bottle of water. 'I was a little mean to you but I wanted you to understand what the basic movements are.'

Vi leaned on the barre, wiped her face and drank deeply

from the bottle. 'If that were the basics, I wonder what the more advanced stuff will feel like.'

'Oh, I don't think we'll be too advanced,' Claire said. 'We'll stay with the basic exercises and just do a little floorwork next time. Movement to music, perfecting what I showed you today. You just need to learn to move with that Kathleen O'Sullivan grace. If you work hard it will eventually come naturally to you. I watched one of her movies online yesterday after our conversation, just to see what we need to do. She was incredibly light on her feet despite being quite statuesque. Straight back and a flexible body with that special walk and the way she held her head and shoulders were her trademark. She made it look so natural too.'

Vi nodded. 'I know. That's exactly what I'm after.'

'Thought so.' Claire walked across the floor with a light step, swinging her hips. 'Like this.'

Vi tried to imitate the walk but failed. She stopped when she saw her image in the large mirror and laughed. 'It'll take a while before I can do it, but I get what you mean.'

'You're tired,' Claire said. 'I think we've done enough for today.'

'Oh, yes.' Vi grabbed her green hoodie from the barre and pulled it over her T-shirt. 'There is so much to learn, though. But now I feel I need to take a break.' Then she put on her tracksuit pants over her leggings, draping the towel around her neck. 'I'll go home and have a long hot shower. And a lie-down,' she added. 'I need to rest before lunch and then try to look my best.'

'Why?' Claire asked. 'I mean, you look pretty good even now.'

'Well, it's... I have a date...' Vi blurted out. 'He's picking me up just before lunch and then we're going for a drive.'

'Just be yourself,' Claire said. 'I've found that's the best policy even with drop-dead gorgeous men.'

'Sweaty with no makeup?' Vi said, laughing as she caught sight of herself in the big mirror on the opposite wall. Her cheeks were bright red, her face shiny and her hair plastered to her head, the rest hanging limply in a ponytail.

'You're glowing,' Claire argued. 'But yeah, maybe tidy yourself up a bit, of course. Just don't lose that natural look you have. I always wanted a face full of freckles like you. It's so cute.'

'Cute?' Vi asked. She shook her head. 'I hated my freckles when I grew up.'

'Kathleen had them too,' Claire remarked. 'Except she must have covered most of them up with makeup and just left a sprinkle on her nose which made her look young.'

'Yes,' Vi agreed. 'I've noticed that too. No problem with that. The makeup artist is a genius. He made me up for that photo that was used in the press release.'

'That's an amazing shot,' Claire agreed. 'I thought it was kind of spooky when I saw it.'

'Oh, that was all Leo's work,' Vi said. 'He made me look exactly like her, except for the prosthetic nose. He did an excellent job.'

'He certainly did,' Claire said. 'So where are you going with this very attractive man you're meeting today? Is he a local?'

'No. He's never been here before,' Vi replied. 'So I thought I'd go over the Connor Pass and have lunch in Brandon village or Cloghane.'

'Or maybe do the Slea Head drive?' Claire suggested. 'That's very beautiful. And you could have lunch in Ballyferriter.'

'That's a great idea. I'll think about it.' Vi took another sip of water from the bottle. 'I have to go. I borrowed my grandmother's car and she'll want it back. Thank you so much for the lesson. When can we do it again?'

'I think you should come once a week and maybe practise at home as well,' Claire said. 'I'd say you'd need my help for a few weeks and then you should have the hang of it.' She paused. 'I have a feeling you really want to get into Kathleen's skin.'

'That's exactly it,' Vi said. 'I need to really *be* her, if you see what I mean. And I only have a few more months to prepare. I need to know a bit more about her too.'

'Well, she did live right here in Dingle for a year,' Claire said. 'Did you know that?'

'No, I didn't,' Vi said, surprised. 'When?'

'Just after she married Don. They lived in a house at the top of the hill.'

'How do you know?' Vi asked.

'Because my grandfather used to own that house. It's gone now, demolished when they started to build the new housing estate.'

'Oh. What a pity. I'm glad to know she was here, though. That makes me feel it's okay to shoot part of the movie around here. It revolves around the time she was married to Don, after all.' Vi patted her face. 'But now I really must run. See you... when?'

'Come back on Thursday at the same time,' Claire suggested.

'That would be grand.'

Vi said goodbye and rushed out of the house, not wanting to let Sylvia wait to get her car back. But then, instead of going down towards Magnolia Manor, she drove up the hill and pulled up beside a row of terraced houses. She got out, looking at the spectacular view of the bay, the ocean and the islands outlined against the sky. This would have been what Kathleen looked at during the time she lived in the house that was no longer there. Vi imagined that there might have been a bay window where Kathleen might have sat, enjoying the vista while she had tea or maybe a glass of wine. What a wonderful place to spend her first year married to the love of her life.

Vi stood there as the breeze blew her hair around her face

and cooled her cheeks, still hot from the dance lesson. She closed her eyes and breathed in the salt-laden air and felt as if she was standing at the top of the world, ready to fly away on the wind. Then she opened them again and laughed at the notion. She got back in the car and drove off, feeling oddly that she had come a tiny bit closer to the woman whose life she was about to recreate.

A red Audi pulled up outside the gatehouse at twelve thirty on the dot. Vi peeped out the window and watched as a tall blond man got out, bounded up the steps and rang the doorbell several times. She opened the door and stared at him. If she hadn't known it was Jack in disguise, she would have thought he was a complete stranger. His blond hair was long and shaggy and his teeth protruded slightly. But there was no mistaking the brown velvet eyes behind the steel-rimmed glasses and the long eyelashes or the wide smile. His green anorak and baggy pants didn't hide his tall, toned body, even if the outfit made him look just like anyone walking around the streets of Dingle or sitting at a bar counter in one of the pubs.

'Hello, Bill,' she said, smirking. 'How nice to see you.'

'And you, m'dear,' he replied and doffed his blue baseball cap. 'I've a nice range of waterproof hiking gear for sale in the car. Would you care to take a look?'

'No, I have plenty of hiking clothes, thanks,' Vi said. Then she pointed at the car. 'Is this what you call incognito?' she asked, relieved she had had the time to not only wash her hair but to put on her best jeans and navy cashmere sweater and to apply a little bit of makeup.

'Yeah, well, the car was the only thing the rental company could offer at short notice.'

'It's very cute, though,' Vi said and opened the front door wider. 'But come in for a bit before we go up to Magnolia.'

Jack stepped inside and looked around the hall and glanced into the living room. 'Nice house. You live here on your own?'

'Yes, I do. It belongs to my grandmother but whichever of us needs a roof over our heads can stay here. My sister Rose and her husband moved out a while ago so I could have it while I'm here.'

'You plan on staying long?' Jack asked.

'Yes. I have nothing much on so I thought I'd use the time before the movie gets going to get to know everything about Kathleen and work on being more like her,' Vi explained. 'I have to put on weight, perm my hair and learn how to smoke, according to Leo.'

Jack looked at her. 'Well, you look nice the way you are. But I get what you mean. I also have to get into Don's persona. Talk like him, walk like him and move like I've been riding horses all my life. They met in Kildare, at a place where you could ride horses. Did you know that?'

Vi nodded and smiled. 'Yeah, it was one of those country house hotels with stables, according to what I read online. I imagine that she was taking a break from filming after having broken her engagement for the second time. I have been wondering if she was homesick and wanted to go riding, so she flew to Ireland and went to this place just to be with horses.'

'And then she met the love of her life,' Jack said, looking at Vi in a way that made her face flush. 'Must have been a very romantic place. Just like the manor up there. She found love at long last.'

'It's a sweet story, but there might be things we don't know,' Vi said, thinking of the beginnings of secrets she was trying to uncover. She wondered if Jack had found out anything inter- esting about Don.

'I know. I think they were both a little damaged by life and lost love.' Jack shrugged. 'But aren't we all in one way or another? Can we go and see the manor now? I'd love to have a look at it.'

'Of course,' Vi said, wondering what he meant. He seemed to know more about Kathleen than she did. She decided to make him tell her during their outing. 'We can either drive or walk up there. Whatever you feel like.'

'Let's walk,' Jack said. 'Then I can get a feel for the gardens and see the house from a distance. But first I have to remove the fake teeth,' he said and pulled them out of his mouth, putting them into his pocket. 'I put them in to make you laugh.' He smiled, showing his own perfect teeth. 'There. Much better, you have to agree.'

'Absolutely,' Vi said, feeling that familiar dart of attraction. Today he was even more charming than before, looking at her with a warmth that hadn't been there the last time they'd met. Gone was the cool, slightly conceited expression of a man who was very sure of his appeal. Was this just his way of getting around her, or was it genuine?

'Let's get going, then,' he urged, moving to the open front door.

'Okay.' Vi shook herself out of her musings and took her jacket from a peg in the hall. 'Come this way. It's not far and it's not raining so we're in luck.'

'It's not a bad day,' Jack said as they went outside. 'Windy but with sunshine now and then. I love the salty smell in the air, the seagulls and the glimpse of the ocean through the trees.'

'Yes, it's really nice,' Vi agreed, zipping up her jacket once they were outside. 'There's nothing like the seaside.' His words made her suddenly realise that it was true. Being by the sea was certainly invigorating. She glanced at him as they started up the avenue towards the manor. 'Did you grow up by the sea?'

'No. We lived in Yorkshire. Near the moors. On a little sheep farm. Real Herriot territory.'

'Wow, I had no idea,' Vi said, surprised. 'I thought you were from London. You speak with that posh boarding-school accent.'

'Oh, that's what I picked up at drama school,' Jack replied. 'A kind of neutral British accent that Americans love. Got me a lot of parts, especially in period dramas. But you should hear me when I'm with my folks at home. Then I'm a pure Yorkshire lad.'

Vi laughed. 'Amazing. A bit like me when I'm here. My Kerry accent just comes out naturally after a day or two.'

'It's very charming and melodious,' Jack remarked, taking her arm. 'I'm so glad I came, you know. It's such a rest from the movie world.' He looked up at the blue sky and took a deep breath. 'This is an incredible place.'

They walked slowly up the avenue and Vi found that seeing the place through someone else's eyes made her notice things she hadn't thought of before. Jack remarked on the lush gardens and the many subtropical plants that grew here in the mild climate, how the sun shining through the foliage of the evergreen trees and shrubs cast a dappled light on the grass and the path. Then he suddenly stopped, awestruck by the sight of the old manor, its Georgian architecture, the mellow stone of the façade and the tall windows reflecting the sunlight. Vi kept glancing at him, thinking again that he was so different from the slightly stuck-up man she had had a drink with in London. Now he seemed relaxed and at ease, deeply interested in both the garden and Magnolia Manor, and enjoying all of the magic Kerry had to offer.

'Tell me the story of this gorgeous house,' he said. 'When was it built and by whom?'

'It was built in eighteen hundred by one of my ancestors, a Fleury who had made a lot of money importing spices from the West Indies,' Vi told him. 'The first Fleurys were Huguenots who came to Ireland in the sixteen hundreds. But they weren't that wealthy until Gerald Fleury made his fortune. Then the house was built as a summer house and later became the main residence of the family. You can read about the later Fleurys on the Magnolia Manor website.'

'I'm going to look that up,' Jack declared. 'Great that all the historical facts are there.'

As they drew nearer, Vi saw people come and go through the big oak entrance door, and getting into their cars parked at the new car park beside the house.

'A busy place,' Jack remarked. 'Despite the fact that the tenants are all quite old.'

'They're all pensioners,' Vi explained. 'People who are still active but want somewhere easy to live where there's a community and certain services, like a library, an infirmary and a communal dining room on the premises. There's an indoor pool now, too, and a gym in that extension on the west side. Don't worry, they're normally quite respectful of our family's privacy with Sylvia still living in the house.'

'Amazing,' Jack said, looking impressed. 'Who thought all this up?'

'My grandmother,' Vi said with great pride. 'It was all her idea. Then this French businessman and his son arrived on the scene and founded a partnership with our family. There was a bit of trouble between the two families at first but it's all sorted now and it's running very smoothly.'

'A bit of trouble?' Jack asked, looking intrigued. 'That sounds interesting. What happened?'

'It's a long story,' Vi said, not wanting to reveal any family secrets just yet. 'I'll tell you later.' She spotted Sylvia driving out from the courtyard at the back of the house and waved. 'There's my grandmother,' she said to Jack as the car slowed down. 'She's coming to say hello.'

The car stopped and Vi saw there was someone sitting beside Sylvia. A distinguished-looking older man with white hair. It was Arnaud, smiling and waving. Vi waved back, shouting: 'Hi, Arnaud. Welcome back.'

Sylvia rolled down her window. 'Hello, Vi,' she said, glancing at Jack. 'Is this a friend of yours?'

'Eh, yes... this is...' Vi hesitated but then decided to come clean. 'It's Jack Montgomery in disguise, actually.'

Jack leaned forward and lifted his cap. 'Hello, Mrs Fleury. How lovely to meet you. I've heard so much about you.'

'Have you now?' Sylvia said, lifting an eyebrow. 'I suppose those movie people called me all sorts of names.'

'Not as far as I know,' Jack replied. 'I just heard that you're an amazing businesswoman and a great negotiator.'

'Hmm,' Sylvia said. 'I'm sure that's the polite version. Your disguise is terrible, by the way. I knew who you were straight away. I'd lose the wig if I were you. That blond shade does nothing for your complexion.'

Jack laughed. 'I'm sure you're right. Anway, I must compliment you on this beautiful house.'

'Well, I didn't build it,' Sylvia countered. 'But thanks. We love it very much.' She turned towards Arnaud. 'This is my fiancé, Arnaud Bernard.'

'How do you do, Mr Bernard?' Jack said. 'Very nice to meet you.'

Arnaud smiled. 'Nice to meet you, too, Jack. Of course I've seen some of your movies. You're a talented actor,' he said in his correct but accented English.

'You're very kind,' Jack said modestly.

'So you've come to see Violet?' Sylvia asked.

'Yes,' Jack replied. 'And to familiarise myself with the area and the setting. We're going for a drive later to see the other side of the peninsula. I'm really looking forward to that.'

'You're driving?' Sylvia asked.

'Yes. I hired a car,' Jack replied.

'Drive carefully,' Sylvia ordered. 'Vi, let me know when you get back.'

'I will, Granny,' Vi promised, wondering why Sylvia looked so suspicious. 'Jack and I are just friends,' she added in order to reassure her grandmother.

'I'll look after her,' Jack cut in.

'Good.' Sylvia nodded, looking mollified. 'I don't mean to appear so doubtful,' she added with a little smile. 'I'm sure you're a perfect gentleman. It's just that my granddaughters are so very precious to me.'

'Of course they are,' Jack said warmly. 'I understand completely. Family is what matters most in life, after all.'

'Exactly.' Sylvia paused. 'But now we'd better get going or we'll be late for lunch at the golf club in Killarney. It's a bit of a drive, you see.'

'Drive carefully,' Vi said. 'I'll send you a text later.'

'Goodbye, Mrs Fleury. So nice to meet you. I hope we'll meet again soon,' Jack said.

'You may call me Sylvia,' she said graciously. 'Bye for now.'

Jack shook his head when Sylvia's car had moved off. 'I feel as if I've just met the queen. What an amazing woman.' He looked at Vi and clapped his hand to his heart. 'I think I fell a little in love with her. It was the way she looked at me with those beautiful eyes just now and told me to call her Sylvia. Before that, I was scared of her.'

Vi giggled. 'Yeah, Granny is something else. There's nobody like her. I love her to bits.'

'So do I from now on.' He took off the glasses and pulled off the blond wig. 'I'll ditch this now as it does nothing for my complexion.'

Vi laughed. 'Oh don't mind Granny. She speaks her mind always and can be a little too critical at times.'

'Nothing wrong with that,' Jack declared. 'I wish more

people would be as honest. But of course she is your beloved granny and so very dear to you.'

'Yes, she is. For so many reasons,' Vi said as they resumed walking.

'How are things with your sisters?' he asked. 'Have you been talking to them?'

Vi sighed. 'Oh, it's complicated. But I've had a talk with Lily, my eldest sister, and we get on better now. I haven't seen Rose. She's still giving me the cold shoulder.'

'I'm sure she'll come around,' he soothed.

'Maybe.' Vi started to walk faster. 'But now I'll show you around and then we'll go back and get in the car and go for our drive.'

'Yes, ma'am,' Jack said with a grin. 'You're a chip off the old block, aren't you?'

'I hope so,' Vi said. 'If I'm just a little bit like Granny, I'll cope with most things.'

'I'd say you'd cope with anything,' Jack remarked. He stopped walking and looked at her. 'Even me. I'm not the easiest man to get along with.'

Vi looked at him and wondered what he meant. 'Yes, but I'm sure you're very professional when you're working with other actors,' she countered. 'What you're like in private is not relevant.'

'Good point,' he said. 'Let's drop it for now and explore this lovely building.'

'Grand,' Vi said and started to open the big entrance door.

As they walked into the house in silence, she wondered what he had meant. Would the making of this movie be more challenging than she had thought? He had hinted at the fact that he could be difficult, and when she thought about how he had behaved when they'd had that drink in London, she realised that there might be many sides to his character. Sides that she might not find easy to accept. The reality might be very different to her dreams.

14

The tour around the ground floor and gardens of the manor took longer than Vi had planned. Jack wanted to see as much as he could. He looked into every nook and cranny of the downstairs rooms, asking questions about the family and its history. As luck would have it, the rooms were empty of residents, avoiding any questions or curious stares. He was fascinated by the library, where the bookcases and oak panelling were still as they had been when the house was built. The old books had been replaced by a modern selection, mostly contemporary literature in paperback. But there were still a few leatherbound volumes here and there, books about the flora and fauna of Kerry with beautiful illustrations that Jack found fascinating. He leafed through them, staring at the pictures, impressed by the detail.

They had a quick look in the dining room that was now furnished with round tables and chairs and had art posters on the walls. 'Nice,' Jack said, 'but I bet the old dining room was a lot more interesting.'

'Of course,' Vi agreed. 'There was a huge mahogany table here that could seat twenty people with matching chairs and a beautiful oriental carpet. And then there were Regency sideboards and a glass cabinet and oil paintings on the walls. The old furniture and some of the paintings were sold off when they created this communal dining room. And the ballroom was also modernised and made into a space for events such as weddings and other festivities. It's very popular for receptions in the summer months because then they can also use the terrace and have drinks outside when the weather is nice.'

Jack looked into the ballroom and agreed that it was a great room and would be perfect for the setting of the movie when they staged the scenes that required a large room. 'Great for dancing the waltz like Don and Kathleen did after their wedding.' He smiled at Vi. 'You know that scene that's in the script, just after they met? We must rehearse dancing together before we start shooting.'

'Good idea,' Vi said, feeling a lot more confident as the day wore on.

They went outside to walk through the Regency garden, Lily's special domain that she had created with the help of a landscape gardener. Within its walls, they were sheltered from the winds, and despite the flowerbeds being bare of flowers at this time of year, it was a beautiful, calm space where the gravel paths wound around shrubs and fruit trees in a pattern designed after the gardens that had been there nearly two hundred years ago.

'Here, the ladies of the house would walk and then take tea in the little pavilion over there.' Vi showed Jack a small building with a roof covered in shingles.

'I can nearly see them,' he said. 'Walking slowly, chatting, their long skirts trailing, holding parasols and then sitting down in the pavilion having tea.'

'Must have been lovely on a summer's day.' Vi walked ahead to the orangery. 'This is Lily's café. It's closed now, but she's going to open it over the Christmas holidays and have a tea party here on Christmas Eve.'

Jack peered through one of the tall windows. 'Looks like a nice space. Very nicely done. What are those paintings on the back wall?'

'Family portraits,' Vi said. 'The café is locked but I know where the key is. Do you want to go in and take a look?'

'Yes, please. I love old family portraits.'

'Okay.' Vi went to the door, lifted a potted plant and found the key underneath it. 'Here it is, as usual.'

Jack laughed. 'What an original place to hide a key.'

'I know, but around here nobody would dare break in. That would bring the curse of the Fleurys on them. In any case, there isn't much to steal.'

'Except the family portraits,' Jack remarked.

'Ah no. Who'd want them?' Vi turned the key in the lock and opened the door. 'Here we are. It's freezing so we won't stay long. But you can have a quick look at the paintings.'

It was certainly very cold in the café as it hadn't been heated since it had been closed for the season in early October. Sylvia had turned on the heating briefly while she was doing the accounts, but it had turned cold again after that. Despite the chill, the orangery was a lovely big space with a tiled floor and tall windows overlooking the garden. A weak winter sun cast beams of light on the floor and there was a faint smell of rose petals and lavender in the air.

'It's like stepping into the past,' Jack said in a low voice as he walked over to the back wall to look at the portraits. Then he gazed at the faces in silence. 'Tell me about them,' he said after a while.

Vi looked at him with a smile, enjoying how enamoured he was. She pointed at the painting of a dark-haired woman with lovely eyes. 'That's Maria Fleury. She married my great-great-grandfather sometime in the eighteen eighties. The tall man standing against the oak tree is Frank Fleury, her husband. The dark man with the moustache and the mischievous eyes is their son Cornelius, the one who gambled away all the money and nearly cost the family Magnolia Manor and the whole estate.'

'Interesting,' Jack said with an amused smile. 'I sense a story that you're reluctant to tell.'

'Oh, I will later,' Vi said.

'Can't wait.' Jack walked on and stopped at the portrait of a beautiful woman in a red dress wearing the famous Fleury pearls. 'Oh how lovely. Sylvia as a young woman?'

'Yes,' Vi said. 'It was painted two years after her wedding.'

Jack kept staring at the painting, looking mesmerised. 'What a beautiful woman. And how lovely she still is. She might have aged, but the charisma is still there. That straight back and the feisty look in her eyes... wow.'

'She's a force of nature,' Vi agreed.

'That's for sure.' Jack had moved on to the last portrait of two men. 'This one is lovely. Father and son?'

'Yes,' Vi said, looking at the painting. 'That's my grandfather and my father. It was painted just before they both drowned in a boating accident. A freak wave hit their sailing boat and...' Tears pricked her eyes as she said it and she didn't know how to go on.

'How sad,' Jack said gently. 'What a horrific tragedy. I'm sorry I asked.'

'It's okay,' Vi said, touched by the sympathy in his voice. 'I was only two years old when it happened, so I don't remember it.' *Except the sorrow,* she thought, staring at the painting. *The crying and sadness creeping into every corner of the house, the tears and sad faces that lasted for years afterwards. And sometimes – just silence.* 'I don't remember my grandfather or my father either. I wish I did,' she said, trying to keep the pain out of her voice. 'This painting and some photos are all I have.'

'Oh.' He put a hand on her shoulder. 'That's perhaps a worse loss.'

'I don't know. Maybe.' Vi moved away from the painting. 'Can we go now?' she asked, suddenly overwhelmed by all the emotions.

'Of course,' Jack said, looking concerned. 'We should walk in the sunshine for a bit, I think. And then go for that drive.'

'Great.' Vi smiled to reassure him that all was well. 'Didn't mean to be gloomy. Not your fault that all these feelings suddenly came to the surface.' Perhaps it was why she had been a little doubtful about coming home, she pondered. Despite her love of this place. the dark shadows of loss and sadness always seemed to come to the surface when she was here. She wondered how Lily and Rose could cope with all the memories, living so close.

'I can't imagine how it must feel. Must be very difficult for you.' He paused, casting a final glance at the portraits.

Vi was happy to step outside and feel the warmth of the sun. Then they walked in silence through the gardens and along the path to the gatehouse and Jack's car.

Vi felt more comfortable in his company after that. She was getting used to being with him and found him a great conversationalist, being knowledgeable about so many subjects, such as history, politics and literature. She was no longer so in awe of him or afraid to contradict him when she felt like it. The schoolgirl crush was replaced by a more mature feeling of friendship and respect for an actor with so much experience. She was attracted to him but she was no longer starstruck and felt calm and content in his presence. He had been wonderful company ever since he had turned up on her doorstep that morning. But deep down, she felt unsure of him as she remembered the stories she had read in the papers and the photos of Jack and all kinds of beautiful women on his arm at red carpet events. That was far from the man she had spent all morning with. Who was the real Jack Montgomery?

15

Later, as they were walking on the vast expanse of Fermoyle beach on the other side of Connor Pass, Jack asked Vi about the Fleurys' connection with the French family.

'I sense an interesting story,' he said, turning towards Vi, his hair ruffled by the strong breeze. 'Or am I stepping on sore toes with my question?'

'Not at all,' Vi said. 'That old story is something we laugh at now. About five years ago, my grandmother received a letter from a lawyer in France representing the Bernard family, claiming ownership of Magnolia Manor and all the lands around it. This was based on an old gambling debt incurred by my great-grandfather Cornelius Fleury about a hundred years ago.'

'The gambler in the portrait?' Jack asked, looking impressed. 'How exciting.'

'Not really,' Vi replied. 'We thought it was quite appalling. Especially as he had given away everything he owned.'

'I suppose. But the whole thing was resolved in the end, then?'

'That's right,' Vi said. 'We finally found a letter from the member of the Bernard family who had accepted the property as payment of the debt, giving it back to Cornelius's wife. So all was well in the end.'

'And you all made friends and then got together to turn the manor into apartments for pensioners?'

'After a lot of toing and froing, yes,' Vi replied. 'It was Granny's idea from the start but Arnaud and his son Henri thought it would work really well and decided to join the business venture.'

'And Sylvia and Arnaud fell in love and became engaged?' Jack said.

Vi laughed, looking up at the blue sky, enjoying the memory. 'Oh yes, they did. That was quite funny, actually. They were arguing about the letter Sylvia had received and she told him off about it and how rude and insensitive it was for the Bernards to claim Magnolia Manor as their property based on an old gambling debt. She gave him hell but he just stood there and took it, admiring her feistiness and her flashing eyes. And then, when she had marched out of the room, banging the door behind her, he told us she was *magnifique* and how much he admired her spirit. She was already quite smitten, too, with his good looks and charm. Then, later, Granny laid her plans of the senior apartments in front of him and he was so impressed with the idea and they became partners both in business and privately. They're quite a power couple in their own way.' Vi drew breath.

Jack grinned. 'What a great story. Proves that it's never too late to either fall in love or start a new venture.'

'That's very true,' Vi agreed, thinking of how worried she had been at turning thirty.

Jack looked out at sea and then across the stretch of golden sand lapped by the waves. 'This is a fabulous beach. I don't think I've ever felt so invigorated.'

'I love coming here,' Vi said. 'Especially on a windy day like today. It raises my spirits.'

'It certainly did something the same to mine,' Jack declared.

They walked on in silence. Whipped by the wind, they watched as flocks of tiny sandpipers skimmed the surface of the water before they soared upwards, turning their bodies this way and that in a graceful ballet, their underbellies like flashes of silver in the brilliant sunshine against the backdrop of the turquoise sea and the bright-blue skies. The air was like cold, crisp white wine.

With the salty wind whipping her hair away from her face and the roar of the sea and the cries of seagulls in her ears, Vi forgot all her worries and breathed in the clean air. She smiled at Jack, who, having taken off his shoes, ran into the waves but pulled back as the water soaked his jeans. His hair was ruffled by the wind, his cheeks pink and his eyes calm. He closed them for a moment and turned his face to the sky, as if drinking in the sensations and trying to keep them in his mind forever. She knew then that the magic of Kerry had captured him. Both glowing, they returned to the car for the drive to Cloghane, the nearby village, for a glass of Guinness and a sandwich by the fire in the little pub.

As they sat by the smouldering turf fire, enjoying a bacon and tomato sandwich and a frothing glass of Guinness, Jack gazed at Vi and smiled. 'You look amazing. Happy, glowing and very beautiful.'

Vi felt her face glow even more. 'Thank you. You're not too bad yourself, you know.'

'That's high praise indeed.' Jack raised his glass. 'Cheers and thank you for a wonderful day. First I fell in love with your granny and now I'm completely besotted with Kerry.'

'Despite the cold wind and the rain showers?' Vi asked.

'Not despite,' he argued, 'but because of it. Don't forget I'm from Yorkshire, where the wind is even stronger in the wintertime. Call me mad, but I love winter, as a matter of fact. Summers are nice, but this time of year, the weather is invigorating.'

'Oh, absolutely.' Vi took a bite of her sandwich. 'Winter is my favourite time of year. Especially now, coming up to Christmas.' She looked at the little Christmas tree beside the fireplace and the decorations hanging from the beams in the ceiling. 'The holidays are very special here. There are lovely Christmas concerts all around the villages and we go to the pubs to meet everyone who's come home from all kinds of places around the world and we have parties and drinks and go for hikes in the mountains.' She drew breath and laughed. 'I'm sure Yorkshire is the same.'

Jack looked suddenly serious. 'Well, yes. In a way. But not really for me. Not any more.'

'Why?' she asked, noticing his troubled eyes. 'Did something sad happen to you?'

'Yes.' He drank some Guinness before he met her gaze. 'I don't really have a family there any more. My father had a serious drinking problem and spent all his money in the local pubs. The debts started to pile up and he ended up having to sell the farm. He and my mother divorced after that and she now lives in a little cottage in the village. My dad died shortly afterwards.' He paused, staring into the fire. 'When I left to go to drama school in London, everyone thought I was abandoning my mother, despite the fact that she wanted me to go. My sister got married and lives nearby with her family, so Mum is well looked after. In any case, she's only in her mid-sixties and works as a nurse in the local hospital. There's no need to feel sorry for her at all. And I do help her out financially too. But my old friends and some of my cousins think I'm stuck-up and won't even speak to me when I go back home to see my mother. So Christmas there isn't much fun, I'm afraid.'

'But your mother and sister must be so proud of you,' Vi

argued. 'I mean, look at all you've done... the awards and the fabulous reviews in the papers.'

'That only seems to make them hate me more. Not my mother and sister, of course. But my old friends and some of my relatives can't relate to me at all.'

'They're jealous,' Vi said.

Jack smiled and shrugged. 'Who knows? I only wish they were proud of me. It's not easy. They see this caricature of me in the papers and assume I like the publicity side of things. But you know the old saying about being a prophet in your own back yard...'

Vi nodded. 'Oh yes. I can understand that.' She stopped, thinking about Rose and how they had yet to make peace. She heaved a deep sigh. 'Oh, I wish...'

'What?' Jack asked.

'That my sister Rose and I were back the way we were. Teasing and stealing each other's clothes. You know, the way sisters are. That was never serious and mostly fun. We always ended up laughing. But now there's this silence between us. I don't know what to do about it.'

'That's a tough one,' Jack said sympathetically. 'Is there any reason for her to be like that?'

'It was this interview last year that turned into something I hadn't planned.' Vi went on to tell Jack what had happened with the journalist while he listened intently.

He nodded when she had finished. 'I can relate. Stuff like that happened to me too in the beginning. I was at a press conference about a movie I'd got a part in. Not the main part, but quite big all the same. One of the journalists threw me a question about my family and I blurted out something about not having had the best childhood, which then came to be blown up into me being the victim of some kind of child abuse. Not true at all, of course, but it must have sold a lot of newspapers of the tabloid kind.'

'Oh no,' Vi exclaimed, appalled. 'That's much worse than what happened to me.'

'Well, yes,' Jack said with a shrug. 'Didn't earn me a lot of brownie points at home, which caused much of the negativity. The media can be such a bog that's hard to get out of. I try to avoid doing too much of that stuff. But, of course, the movie companies want you to make headlines all the time to sell tickets at the box office. They sometimes even encourage controversy.' He grinned. 'You'll see. It's only starting for you. Wait till our movie comes out. Then it'll really be tricky to stay out of the limelight.' He looked around the little pub. 'And then...' he whispered into her ear, 'of course there are the fans out there with their phones. Someone will take a snap of you with someone and then, boom, you're in a "relationship" with whoever you happen to sit beside, or walk out of a bar or restaurant with. Even if it's not true at all. Happens all the time, everywhere.'

'I don't think that would happen here,' Vi said. 'Kerry people are discreet and kind.'

'Yes, but there might be someone not from around here who has no scruples,' Jack suggested, draining his pint. 'Except here, in this cosy little pub, I don't sense any excitement about either of us.'

'No,' Vi said, also looking around the sparsely occupied room. 'Not many people here as it's a Tuesday at the beginning of December. But everyone here knows who we are, of course. That's the way it is in small villages and towns in Kerry.'

'Oh, I know,' Jack agreed and drained his glass. 'Same thing where I come from. There is this knowledge, like a whisper in the wind. Nobody says anything, but they all *know*.'

He looked so comical, Vi started to laugh. 'Yes, exactly. Scary, isn't it?' A phone rang, making them both give a start.

Jack pulled his phone out of his pocket. 'Not mine.'

'It's mine.' Vi groped for her phone in her jacket. 'Hello?'

'Hi there,' a voice said. 'Violet, this is Finbarr at On Your Toes. We chatted recently about Kathleen O'Sullivan, remember?'

'Oh yes,' Vi said, suddenly back to the conversation she had had with him. 'Fidelma, wasn't it?'

'That's right. She knew Kathleen back in the day. Anyway, it appears that old Fidelma has had to go into a nursing home.'

'I'm sorry to hear that,' Vi said, feeling sad for the old lady.

'Yes, it's a bit of a blow for her,' Finbarr agreed. 'Now, the thing is that she sent a package for you to us. Some mementoes of Kathleen she found when she was clearing her house before going to the nursing home.'

'Oh, how kind of her to think of me at such a difficult time,' Vi said.

'I think she felt that you would like to have these things, whatever they are. Letters and cards and such by the looks of it. But what do I do about the package? She sent it to us because she didn't know your address. Can I send it on to you?'

'Of course. That would be great,' Vi said. 'Send it to The Gatehouse, Magnolia Manor, Dingle, County Kerry.'

'Got that. I'll send it off as soon as possible. Not a large package, just some letters and cards and a few other little items. Could be interesting for your research.'

'Thanks a million,' Vi said. 'That's very kind.'

'Not at all,' Finbarr replied. 'I'll expect tickets to the premiere in return.'

'Of course,' Vi promised. 'Front row seats and an invitation to the after-party.'

'Looking forward to it,' Finbarr said. 'Let me know you got the package.'

'I will,' Vi promised. 'Bye for now.' She hung up and looked at Jack. 'Nice guy. Very helpful.'

'With what?' he asked.

'I had a chat a while ago with an old lady who knew Kathleen in the early days – at the time she was discovered by the talent scout. She told me they kept in touch after Kathleen went to Hollywood. She has sent me some correspondence she had with Kathleen back in the day. I can't wait to read them.'

'Sounds interesting,' Jack said. 'Should give you a feel for who Kathleen was in private.'

'Exactly,' Vi agreed. 'You see, I'm trying to find out more about her than what's written in the biographies. That will help me get more depth into her persona when I play her. Not that it would change the screenplay in any way, of course.'

'I don't see why not.' Jack looked thoughtfully at Vi. 'Right now I find the dialogue a little bland and clichéd. Maybe we could jazz it up a bit with some drama?'

'Yes,' Vi agreed. 'I did like the dialogue, it's very well written. But yeah, it's a little run of the mill. But I never thought I'd have any influence on what's in the script. I don't want to make trouble.'

'I'd make it for you,' Jack remarked, waggling his eyebrows. 'Maybe we could go through the script together and see what needs to be done? Rehearse the dialogue and get the feel for it, maybe to see how we click. What do you think?'

'Yes,' Vi agreed. 'That'd be great. Let me know when you're free to do that.'

'We could do it on the phone,' he suggested. 'Anytime at all when I take a break.'

'I'm free most evenings. And maybe once I get more information about Kathleen, we might work that into it,' Vi said.

He nodded. 'Good idea. I think it's terrific that you're doing a bit of digging into Kathleen's personal life.'

'I just wanted to get to know the woman behind the glossy image,' Vi explained. 'I want to have a real feel for what was in her mind at the time. Things nobody would know except close friends like Fidelma. Or maybe you?' she asked.

Jack looked surprised. 'Me? I don't know much about her.

Except one or two hints that she was hiding something from the press. But I'm not sure what it was. Just old Hollywood gossip that might be made up.'

'Could it have been something personal and embarrassing?' Vi suggested.

'Stuff she wouldn't have told journalists in interviews, you mean?' he teased.

'Yeah,' Vi said, feeling embarrassed herself. 'I bet she never made that mistake.'

'Probably because she was coached to say what would look good,' Jack mused. 'And by the way, talking about stuff nobody knows...' He suddenly looked awkward. 'I'd appreciate it if you didn't tell anyone what I said about my father. That's not out there in public and it would hurt my mother and my sister if it came out. The official story is quite different.'

'Of course, I won't tell anyone,' Vi promised.

'Great.' Jack rose from his chair. 'I think it's time we went back. It's getting dark and the drive across that mountain pass was scary enough in daylight.'

'We could go the longer way,' Vi suggested.

'I'd rather take the short sharp one,' Jack said. 'And I have a feeling the skies would be amazing up there just after sunset.'

Vi got up. 'Yes, that's true. Let's go.'

When Jack paid the bill at the counter, the waiter smiled at them. 'Nice to meet the stars of the next big hit,' he said. 'Good luck with the movie, lads.'

They smiled and thanked him. Jack looked curiously at Vi when they were outside. 'So he knew who we were but didn't say anything or ask us any questions. That's classy, I have to say.'

'That's the Kerry way,' Vi said as she got into the car.

'I'm impressed.'

They didn't talk much during the drive, only stopped briefly at the top of Connor Pass and looked at the sky, a riot of orange and pink in the west and stars twinkling above them. 'Incredible,' Jack said and then slowly drove down the steep road on the other side where they could see the lights of Dingle below them.

He pulled up outside the gatehouse and turned to look at Vi. 'Thank you again for a wonderful day. You have changed my view of Ireland and Kerry in particular. Not to mention everyone we've met. It's been such a day full of wonderful things to remember. I'm looking forward to shooting this movie with you.'

'Me too,' Vi said, noticing the warm expression in his brown eyes. 'I think we'll work well together.'

'I hope so.' He paused for a moment. 'So how are you going to fill your days until then?'

'Oh, I'll be busy,' Vi replied. 'Dance lessons, sessions with the voice coach, looking at Kathleen's movies and then reading these letters. I'll also spend time with my grandmother and help my sister Lily with babysitting.'

'Sounds like a lot. So Lily is the older sister?' he asked. 'She's not holding any grudges, then.'

Vi shook her head. 'Not any more. We had a chat and she seemed to understand what happened. Rose is a different story.'

'The kind who can't let go of anger?' Jack suggested.

'Something like that.' Vi opened the passenger door, not wanting to continue discussing Rose and what was going on between them. 'I'd better go. Thanks for the drive and lunch. It was fun.'

'Yes, it was,' Jack said, looking at her in an odd way. 'I'd say you'll find those letters Kathleen wrote very interesting.'

'I hope so.' Vi looked back at him. 'It'll be fascinating to read her own words.'

'I'm sure it will,' Jack agreed. He paused for a moment. 'Violet... Would it be okay if I called you sometime? Just for a chat, apart from working on the script, I mean. I felt that we clicked today.'

'I think I know what you mean.' Vi nodded, touched by the earnest look in his eyes. She felt a connection to him that had nothing to do with the crush she had had on him for so long. It was as if she had seen a little bit of the real Jack today: a vulnerability and a love of nature she herself felt so strongly. 'Of course you can call me any time.'

'I'll text you first to see if it's a good time,' he suggested.

'Perfect.' Vi got out of the car. 'Have a good trip to Scotland.'

'Thanks. I really enjoyed the day. I'm looking forward to Scotland.' He shot her a dazzling smile that made her heart flutter. 'The winds will be even colder there than here. But it will be refreshing. I'll be in touch. And hey, let me know if you find anything interesting in those letters.'

'I will,' she promised. 'Can't wait to read them. I feel they'll bring me closer to her somehow.'

'You might find out things you don't want to know,' Jack said through the open window of the car.

Vi stared at him. 'What kind of things?'

He shrugged. 'Oh nothing. Just... be careful what you wish for. Bye, Violet.'

Before she had a chance to ask any questions, he drove off. She stood rooted to the spot, wondering what on earth he had meant. Did he know something about Kathleen that might be bad? Something nobody else did? He had said he had heard a hint here and there, but not what it was about. He was difficult to figure out and sometimes said things that seemed innocent but could mean something else. *A mysterious man with a lot of baggage,* she thought as she walked up the steps to the house. It would be best not to get too involved on a personal level. But how could she avoid it? She realised she was starting to like him more and more.

16

The padded envelope arrived in the post a few days later. Vi had just ended an online session with the voice coach when she heard the doorbell. Still in her pyjamas, she peered through the half-open door and found Joe, the postman, standing on the doorstep. 'Couldn't get this through the letterbox,' he said and handed her the package. 'And it's registered post, so you have to sign for it.' He gave her a form and a pen. 'Just scribble your name and we're done.'

'Okay. Thanks, Joe.' Vi signed the form and took the package.

'Big script, is it?' he asked as he handed it to her. 'For the film you're going to shoot here, I mean.'

'No something else, but yes, connected to the movie.' Vi smiled at him. 'Not much excitement yet with the movie stuff. It's still early days.'

'But when the film crew arrives, the town will be hopping, I bet,' he said. 'Everyone is talking about it already. I saw Jack Montgomery was in town, too. And you were out on a date and all.'

'What?' Vi asked, startled. 'A date? When?'

'The other day. At a pub somewhere,' Joe replied. 'I saw the picture in the *Mirror*. A bit blurred but it was definitively you – and yer man.'

'Eh, okay,' Vi said, trying to compose herself. 'Well, it wasn't a date, exactly. Just an outing to show him around. Someone must have taken a shot of us with their phone.'

Joe nodded. 'I see. Well, I'm sure some nosey lad will always try to blow up everything to make it look more interesting. Just ignore it would be my advice.'

'You're right, Joe. I'll do just that. Thanks for the heads-up about it, though.'

'No problem, pet,' Joe said. He ran down the steps and got into his green van, waving as he drove off.

Vi smiled and waved back. Joe was a darling. He had been delivering their post ever since she could remember. He must be near retirement by now. She'd miss him when he finally stopped working. So nice of him to tell her about that photo in the *Mirror*. It was annoying to find out that someone had taken a photo of her and Jack, but in this case it was something to simply ignore. She wouldn't comment on it and if asked, she'd just shrug it off. She knew things like this came with the territory of having been cast in a movie to be shot on her own doorstep. A place where everyone knew everyone and liked to talk about it. Not much harm done – yet.

Vi sighed and went into the living room to look through the items in the package. It was so kind of old Fidelma to send it. Vi wondered if she could visit the old lady in her nursing home in Dublin once the filming was over. It would be nice to meet face to face.

Excited, she sat down on the sofa and opened the package. There was a note on the top of the stack of letters and cards that said:

Dear Violet,

My mother asked me to send these letters and cards to you c/o the dance studio as we didn't have your address. My mother is a little feeble in her mind these days but she was adamant that you would want to read them. We were tidying up her house prior to selling it as she is moving to a nursing home where she can get the care she needs. She had such lovely memories of Kathleen O'Sullivan and now that you are going to play her in the movie, you might want to know more about her. I haven't had time to read the letters, so you will be the first to see them after all these years. I hope you will like them.

Best wishes,

Emma Murray (Fidelma's daughter)

Vi put the letter to the side, feeling grateful she had been able to contact Fidelma before the move to the nursing home. The letters might have been thrown in the bin during the move if Fidelma hadn't asked her daughter to send them on. Vi didn't quite believe that Fidelma was 'a little feeble in her mind' as her daughter had put it. She had seemed quite the opposite during their conversation. But perhaps she couldn't cope on her own any more and that was why she had to move in to a nursing home. What a pity she couldn't move in to the senior apartments at Magnolia Manor, Vi thought fleetingly. Then she looked at the pile of cards and letters before her and forgot all else as she picked up the first one. Vi's hand shook as she realised that she was holding a Christmas card written by Kathleen herself.

The card was dated Christmas 1950 with a Christmas tree and a Santa Claus on the front. Vi opened it.

Merry Christmas, Fidelma! My very first one in Hollywood! It's very strange to look at palm trees and feel the hot sun at this

*time of year. But this is California and not Ireland, so I have to
get used to it. And – I'm going to be in a movie with Henry
Fonda! A small part but it's a beginning. My agent says it'll be
very good for my career. I hope you have a wonderful
Christmas and congratulations on your engagement. Brendan
seems to be a lovely man with great prospects in the civil
service. I wish you both the very best life together.*

Love,

Kathleen

The handwriting was indeed a little difficult to read but Vi
soon got used to the scribbles as she continued to look through
the correspondence. Kathleen seemed quite impulsive and
appeared to have scribbled the messages down without paying
much attention to a nice style.

Most of the letters were short, some consisted of just a few
lines, wishing Fidelma a happy Christmas or Easter and
contained little information about her life and acting career in
Hollywood. Frustrated, Vi leafed through the pile of papers,
skipping the Christmas cards, while she looked for anything of
importance. As the cards and letters were sorted in chronolog-
ical order, starting with the cards dating from Kathleen's first
years in Hollywood to the years just before her death, it was
fairly easy to get through to what looked like longer messages.
Some of them, in the later years of the 1950s, were more
detailed, describing incidents during filming, descriptions of
some of Katheleen's co-stars in various movies and the fights she
had had with some of the movie people about her rights. Kathleen hadn't minced her words and was often threatened with
dismissal if she insisted on her demands being met. Fun reading, which Vi enjoyed, but it didn't tell her anything she didn't
know already from the biographies she had read online.

It wasn't until Kathleen had met Don, who was to become her husband and the love of her life, that she had started to write to Fidelma in more detail, pouring her heart out to the person she described as her 'only real friend that I can trust completely'.

It appeared that Kathleen and Fidelma had met from time to time when Kathleen paid occasional short visits to Ireland, and they seemed to have had a close friendship that continued until Kathleen's untimely death from lung cancer in 1995 at the age of sixty-six. She had met Don when she was thirty years old and had been through two broken engagements after short relationships with men with either anger issues or problems with alcohol. *I'm not the best picker of men*, she had written to Fidelma and had said she had gone to a country house hotel in Kildare to ride as her father had kept horses on the farm in Kerry and she had always loved riding. *A horse is the best companion*, she wrote. *They always listen and seem to understand when you're sad. I met some terrific horses, especially one called Peggy, a mare who is gentle and kind and never breaks into canter even when she's startled by something. We have been on some lovely trips through the Kildare countryside and it's been so soothing and comforting, taking me away from all my troubles. I hope you and Brendan are well and the children continue to thrive. I will write again soon as I have some lovely news (about a person I've just met) to share with you (if this is what I hope it is).*

Vi smiled as she read the letter, knowing what would come. Kathleen had obviously just met Don but was being careful, having been through two failed relationships. She was also probably careful not to have anything leaked to the press as it looked like she had gone to the country house hotel to escape the media coverage about her recent break-up. Any new man in her life would attract immense attention from the journalists of the gossip columns. Vi suddenly felt a strong connection to

Kathleen, trying to imagine what it would have been like to be so famous. Would the movie Vi was about to star in also bring with it a lot of media attention of the kind she was afraid of? With social media the way it was today, it might possibly be a lot worse than it had been for Kathleen.

Feeling a little stiff after sitting on the sofa for over an hour, Vi jumped up and decided to go for a walk. She put the letters away and went upstairs to have a shower and get dressed. Jeans, a warm sweater and her windproof jacket would be the best outfit today as it was both wet and windy outside. All showered and warmly dressed, Vi was ready to go outside, deciding to walk through the park down to the shore and then take the path across the bridge and then on to Dingle town where she'd have a coffee and a bun in one of the cafés overlooking the harbour. It was a well-worn path for her and her family.

She might even bump into someone she knew on the way and have company in the café. She hadn't seen any of her old friends since she arrived. She assumed most of them were either working full time or had moved to live somewhere else. She hadn't kept in touch with anyone, feeling her sisters were all the company she needed. But now, as one of her sisters – Rose – was still not talking to her, she felt a sudden need to confide in someone who was not family. Maybe it was reading the correspondence between Kathleen and Fidelma that sparked this feeling of needing a friend she could trust. They had seemed so close, even though they didn't meet in person that often.

Vi zipped up her jacket, put on a woolly hat and gloves and walked out of the house. The wind that brought with it a smell of the sea was cold but invigorating and she walked swiftly down the gravel path that wound around trees and bushes through which she could glimpse the sea glittering in the distance. The clouds parted from time to time, permitting the sun to shine through, providing a moment's light and warmth before the sky darkened again. *Typical December weather*, Vi thought, enjoying the fresh air despite the cold nearly gale-force wind.

She turned a corner behind a large oak and was startled to come face to face with a woman pushing a buggy. Vi stared at the woman and blinked.

'Oh, it's you,' she said, stuck for something better to say as the shock of the sudden meeting made her heart contract.

17

'Yes, it's me,' Rose said. Her blue eyes were cold as she looked back at Vi. 'I wasn't planning to meet you like this,' she continued. 'Or at all, really.'

'Well, I...' Vi started. 'I mean, I was hoping we could get together and talk or something.'

'I'm not ready,' Rose said.

'I see.' Vi put her hands in her pockets and stepped back. 'I thought I'd see you around town maybe.'

'Well, we live on the outskirts of town,' Rose said stiffly. 'And I've been stuck at home with Sophie, who's been quite sick.'

'That must be hard,' Vi said, trying to sound sympathetic. Then she looked at the little girl in the pram. 'Hi, Sophie.' She leaned forward and smiled at her niece. 'How you have grown. I haven't seen you since last year. Remember me? I'm your auntie Violet. What a pretty girl you are.' Sophie, at around a year and a half, was indeed enchanting, with deep blue eyes and curly blonde hair and a small, upturned nose. She stared at her aunt for a moment, and then her face broke into a wide smile, showing tiny teeth. Then she pointed to Rose and said: 'Mamma.'

'I know your mamma.' Vi pointed to herself. 'I'm Violet.'

Sophie let out a delicious laugh like little bells. 'Vilet,' she repeated and then chuckled again.

'Aren't you a clever girl,' Vi said. Then she straightened up and looked at Rose. 'She's lovely, Rose. And the spitting image of you.'

'Thank you,' Rose said stiffly and started to move past Vi. 'I have to go now.'

'No you don't.' Vi grabbed the handle of the buggy, staring at Rose. 'Just one question. Are you going to keep this up forever? Or are you waiting for hell to freeze over? Or that I will do – whatever – so you'll forgive me?'

'That was three questions,' Rose remarked.

'I know. But can you answer any of them?' Vi demanded. 'I mean... hey, we're sisters. We should stick together. Have you listened to any of my voicemails? My apologies? I meant it. I'm truly sorry, Rose.' Vi drew breath and looked levelly at Rose while she waited for an answer. She knew Rose was always slow to forgive any kind of slight and that it would take her longer than usual to soften towards Vi. But she was tired of waiting and feeling guilty. She also noticed that Rose looked pale and tired and that she had lost weight. 'It's nearly Christmas,' Vi said. 'And Granny is having her traditional dinner as usual. We'll all be there together. Wouldn't it be nice for us to sort this out before then? If only for Granny's sake.'

Rose looked away while Sophie bounced up and down in the buggy. Then she looked at Vi again and heaved a big sigh. 'I didn't realise,' she said. 'I thought you were just going to defend yourself all over again. Well, I accept your apology.' Violet smiled, feeling relieved. 'For Granny's sake,' Rose added. 'That's all. I need to think about all this before we can be back to what we were. But it's okay. Relax. No more aggro from me. We could maybe talk some more before Christmas. Try to understand each other and then... maybe.'

Vi felt that there was a ray of hope. There was a long way to go yet, but at least Rose had softened somewhat. 'Life is too short to fight,' she said. 'Especially with your sister. I'm here for quite a while, so we can spend some time together and I'd love to help with babysitting or anything else you need.'

'You'll be too busy with the movie and your new boyfriend,' Rose said with an edge still in her voice.

'New boyfriend?' Vi asked. 'Oh, please, don't tell me you read the tabloids now.'

Rose shrugged. 'No, but the butcher does, and the woman in the dry cleaners and the check-out girl in the supermarket.'

'I see.' Vi suddenly remembered that she was living in a small country town where people liked to gossip. 'Whatever they said, it wasn't a date. I was showing Jack around and we were talking about the movie and how we'd portray the various characters and so on. There's no romance between us.'

'Yet,' Rose said.

'Never,' Vi protested. Suddenly, Violet realised why Rose was so angry. She and Rose used to share everything together: there wasn't a single man Violet had ever dated that Rose hadn't had an opinion on because she had been so protective. Rose had been the older sister who knew Vi's best interests, she had said then. 'No matter what the tabloids say, it's not true. They try to make up stories all the time. So you can tell the butcher and the dry cleaners and the girl in the supermarket and whoever else wants to know that there is nothing going on between me and Jack. Could you check with me in future before you believe anything you read? And tell others to do the same.'

Rose nodded and her eyes softened. 'Okay. Fair enough. I see what you mean. But...' she started. Then her face suddenly brightened and she shot Vi a mischievous smile. 'I would like to make one exception. Remember Sinead Morrisson?'

'From boarding school?' Vi asked, as the memory of the girl who had been so mean to her popped up in her mind. 'The girl who was always teasing me about my hair?'

'Yeah. Her,' Rose replied. 'She lives in Dingle town now and she hasn't improved with age. Always saying nasty things behind people's backs. I think she's green with envy that you've done so well. And now, to top all that, dating the brightest shining star in the world of cinema that we all fancy. Do you mind if I don't tell her there is no romance?'

Vi had to laugh, feeling the ice was broken between them at last. 'That's okay. Tell her anything you like. I don't mind if that stuck-up biddy is jealous of me.' She paused and looked pleadingly at Rose. 'So then we're okay? You and me?'

Rose looked suddenly contrite. 'Yes, we are. I'm sorry I've been so slow to forgive you. The more I've heard about this movie the angrier I've become. I want us to be back to where we were before. Arguing about silly stuff, but being sisters.'

'Oh, great. That's a huge relief,' Vi said, touching Rose's cheek. 'I understand that it was hard for you to forgive me. That journalist just wanted to make it into a juicy story.'

Rose sighed. 'Yeah, I get that. But it's been a hard year for me. Sophie's been sick so many times that I had to take time off work and leave everything to Henri which he hasn't liked one bit. And Noel and I didn't get much sleep while the baby was sick. I had to do most of the minding because Noel just can't take much time off. Then there was you with your glammy life and then getting that part. Hearing the news of you dating Jack Montgomery was kind of annoying, too, I have to say. But now that you've told me the true story, I feel stupid to have believed it.'

'You're not stupid, Rose. You're the smartest person I know.

I'm really sorry I haven't been here to help out when you've had all these problems. But hey, let's forget it and move on, okay?'

'Deal,' Rose said and leaned forward to hug Vi. They squeezed each other tight for a long moment, their eyes brimming with tears. Then they sprang apart and laughed, wiping their eyes.

Vi looked at Sophie to see her reaction, but the little girl had fallen asleep in her buggy, hugging her teddy. 'She nodded off,' Vi remarked.

'Thank goodness,' Rose said with a sigh of relief. 'I was up at Magnolia to see Granny, but Sophie was so cranky I decided to take her for a walk to see if she'd fall asleep. So that worked. And now you and I are friends again, so win-win, I'd say.'

'It's a lucky day,' Vi agreed. 'Sophie looks okay, though. Is she getting better?'

'Oh yes, finally better,' Rose said. 'Not sleeping that well at the moment because she's teething again. But we're over the worst and we have a great doctor who has put her on a special diet to deal with her food allergies. I think I can go back to work as soon as she settles into the crèche.'

'That's good news. Babies must be hard work,' Vi remarked.

'Even when they're well,' Rose agreed. 'But let's keep walking. Where were you going?'

'I'm just out for a walk,' Vi replied. 'I thought I'd go into town and have a coffee. But we could go up to Magnolia to see Granny, if you like. I'm sure she'd love to hear that we've made up.'

'She would,' Rose said and started to push the buggy up the path. 'She was just telling me off about being in a snit for so long. So let's go and tell her the good news.'

They turned and walked back up the gravel path towards the manor, chatting and laughing and enjoying being sisters again. Vi told Rose about Jack's visit and how he had been so taken with Kerry. Rose shared the ups and downs of being a mother for the first time, which seemed exhausting to Vi. When they rounded the corner to the courtyard, Sylvia opened her door and looked at them in surprise.

'Rose and Violet,' she said. 'Together. Have you made up at last?'

'Yes, we have,' Rose said. 'And we've decided it was both our faults.'

'Good,' Sylvia said and opened the door wider. 'Now get inside out of the cold and we'll have coffee and a chat. You could both stay for lunch if you like. Arnaud is at a meeting in the main office with Henri and some of the members of the board. They're discussing the maintenance of the building and what needs to be done.'

'Maybe I should be there, too,' Rose suggested as she got the buggy with the sleeping little girl inside with Vi's help. 'I need to get back to work. I haven't been at a board meeting for ages.'

'If you like,' Sylvia said. 'We'll mind Sophie. Could be a good opportunity to find out what's been decided since you've been away.'

'Brilliant,' Rose said, smiling at Sylvia. 'It'll be great for Vi and Sophie to get to know each other too.' She went into the kitchen and parked the buggy in the alcove behind the dining table. 'There. She might wake up but I'm nearby so you could give me a shout if she's upset.'

'No, we won't,' Sylvia said to Vi when Rose had closed the door behind her. 'We'll let her have a break and get connected to work again. She needs that more than anything. Sophie will be fine with us even if she kicks up a fuss. Now, let's have coffee.'

'Good idea,' Vi said and went to the Nespresso machine on the kitchen counter. 'Do you want me to make the coffee?'

'Yes, please.' Sylvia sat down on a chair at the table. 'There are some of Nora's oatmeal cookies in the cupboard.'

'Yummy.' Vi proceeded to make two cups of coffee and put

several of the cookies on a plate and brought it all over to the table. Then she sat down and smiled at Sylvia. 'Hey, I can't believe Rose and I are back together. What do you think of that, then?'

Sylvia stirred sugar into her coffee. 'I think it's a huge relief. I couldn't imagine what Christmas would be like with you two glaring at each other over the plum pudding. Now you'll just be teasing each other the way you used to. That's very good news indeed.' She took an oatmeal cookie from the plate. 'So what is this I hear? You're going out with your co-star? That young man I saw you with the other day?'

'No, I'm not,' Vi protested. 'That's just a rumour. We're friends and colleagues, that's all.'

'I'm glad to hear it,' Sylvia said. 'I didn't really believe it anyway.'

'Of course you didn't.' Vi took a bite of her cookie. 'You're too smart to believe stuff like that.'

'And you're too smart to be taken in by a pretty face,' Sylvia retorted.

'Yes, I suppose,' Vi said, trying not to show how she really felt about Jack. She couldn't help being attracted to him, especially now that he had revealed things about himself that nobody else knew. It had made him more real, somehow.

'But forget about him,' Sylvia said. 'What have you been up to lately? Other than taking ballet lesson from Claire Ryan, that is.'

Vi laughed. 'I had forgotten what a goldfish bowl Dingle is. Everyone knows what you're doing minutes after you've done it. Well, they don't know what I do at home, do they? I've done some research into Kathleen O'Sullivan's background. And as luck would have it, I found an old lady called Fidelma Sheridan who knew Kathleen in the early days in Dublin. Around the time she was discovered.'

Sylvia looked startled. 'Well, that was a real stroke of luck, wasn't it? What did she tell you?'

'Not much.' Vi finished her cookie and took a sip of coffee. 'But then I was sent a whole stack of letters from Kathleen to Fidelma that I'm reading through right now. So far, I haven't found anything new.'

'I hope you don't,' Sylvia said. 'It might compromise your role.'

'In what way?' Vi asked.

'What if you don't want to play her any more?' Sylvia said.

'Oh, I'd never change my mind,' Vi exclaimed. 'I want to know Kathleen deep down, not the clichéd Irish sweetheart she was supposed to be.' She studied Sylvia for a moment. 'You know something about Kathleen, don't you?'

Sylvia evaded Vi's gaze. 'No, not really. I know about rumours that were flying around at the time, but not if they were true.'

'What rumours? Granny, please tell me what you heard,' Vi pleaded. 'Jack has said some odd things too.'

'No, love,' Sylvia said. 'I don't want to say anything. Facts are one thing, but idle gossip is something I hate with a passion. You're going to play Kathleen in a movie about her life. It has to be a true story, not anything based on what could simply be vicious lies told by people who resented her fame and fortune. Do your research, read the letters and find out what the truth is. The real truth, I mean.'

Vi thought for a moment. Then she realised that her grandmother was right. There must have been something in Kathleen's past that had been hidden all this time. Something Kathleen herself didn't want anyone to know. But if Vi found out what it was, it had to be based on real facts, not made-up stories or rumours. 'Okay, Granny. I see what you mean. I'll go through the letters and if I find anything, I'll use that and tell the researchers and if not, I'll just follow the official story and leave it at that.'

'You could perhaps go and see Fidelma,' Sylvia suggested. 'You never know. She might be able to solve the mystery.'

Vi nodded. 'Yes, I think you might be right. Thanks, Granny. You've been a great help.'

'Well, I didn't tell you anything,' Sylvia said.

'Exactly. That's the best thing you could have done. I don't need gossip. I need the truth,' Vi said. 'I know that better than anyone now.'

18

During the following week, Vi continued to search through the letters, now finding them more interesting as the love story between Kathleen and Don became more and more intense. There was no doubt that they were deeply in love and also that they were careful not to rush into anything too soon. They had dated in secret for over a year, and Kathleen wrote to Fidelma that she had never been happier.

All the pain of the past is disappearing and I feel as if I'm walking on clouds rather than through fields of barbed wire. I rushed into relationships with the wrong men for the wrong reasons twice, and I'm being careful not to do it again. Don has been married before, not happily at all, so he is just as nervous as me. We're not always in tune, we have a lot of arguments from time to time. I get so mad at him I want to scream sometimes, especially when Don accuses me of being attracted to my leading men. But then, when my temper cools, I regret my outbursts and have to apologise profusely. Sometimes Don blows up and has to do the same while I sulk for a while before I forgive him. Making up is very sweet! Despite all that, we're

*slowly getting to know each other and feeling our way, having
lots of fun meeting in secret. My agent and some of the people
at Paramount have been very kind and have not told the press
about us, as we have promised to go public as soon as we're
ready. If we ever are.*

Vi put the letter away, thinking that the love story on the
screen would have to be as deep and real and true as Kathleen
described it. And as wild. She had no problem imagining how
she would tackle the part and those scenes, but then... How
could she stop being Kathleen off-set? She was very attracted to
Jack, especially now after their trip to Cloghane, when he had
shown a vulnerability that had surprised her. She had never
been in this situation before as the roles she had played had not
involved her characters falling in love.

As if reading her thoughts, Jack texted late that night, asking
if he could call.

*Sorry for the late message. We ran into problems shooting the
last scene. Hope you're still up.*

Vi, sitting up in bed, about to turn off the light, texted back
to say it was fine to call as she was still awake.

'Hi,' he said when she answered. 'Thanks for taking the
call.'

'You're welcome,' Vi said. 'Tough day?'

'To say the least. I'm trying to forget it over a shot of Glen-
fiddich. Several shots, actually. The hotel is terrible too. Can't
wait to get out of here.' He let out a grunt. 'Sorry to be such a
grouch. How are things with you?'

'Not too bad. In fact, pretty good. Except...' Vi hesitated,
wondering if she should mention the photo but then felt she
had to. 'Someone took a shot of you and me coming out of the
pub together and it was in one of the Irish tabloids.'

'Oh. Well, that's no big deal, is it? Has it caused you any embarrassment?'

'Not really. It just gave me a bit of a jolt. I realised what a public figure you are.'

'Yeah, well, I'm used to it. If all the tabloids do is reveal I was in a pub with a pretty girl, then that's nothing to worry about. Is this all over your home town now?'

'Yes, but I don't think it has caused huge excitement, actually. Everyone knows about the movie anyway.' Vi smiled as she remembered how Rose thought it would annoy Sinead Morrisson. 'I just thought I'd mention it since you went to such trouble to hide your identity.'

'Okay.' Jack seemed to take a sip of his whiskey.

'I got Kathleen's letters,' Vi said. 'They're very interesting.'

'Anything in them to add to the script?' Jack asked.

'Yes, actually. I think so.' Vi paused. 'Don and Kathleen were constantly arguing, it appears. Don was sometimes jealous of Kathleen's leading men. They both had hot tempers which resulted in screaming matches, door slamming and sulking and near break-ups. Then they made up and all was well again. Until the next row.'

Jack laughed. 'That sounds great. I must get on to Liz and tell her the script should be adjusted to add a few ding-dong fights. In fact, I'll put in some suggestions and email them to you for a start. And then we could read the new material together to see how it feels. And then do the make-up scenes, of course. Won't that be fun?'

'Maybe.' Vi felt her face flush as she thought of the make-up scenes. 'It's all a big challenge for me. But there is still time to get used to the idea. In any case, I'm getting a handle on Kathleen just by reading these letters. I'm beginning to like her a lot.'

'At least she wasn't boring.'

'Anything but,' Vi agreed. She stifled a yawn. 'Sorry. I'm very tired.'

'I know. It's late. I'd better let you go. I'm still feeling wide awake, though, so I'll work on the script and then you should have the new stuff in your email tomorrow morning. Let me know what you think of it.'

'That would be great,' Vi said, excited at the thought of working on the script with him.

'Good. I'm glad we had this chat. I really just called to hear that lilt in your voice and to tell you how much I enjoyed seeing you. And meeting your grandmother. Wonderful woman.'

'She is,' Vi said proudly. 'She's having us all over for Christmas dinner in the big dining room. She has invited any of the tenants in the apartments who are alone to join us.'

'That's very kind,' Jack remarked. 'I'd say you'll have a wonderful day with all your family.'

'Yes, I'm so looking forward to it,' Vi said. 'And Rose and I have had a talk, so all is well between us again. Lots of things going on beforehand, too, like the ballet school's Christmas show. My little niece will be a fairy. I have promised to go and watch her and that is something I mustn't miss.'

'You'd better not,' Jack agreed. 'I'll be going to Yorkshire to spend the holidays with my mother and sister and her family. Haven't seen them for a while. Looking forward to going there and closing the door to the big bad world out there.'

'I'm sure that'll be lovely,' Vi said.

'Yes, it will. Well,' Jack continued, 'I'd better let you sleep. Thanks again for taking the call.'

'No problem. Nice to talk to you.'

'It was. I'll be in touch. Goodnight, Violet. Sweet dreams,' he said softly and hung up.

But after turning off her phone, Vi found she couldn't go to sleep. Jack hadn't said anything important or startling, he was just lonely and needed to hear a friendly voice. But his warm voice had made her feelings for him stronger and now she wondered if he felt anything at all for her. These thoughts made her worry even more about how she was going to deal with him when the cameras stopped rolling. How was she going to handle all this confusion?

There were no manuals on this, or any tips in any acting courses about how not to fall for your co-star. She knew this happened from time to time between actors and that the relationships then crashed and burned afterwards, more often than not. She didn't want that to happen to her as she was sure it would eventually end in tears. But then she pushed all those thoughts away, chiding herself for being so unprofessional. She would have to do what other actors did – be cool off-set. That was probably what Kathleen herself had done, so Vi would have to do the same – if she could.

Vi checked her email as soon as she woke up and found a message from Jack with an attachment.

Just a quick sketch, he wrote. *A scene I thought would work. An argument between Kathleen and Don where he is jealous of her leading man, as you hinted that that was an issue with them. Read it through and then we'll discuss it when I call you tonight.*

The scene he had written was very well done, the dialogue snappy with an undertone of distrust from Don and huge distress from Kathleen when she was trying to explain that she only loved Don and that her attraction to her leading man was simply good acting and not real in any way. The subsequent storming out by Don was dramatic and true to the impression Vi had had from reading Kathleen's letters to Fidelma. It felt very real to Vi and she was amazed at Jack's writing skills.

'You're so good at writing dialogue,' she told him when he called that night on FaceTime.

'I just had that gut feeling about Don and Kathleen based on what you told me,' Jack replied, smiling at Vi. 'But thank you.

So... are you ready to read this with me? Starting with the first line on the top of the page.'

Sitting on the sofa, Vi picked up the pages she had printed. 'I'm ready.'

'They are in her trailer during a break from filming,' Jack explained. 'Kathleen is in period costume, including a very tight corset. You need to feel that as you say the lines.'

'Great image. I'll bear that in mind.'

'Good. So... action!' Jack exclaimed.

'"What do you mean I must be in love with him?"' Vi said in the Kathleen-voice she had practised. '"It's not real attraction. It's called acting."'

'"If that's only acting you're doing an Oscar-winning performance,"' Jack/Don growled in a slight Texan accent. '"I could tell that you're more than acting in that last scene. It was in your eyes and in the body language."'

'"Are you saying I'm lying?"' Kathleen asked.

'"If that's what you want to call it,"' Don drawled.

Vi felt suddenly angry on Kathleen's behalf and she read the rest of the lines in the scene with such fervour Jack started to laugh. 'I'm glad we're not in the same room,' he said. 'Or you might hit me.'

Vi, feeling breathless, looked at Jack on the screen of her phone. 'Yes, I might have. Sorry, I felt so into it I thought I was her for a while.'

'That's brilliant,' Jack said, smiling back at Vi. 'But maybe you should try to take a step back now. Try to think of something else just to get back to yourself.'

'Okay. We could just chat,' Vi suggested. 'How is the filming going over there in Scotland?'

'It's okay. A bit of stop-start as the weather changes all the time. But enough about me. I want to hear all about those letters you're reading. Anything else startling?'

'Nothing much,' Vi said. 'Just that Don and Kathleen didn't

speak for a long time after that row. And then he called her and they started seeing each other again. He was a little bit cool and distant for a while until they made up and then everything was fine.'

'So no more hints about her background or early life that might explain her insecurities?'

'Nothing so far.'

'I might look up some of the archives at Paramount,' Jack suggested. 'I have a friend who works there. A long shot but you never know.'

'Yes, I think we have to search everywhere to get a handle on her true persona,' Vi said.

'You're so dedicated,' Jack remarked, smiling warmly at her. 'I like that.'

'Thank you,' Vi said, the compliment making her blush.

'But now I will let you go,' Jack said, stifling a yawn. 'I'm falling asleep here. That was great reading by the way. I'll be in touch about the script, and you must let me know if you find anything else we should include. Bye, Violet,' he mumbled and then hung up.

Vi blinked and stared at the screen, wondering why he had been so abrupt. Had she revealed too much of how she felt about him, or was he just tired? Vi put her phone away, confused, worried and still wound-up after the intense scene she had just rehearsed. She would never really get a handle on Jack and his feelings. It would be best not to try too hard and put him out of her mind as much as she could. If that was even possible.

But she couldn't get Jack out of her mind now no matter how much she tried. When they had rehearsed the scene, she had felt such passion, not for Don and Kathleen, but for herself and Jack. He had complimented her on her acting skills, but she hadn't been acting. She had used her feelings for Jack and imagined him being jealous and not believing that she wasn't interested in flirting with other men. She had imagined how it would feel if Jack didn't trust her and she had felt Kathleen's anger as if it was her own.

When she went to sleep after their FaceTime session, Jack's face floated in front of her, his beautiful eyes warm and loving as he looked at her. In her dream, Jack told her he was falling in love with her as they walked on the beach, their arms around each other, looking at the sun setting into the ocean, bathing the sky and everything around them in a rosy glow.

Vi woke with a start in the middle of the night, realising it had only been a dream. She had been intent on not having any kind of romantic notions about Jack, but here she was dreaming about him like a besotted schoolgirl. *How unprofessional*, she thought, turning her pillow to the cool side and punching it into shape, at the same time mentally slapping herself for being such a twit. *Grow up*, she told herself sternly. *He doesn't care about you in that way at all.* But still, she couldn't help trying to imagine what it would be like to kiss him...

During the following week, Vi tried her best not to overthink it and concentrated on her ballet lessons and voice coach sessions. She told herself sternly that Jack had just wanted to rehearse the scene he had just written. It was all about the movie and not about Vi personally at all, she told herself sternly. She tried to distract herself and turned to her family in order to keep busy. She spent many afternoons helping Lily with the children, enjoying getting to know them. Rose said she was now back at work as Sophie was settling in well at the crèche and sleeping much better.

Christmas was fast approaching. Vi helped Sylvia to prepare for the big family dinner and also bought presents for everyone, foraging in the lovely little boutiques in Dingle town for all kinds of hand-crafted goods. The toy shop was a delight and Vi indulged in spending a lot of her money on presents for Naomi, Liam and Sophie. She also bought woolly hats for her brothers-in-law. She found a little shop selling jewellery made of sea glass and bought lovely earrings for both Lily and Rose. Sylvia would get a cashmere pashmina and Arnaud a silk cravat. Henri was the most difficult person to find a present for, but she finally decided on a dry robe to put on after surfing.

Vi then went searching for a present for her mother, who was in Donegal sorting out Vi's stepfather's estate after his death over a year ago. It was so sad to think of her mother having to cope yet again with losing a husband and Vi had been trying her best to help in any way she could. There wasn't much she could do, except keep in touch by phone and FaceTime. Patricia had visited Lily and Rose during the summer and now she was hoping to come and spend Christmas with them all, her first in many years. But what to get a woman who was going through a tragedy for the second time? Then Vi found a beautiful blue cashmere sweater with a matching scarf which seemed perfect for wrapping around her mother, like a permanent hug. It was very expensive, but Vi dug into her savings as she knew her mother would love the sweater and the thought behind it.

That done, Vi went back to the letters, deciding to get through the last ones before the holidays so she could get a final take on the relationship between Kathleen and Don.

Vi had to go back to London at the beginning of January to rehearse and prepare for filming that would start at the beginning of March. Some of the interior scenes would be filmed in London before they started shooting outdoor scenes in Kerry later that month. Vi decided to go back to the letters so she could finally get a clear picture of Don and Kathleen and their marriage. She picked up a letter at random to read while she had a mug of tea in front of the fire in the living room. It was dated 2 May 1960 and started with the usual *Dear Fidelma, I hope you're well, I'm fine and working on the script of a new movie. But I have some exciting news, so get ready for a scoop.* The next few sentences made Vi sit up, her heart beating faster as she read on.

> *Don has proposed! We're coming back to Ireland to get married in Kerry and then we're spending a year in Dingle town. I am taking a full year off filming and Don will be taking a sabbatical leaving his associate in charge of the business.*
>
> *I can't tell you how happy I am. I feel that this time, it's the real thing: true love that will last forever. We have been dating for over a year and now we truly know each other inside out. Despite our occasional rows, we're very much in love. Don is a wonderful man, kind, loving – he's a little domineering but I think I need someone to be solid and strong. I have told him everything, even the secret about my identity that only you know. And now Don knows too. He wasn't shocked at my revelation, only said that every actor creates an image in order to give the public what they want. I think this is true, and I'm so happy he understands and doesn't think I'm living a lie.*

Vi put down the letter and stared into the fire as she digested what she had just read. *Living a lie? What was that all about?* Only Fidelma and Don knew and now only one of them was alive to tell the tale, Don having passed away shortly after Kathleen. Vi knew instantly what she must do: go to Dublin and see Fidelma as soon as possible. But there was only a week until Christmas and she had promised to help Lily with the children so she could prepare for the Christmas tea party in the orangery. Vi couldn't possibly let her sister down and now that Naomi and Liam were getting so fond of their auntie Vi, they would be disappointed if she didn't turn up. And then there was Claire's dance studio's Christmas show. Naomi was dancing the part of a fairy and Vi had promised her to be there to watch. She couldn't possibly miss that.

Vi decided to put off the visit to Dublin until after Christmas. She had to go to London soon after that anyway, so she might visit Fidelma a day or two before her trip. That seemed the best solution. But first she had to find out which nursing home Fidelma was in. Vi called the dance studio in Dublin, hoping Finbarr might give her a clue, as he had been in touch with the old lady's daughter. But when Vi rang the number, all she got was a recorded message that said the dance studio was closed for the holidays and would open again on 4 January. Frustrated, Vi hung up, deciding it would be better to wait until January to pick up her research again.

Her phone rang just as she put away the letters. It was her agent Hugh calling from London.

'Hi, Hugh,' Vi said. 'How are things with you?'

'Not too bad,' Hugh replied. 'But there's something I want to go through with you before the holidays. I suppose you'll be with your family in Kerry during Christmas?'

'Yes,' Vi replied. 'I'm looking forward to it. So what was it you wanted to discuss?'

'The publicity people at the movie company have been in touch with me. They want you to raise your profile a bit before the shooting starts. Create a bit of a buzz, they said. They saw the photo of you and Jack at the pub a few weeks ago and now they think you should post it on your Instagram profile. You don't need to say that the two of you are an item or anything, just that you had a good time and are looking forward to working with him. That kind of thing.'

'That kind of thing?' Vi repeated. 'Oh, please, Hugh, you know I don't like social media much. I have a Facebook account and an Insta profile but I don't have many followers apart from my sisters and my granny and a few stray friends. I think it amounts to about thirty-five or so on each of them.'

'So get going and get some more,' Hugh insisted. 'Most big stars have thousands of followers, especially on Instagram.'

'Yeah, but...' Vi paused, thinking Hugh might be right. She should raise her profile a bit and go out there in the world of social media. But it seemed scary and not at all her thing. 'What about all the negative publicity?' she asked. 'I've heard so much about trolls.'

'Just ignore them,' Hugh said, sounding a little fed up with her hesitation. 'Don't think you have to expose all the details of your private life or your family. You can be outgoing and still retain your privacy. Just talk about your job as an actress and hold back on the personal stuff. That's what the big stars do, so why can't you?'

Vi sighed. 'Okay. I'll do my best. It won't be much in the beginning, but I'll try to get more followers. Maybe I can find someone to help me out with it? So is that all you wanted?'

'Yes, and to see how you're getting on,' Hugh said. 'Rehearsals start in London on the fifth of January. You'll have to go through the script and learn your lines over the holidays.'

'That's no problem,' Vi said. 'I'm already doing that. Jack and I have been in touch and read some new material together.'

'Good. I'm looking forward to seeing your Instagram posts. Maybe you could do TikTok as well? Post a video or two, perhaps.'

'Maybe,' Vi said. 'Anyway, Hugh, I have to go. Have a very happy Christmas. I'll be in touch before I get back to London. Cheers.' Vi hung up before Hugh told her to do anything else. She wasn't thrilled at the prospect of raising her social media profile, but if that was part of being a mainstream actress, that's what she would do.

But the problems with the script were more important. The more Vi read Kathleen's letters, the more she felt that the whole story should be changed. How could she possibly make that happen? She knew Jack was positive to the idea of rewriting a few scenes, but the whole script? That might be impossible. Vi began to wonder if she could play the part the way it was written now. Or... should she quit rather than portray a false image? Kathleen's story deserved to be told truthfully. Or not at all.

19

'It's such a huge pain,' Vi said later to Sylvia as they were having afternoon tea together in her granny's cosy living room. The curtains were drawn against the wet and windy afternoon and a turf fire glowed in the lovely old fireplace. The lamps dotted around the room cast a warm glow on the beautiful antique furniture and the multicoloured oriental rug. Vi pulled her legs under her and cradled her mug of tea, taking small bites of a freshly baked scone with blackberry jam. 'I mean, going out on social media. I hate that stuff and I'm terrible at it.'

'I enjoy it,' Sylvia said. 'I love posting photos on Instagram and then getting comments from all kinds of people. If you use the right hashtags, I mean.'

Vi sat up and stared at Sylvia. 'You're on Instagram?'

Sylvia nodded and spread jam on her scone. 'Yes. I thought you knew.'

'I had no idea.' Vi kept looking incredulously at her grandmother. 'And hashtags? I kind of know what they are but I don't know how to use them properly. It's so tedious to fill all of them in. So I don't use them.'

Sylvia shook her head. 'And I thought you were really social media savvy.'

'I'm not. But you obviously are,' Vi remarked. 'Amazing.'

'Why?' Sylvia asked coolly. 'Just because I'm old, you mean? But I have been on Facebook since it started and then on Twitter, but now that it's become X, it's a different story over there. So I do Facebook and Insta and have a lot of fun with it. Better than jigsaw puzzles and that boring Sudoku us old folks are supposed to do to stop our brains rotting.'

Vi burst out laughing. 'You're a gas woman, Granny. Hey, do you want a job? You could be my virtual assistant and do my Insta posts. What do you say?'

Sylvia smiled. 'I say that it would be a blast, pet. I was looking for something to while away the hours in the winter now that Rose is back at work and I'm not needed much at the office any more. So, yes, that would suit me very well. And it would help raise our profile too. I mean the Magnolia profile, of course.'

'I like that idea. But I want to see your Insta stuff first before I decide,' Vi said and picked up her phone. 'What name do you use?'

'@Sylviamagnolia. I thought you followed me already.'

'No, I don't think so. I didn't even know about it.' Vi logged into Instagram and searched for Sylvia's profile. 'Oh wow, I see it now,' she said, staring at the screen. 'You have three hundred followers too. Who are they?'

'Lots of locals,' Sylvia replied. 'And then potential tenants for the apartments and also people who love Kerry and might come and visit the Regency garden, the nursery and the café. I use hashtags to target different people and advertise events like Lily's Christmas tea party. That's #magnoliaxmasteaparty, by the way.'

'The photos are great,' Vi said, scrolling through lovely pictures of Dingle town and its surroundings.

'All taken with my iPhone,' Sylvia said. 'But Henri took some of them, too, like the surfing and beach shots.'

Vi put her phone on the coffee table and turned to Sylvia. 'Granny, you're officially hired.'

'We haven't discussed my fee,' Sylvia said. 'You might not be able to afford me.'

'So what is your fee?'

'A hundred a month and free tickets to all your movies, plus an invitation to any premieres either in Dublin or in London,' Sylvia stated.

'No problem,' Vi said, smiling. 'We have a deal.'

Sylvia held out her hand. 'Let's shake on that.'

They shook hands and laughed, then had more tea and scones while they chatted about what Sylvia could do. She said she'd draw up a plan and show Vi before she got started.

'Brilliant, Granny. I wouldn't know where to start, to be honest.'

'I think we should concentrate on the movie,' Sylvia suggested. 'Draw attention to that, take some photos of you in all kinds of beautiful places around Dingle and emphasise your role. Maybe also post photos of Kathleen all through her career. Create a special hashtag for it and tell Jack Montgomery to do the same. No need to get into your private life at all. It has to be professional and not a lot of blather that would invite nastiness.'

'Oh, Granny, that sounds perfect,' Vi exclaimed, feeling a rush of relief. She hadn't expected help from this quarter and it had come as a huge surprise to learn that Sylvia was so familiar with the ins and outs of social media.

Sylvia nodded, looking satisfied. 'Good. And you know I think we might tackle TikTok a little later. I'm really interested in what it does. But let's get going with Facebook and Instagram first. No need to get into that X thing. I think it's had its day.'

Vi nodded. 'That sounds great. We can start after Christmas.'

'What's wrong with right now?' Sylvia asked. 'We should get started as soon as possible. Give me your password to Instagram and I'll get going tonight.'

'What... when... Oh...' Vi stammered, feeling she was suddenly caught in a tornado. 'I have to look it up. It's on my phone.'

'I think we have to come up with a new one,' Sylvia said. 'A strong password, I mean. I bet yours isn't that safe.' She put her hand on Vi's shoulder. 'Don't worry. I know what I'm doing. I think the best idea is to create an image for you that is strictly about your acting career. Nothing to do with your real life or anything that you don't want to share.'

'I think that's what Kathleen did too,' Vi said, remembering that last letter she had read. 'The real Kathleen was a different person.'

'Yes,' Sylvia said. 'That would have been the best thing for her to do under the circumstances. But back to you and your social media profile...' Sylvia went on to lay out a plan for the Instagram posts and the hashtags while Vi looked at her grandmother in awe. It was incredible to her that someone of Sylvia's generation was so clued-up about marketing and how to raise visibility on the Internet. And then, Vi realised she had missed something. *What was that about Kathleen's circumstances?* she wondered. *Does Sylvia know about Kathleen's hidden identity?*

As there was no point in worrying about Kathleen's big secret, Vi decided to wait until she could speak to Fidelma. She took a break from her research, dance and voice lessons and concentrated on the preparations for Christmas: wrapping presents, helping to decorate the big Christmas tree in the entrance hall of Magnolia Manor and the smaller one in Sylvia's living room. Then they threaded a garland with green leaves and red berries all the way up the stairs to the top floor, making the house look festive. Some of the tenants who had no families to go to were happy to accept the invitation to dinner on Christmas Day.

Leo called one morning just as Vi was rushing out the door to do some last-minute Christmas shopping. 'Hi,' he said. 'Sorry not to have been in touch before. I just arrived in Cork and then I went on to Kinsale to celebrate Christmas with my uncle and his family. Thought I'd call to wish you happy holidays and all that and ask if you'd like to come to a party here on New Year's Eve?'

'Oh,' Vi said, surprised to hear his voice. She had nearly forgotten that he was supposed to come to Ireland around this time. 'Thanks. Eh... oh, a party? In Kinsale? But I won't know anyone.'

'You'll know me,' Leo said. 'And it won't take you long to get to know my cousins. They're dying to meet you. It'll be held in a pub, so very casual. No need to dress up. They are all sailing buddies and will be in sweaters and jeans. And there will be a few movie people here that will be working on the Kathleen movie, so you'll have a chance to meet some of the crew. Please say you'll come. It'll be great craic, they said.'

Vi smiled. She wasn't too keen to go to a party full of strangers, but she couldn't resist Leo's warm voice. 'Oh, okay,' she said. 'I'll come. I'll need a break after all the family stuff here.'

'Fabulous,' Leo exclaimed. 'I'll text you the details and the address of a great B&B nearby. See you then, Vi.'

'Looking forward to it. Happy Christmas,' Vi said before she hung up. Then she raced out the door to go to town before the shops closed for the holidays. So much to do and so little time left, as usual. Lily's Christmas tea was hugely successful and everyone made her promise to do it again next year.

Then there was the Christmas ballet show the day before Christmas Eve. It was very well attended and all the tickets were sold out. As they were going into the communal hall to find their seats, Lily told Vi that Naomi had been so excited she hadn't been able to sleep for several nights. 'Then we decided to let her sleep in her costume,' Lily said, laughing. 'It calmed her down and she slept like a log last night. I spent an hour ironing it this morning and trying to get the wings straight after being slept on.'

'Can't have been comfortable,' Vi suggested.

'No but she said she had to be a fairy all night to get ready,' Lily said, putting little Liam on her lap. 'He had to come,' she whispered. 'I hope he'll be quiet.'

'I'll bring him outside if he kicks up a fuss,' Violet suggested. 'But you'll be a good boy for Mummy, won't you?' she said to him, kissing one of his little hands.

Liam nodded, looking solemn. 'Liam good boy for Mummy,' he repeated.

There was a commotion at the door just before the show started. Someone had arrived late and was looking for a seat. *Why can't people arrive on time?* Vi thought, giving the late-comer an irritated glare. But then there was a whisper through the audience and she realised it had to be someone important.

20

'Holy mother, it's Jack Montgomery,' Lily hissed as he walked down the aisle. 'And he's coming this way. The seat beside you is free. Quick, get him to come and sit there.'

'But I thought that was Dom's seat,' Vi protested. 'I was holding it for him.'

'Never mind. He'll find another one,' Lily insisted. She waved at Jack and shouted: 'Hello, there is a seat free here beside Vi.'

Jack, who had been looking a little uncomfortable under the stares of so many people, seemed relieved as he pushed in and sat down beside Vi. 'Thanks.' He held out his hand and leaned over Vi to shake Lily's. 'Hi, I'm Jack.'

'I know,' Lily said, blushing. 'Hello. I'm Vi's sister Lily. How marvellous to meet you in person.'

'And you.' Jack smiled at Liam. 'And who is this?'

'It's me,' Liam said.

'Of course it is,' Jack said, taking Liam's hand and shaking it. 'Hello there. I'm Jack.'

'Jack,' Liam said and then pointed to his round little tummy. 'Liam.'

'What on earth are you doing here?' Vi interrupted.

'I came to watch the show,' Jack replied. 'I thought it might be something unique not to be missed.'

'A performance by five-year-olds?' Vi stared at him. 'I thought you were in Yorkshire for Christmas.'

'No, that didn't really work out,' Jack said. 'I'm going to go to New York to stay with friends instead but then I thought I'd stop off here on the way to see this.' He turned to look at Vi. 'I just wanted to see *you*, to tell you the honest truth.'

'Why?' Vi asked, her heart beating as he looked at her. She suddenly remembered her dream and felt her cheeks blush.

'Shh, the curtain is going up,' Jack said as the lights dimmed.

'Shh,' Liam echoed, putting his finger to his lips.

'You heard,' Jack whispered and took Vi's hand. 'We'll talk later.'

His warm hand holding hers made it hard for Vi to concentrate on the performance. But when Naomi fluttered onto the stage looking enchanting in her tulle skirt and matching wings, Vi pulled her hand from Jack's grip. Naomi's dance was lovely and the whole group of little fairies danced perfectly in time with the music. When they had finished, the audience gave them a standing ovation, shouting, 'Bravo,' over and over again, Jack among them.

He turned to Vi, his eyes shining. 'That was the most beautiful dance I've seen in a long time. Those little girls are the cutest.'

'Oh yes.' Vi smiled as she glanced at Liam, who had fallen asleep on Lily's lap. 'But some of us found it very tiring. I think he slept through most of it.'

'Thank goodness that's all he did,' Lily said. She turned to Jack. 'We're all going to Granny's for a drink and a bite to eat after the show. Mulled wine and mince pies. Would you like to come?'

'I'd be honoured,' Jack said. 'Thank you.'

'You can go with Vi in Granny's car,' Lily said.

Jack gathered up his coat. 'Thanks, but I have a car. Violet, do you want to come with me?'

'Thanks, but I'll go with Granny,' Vi replied, feeling flustered. She wanted to ask him what he was doing, arriving unannounced like this at her little niece's ballet show and why he was holding her hand and acting as though they were in some kind of relationship. Was he doing it for a bit of distraction, or was there another reason?

'But where is Sylvia?' Jack asked, looking around.

'I think she went outside,' Lily said. 'I saw her walking out with a friend. She'll be in the car waiting for Vi.'

'I'd better go,' Vi said. 'I'll see you there, Jack. You can park in the courtyard.'

Jack nodded. 'Okay. See you at the manor.' Then he looked around as someone called his name, asking him for his autograph while other people took photos of him with their phones. 'I'll try my best to get out of here alive,' he joked as Vi left.

'Good luck,' she shot over her shoulder as she left him to deal with the attention. He seemed perfectly at ease and chatted and smiled while he signed autographs and agreed to do selfies. Vi walked to the car where Sylvia was waiting, still wondering why Jack had arrived like that.

The dining room at the manor was buzzing with the news that Jack Montgomery was in town. But then the guests started on the mulled wine and mince pies and talked about the show and how lovely it had been. Naomi, still in her costume, walked around with a plate of mince pies and Vi passed around glasses with mulled wine. By the time Jack walked in the door, the party was in full swing and nobody except Vi and Sylvia noticed him.

'There's Jack,' Sylvia said to Vi and waved at him.

He immediately came to their side and took Sylvia's hand. 'Hello, Sylvia, thank you for inviting me to the party. I have to say the show was lovely. Such talented children.'

'Yes, they were very good,' Sylvia agreed. 'You should tell their teacher how much you enjoyed it.'

'Of course,' Jack agreed.

'Violet will introduce you,' Sylvia said. She paused, studying him for a moment. 'But tell me, how did you find out about the show? I don't imagine for a moment that you went to see it because you enjoy watching five-year-olds dancing. You just wanted to see Violet, didn't you?'

Jack nodded, looking oddly shy as he glanced at Vi. 'Yes, I did. We had such a good time together when I was last here, and then – as I was on my way to New York – I thought I'd stop off to wish her a happy Christmas. And you, too, of course.'

'Of course,' Sylvia said, looking amused. 'But now I have to look after my guests,' she continued and started to move away. 'Violet, get some mulled wine and mince pies for Jack, will you?'

'I will.' Vi didn't move from her spot. 'In a minute. I just want to know... well, what Granny just asked. How on earth did you know where to find me?'

Jack smiled. 'Detective work. I remembered how you said you didn't want to miss your niece's ballet show. Then I googled a bit, found the ballet school and saw the notice about their Christmas performance. But it's true what Sylvia said. I just wanted to see you before we got caught up with Christmas and everything. Please don't ask me why.'

'I'm afraid I have to ask just that.' Vi pulled at his arm. 'But I see people are getting excited now. They'll want to be introduced. We could go somewhere more private to talk for a minute.'

'Good idea. Where?'

'Granny's study. Come with me.' Vi went out through the door and down a corridor, Jack following close behind.

Once in the study, Vi turned on the light and faced Jack. 'Okay. Now we can talk. Or you can.' She stood in the middle of the floor and folded her arms, looking at Jack.

'What do you want me to say? Explain why I'm intruding into your private life? Trying to get to know your family, especially your grandmother?'

Vi nodded. 'Yes. All of that.'

Jack sighed, looking awkward. 'Now you make me sound like some kind of stalker. I shouldn't have barged in on the show like that. But...' He paused. 'I'm not sure you'll understand what I'm going to say, or even believe it.' He looked around the room. 'Can we sit down?'

'Okay.' Vi sank down on a chair beside the antique desk while Jack sat on the little couch in front of the fireplace. 'Go on, then,' she urged. 'What made you come back here?'

'Kerry,' he said. 'This magical place. I only spent a day or two here but I fell in love with it, with the mountains and the ocean and the light and the air and...' He stopped and laughed. 'It sounds crazy when I say it like that. But I felt so good that day we spent together.' He looked at her for a moment. 'And then there's you and your fabulous granny and your sister Lily and that tiny tot in her lap. And this manor with all its history. The people here are also something else. Warm, kind, funny but with great integrity and grace.' He drew breath and looked at his hands. 'It's all a very beautiful package. I've never felt such peace as here. Not even in Yorkshire.'

'Oh. I see. I do understand. I really do,' Vi said softly, oddly touched by his little speech. 'That's what I love about it too. I had forgotten how unique it is – forgotten what family really means, but now it's all coming back to me.' She laughed. 'You know what they say around here? "A day out of Kerry is a day wasted,"' she quoted.

'Great saying. I'm envious of you,' Jack confessed. 'You can always come back here and be with family. Do you know how lucky you are?'

'I do now.' Vi thought about how much she loved everything: the ocean and the mountains, the rain and wind, the sunshine and the green grass and how impossible it would be to live without ever seeing it all again. She had been away for a long time, chasing her dream of a great career, but now she was falling in love with her old home at the same time as he did. Tears suddenly welled up in her eyes as she met Jack's gaze. 'I believe you. And I think it's wonderful that you feel like that after just one day here.'

'Thank you.'

His eyes met hers and for a moment, it was as if time stood still. Jack took her hand and squeezed it, then he leaned forward as if to kiss her. But a sudden noise outside made him pull back and the moment was lost.

He stood up, looking dazed. 'After all this, maybe we should join the party? They'll be wondering what we're up to.'

'I know.' Vi got to her feet, disappointed that the spell was broken. 'Let's go back. Everyone will want to meet you.'

'They'll want to meet Jack Montgomery,' he remarked. 'The film star. Not the scared little boy I am inside.'

'We all have fears and doubts and sadness,' Vi said. 'But it's not a good idea to show it. Let's go out there and be – whatever they want us to be. The package has to shine. Never mind what's inside.'

Jack laughed. 'You're very wise for one so young.'

'It came to me just now,' Vi said. 'It was something in one of Kathleen's letters that made me think. She had told her husband something about herself nobody else knew. I think it's something that might have shocked people. But he wasn't shocked at all and said that all famous people have to create a public persona that has nothing to do with who they really are.'

Jack nodded and opened the door. '"Everyone wants to be Cary Grant. Even I want to be Cary Grant,"' he quoted. 'That's a famous line he said in an interview once. And I think it was true. The real Cary was actually Archie Leach with a very sad backstory.'

'Maybe Kathleen had a very sad backstory too,' Vi suggested, feeling a frisson of doom. 'I hope it's not something we will have to hide.' She walked through the door and started down the corridor. Jack closed the door of the study and followed her. 'I'm trying to figure out what kind of persona I should create,' she said as they walked towards the dining room from where they could hear that the party was still going. 'Don't get me wrong, it's not that I'm expecting to get really famous or anything, but all of this is making me realise I'm quite a private person.'

'Don't be the girl next door,' he suggested as he opened the door for her. 'Sweet, kind, outdoorsy. That's the real you. But your other persona has to have more attitude.'

'What kind of attitude?' Vi asked, hovering on the doorstep.

'Be mysterious,' he whispered in her ear. 'Don't be available for interviews. Don't pose on the red carpet.'

'Is that an option?' Vi murmured back. 'It sounds like a good one.'

'Thought it would suit you,' he said before they joined the party that was promising to go on all night, now with more food and sparkling wine that Arnaud provided. Jack was soon invited to do selfies and to join groups of people who wanted to meet him and tell him how much they admired him. Vi enjoyed watching him being the charming, glamorous film star she now knew was only an act. The real Jack was a different man altogether, a man she was beginning to feel a spark with. It frightened her. But she had never felt so alive in her life.

21

As always, Christmas was over in a flash. After weeks of preparations, the actual day went by very fast, and then St Stephen's Day seemed to follow in the same fashion. It had been a lovely Christmas with the usual mishaps in the kitchen, a few arguments, children getting overexcited, too much food and drink and everyone falling asleep in front of the TV. Violet was so pleased it had been a normal Christmas, not one overshadowed by her spat with her sisters. Her mother, Patricia, had arrived from Donegal and the three sisters enjoyed spending a few precious days with her before she had to go back to continue sorting out her late husband's estate. Vi had even found a few moments to ask Patricia about her father, and they'd spent one long evening huddled over photo albums.

In all, it had been a lovely two days that Vi enjoyed enormously. Sylvia was exhausted but happy and had to stay in bed a whole day to recover, she said, even though they all knew she was using it as an excuse to binge-watch all the episodes of *Downton Abbey*, like she did every Christmas. Lily, Rose and Vi served her breakfast in bed and then went to Logan's Pub in

Dingle to sample their famous brunch buffet, leaving Dominic and Noel to look after the children. It was the first time for over a year that the three sisters were together and this time Vi was determined that they would get on and there would be nothing at all to argue about, not if she could help it.

They went straight to the buffet table and helped themselves to smoked salmon, pork sausages, bacon, grilled tomato and an array of bread fresh from the bakery. Then, after ordering a glass of Guinness each, they sat down at a round table beside the window that overlooked the harbour and the Blasket Islands beyond.

'So... Jack Montgomery,' Rose started as she dug into her plate of smoked salmon and scrambled eggs. 'I could have fainted when he arrived at Granny's party. I missed his arrival at the ballet show. Couldn't get Sophie to settle and then Noel had to work late so I had to make something for him before I went out. I arrived at Granny's just as Jack walked in. Funny, but there wasn't much of a commotion but then most people would have seen him at the show. I was the only one who was surprised. And totally starstruck, I have to admit.'

'Aren't we all?' Lily cut in.

'Oh yes,' Rose said with feeling. 'He's even better looking in real life. I was so mesmerised I couldn't say anything clever when Granny introduced us. All I managed was, "Hi, welcome to Magnolia," in a squeaky voice. He laughed and said thank you and that he had heard so much about me. And then I asked, "Like what?" and he said just that I was a wonderful sister to Vi.' Rose drew breath and laughed.

'He's really nice,' Lily said. 'Not full of himself at all.'

'He liked being here,' Vi said. 'He said he's falling in love with Kerry.'

'Is he falling in love with *you* as well?' Rose looked at Vi.

'No, not at all,' Vi protested, trying her best not to show her real feelings. 'We're just going to work together on the movie and then we'll maybe stay friends, but that's all.'

'Really?' Rose looked doubtful. 'I'd say there's some chemistry going on, though. I thought you looked very cosy over the plate of mince pies.'

'It was the mulled wine going to your head,' Vi tried. 'Made you imagine all sorts of things.'

'I didn't imagine the way he looked at you,' Rose said.

'But he left early,' Lily cut in. 'Did he have something else on?'

'He was going to Shannon,' Vi explained. 'To catch the flight to New York early the next morning. He was staying with friends over there for Christmas. Then he's going back to Scotland to finish shooting the movie he's in. Some kind of thriller. And then we'll be rehearsing in London in January.'

'Oh, so that's what he's doing in New York,' Lily said. 'I thought...' She stopped.

'What?' Vi asked.

'Oh, nothing.' Lily sipped her beer. 'Probably not true at all.'

Vi put her fork with a piece of sausage down and stared at Lily. 'You're trying to tell me something.'

Lily and Rose looked at each other. 'There was a photo...' Rose said.

'In *The Irish Times*,' Lily cut in. 'Of Jack and a blonde woman sitting in a car outside a restaurant.'

'Looking very... close,' Rose said. 'We weren't going to tell you, but then we thought we should before anyone else did.'

'Oh,' Vi said, knowing it would take all her acting skills to appear not to care. She shrugged. 'So what? If he has a girlfriend, that's terrific for him. Why should that bother me? We're friends and colleagues, that's all. Whatever else you hear, it's not true.' She took a bite of sausage, feeling it might choke her, and it took a lot of effort to chew and swallow. 'Fabulous sausage. Is it from a local butcher?' she said in a casual tone that was just a tad squeaky with shock.

'Yeah. They're from Donlon's,' Lily said, looking at Vi with concern. 'Sorry if we sounded as if we believed what it said in the newspaper. It was just a photo taken out of context. Probably happens to him a lot.'

'Must be hard to be stared at and photographed all the time,' Rose said. 'It's bad enough that journalists do it, but people with their phones at the ready all the time must be such a pain in the neck.'

'It is,' Vi agreed. 'But I think he's learned to ignore it. I'm certainly not going to rush to look up that photo,' she lied, knowing that's exactly what she'd do as soon as she had a chance. 'And I'm also going to ignore anyone aiming their phones at me if that ever happens.'

'I'm sure it will once the movie is out,' Lily said. 'Or even before, if Granny has anything to do with it.'

Vi laughed and shook her head. 'Oh yes, she will. I already have several hundred new followers on Instagram. She has been posting lovely photos of the surrounding areas she took with her new phone. I told her there was no rush, but she is having fun, so who am I to stop her?'

'The shots she took of you on Ventry beach are also fabulous,' Rose agreed. 'I've shared some of them and used a lot of the hashtags she used. Especially #violetfleury and #kathleenosullivanstory.'

'And I've got a lot of queries about the orangery café,' Lily added. 'It was the hashtags Granny created that did it: #orangerycafe and then #magnoliamanorgardens. I think I'm going to have to open soon. Maybe February. That's two months before the usual opening. But Gretel, my au pair, is coming back from Germany next week, so that should work well.'

'I'm going to tell Noel to get a temp whenever Vicky is off sick or on leave,' Rose cut in. 'It's a bit inconsiderate of him to be calling on you all the time. But he misses you so he likes having you there from time to time to put a bit of order into the files.'

'I know, but I'm going to put my foot down,' Lily declared. 'It's hard when he's so sweet and asks so nicely but as Vi says, I have to learn to say no and not take on too much.'

Vi looked at her sisters and felt a dart of happiness that the three of them were together like this, chatting, helping each other and having fun. But the thought that Jack was over in New York because of some blonde woman he was possibly dating niggled at her so much she felt her stomach churn, which ruined her enjoyment of the food and being with her sisters. She had thought he felt as attracted to her as she was to him but then told herself sternly she had been reading too much into what he had said to her. She felt his feelings for Kerry were genuine and that he had truly found real peace here in this beautiful place. But that had nothing to do with how he felt about Vi. She had read too much into what he had said, misunderstood their almost kiss, and maybe that was her mistake. After all, they had only met a few times, even though they had shared a lot of things about themselves that day they spent together. She was rushing ahead, imagining a romance that would probably never happen. *I have to slow down, be more professional and stop thinking of Jack as some romantic hero*, she told herself. *He's not my boyfriend and never will be.* She smiled at Lily and Rose and raised her half-finished glass of Guinness. 'Here's to us and the great time we're having. Together and no fighting.'

'Cheers to that,' Lily said and clinked her glass to Vi's.

'Such happy holidays,' Rose agreed and clinked her glass with Vi and Lily in turn.

'Best Christmas ever,' Lily declared. 'And our little Violet a big star.'

'What are you doing for New Year's?' Rose asked.

'We're going to a party in Killarney,' Lily said. 'And we're taking the kids. Granny and Arnaud are going to some glam party in Tralee, I heard. Black tie, long dress and all that. Granny will be in her element. How about you?'

'We're staying at home,' Rose replied. 'Just having dinner and a little bit of bubbly in front of the TV. We need some peace and calm after all the upsets with Sophie. She's sleeping through the night now, thank goodness.' She turned to Vi. 'You can join us if you have nothing else on.'

'Thank you, that's very kind,' Vi said. 'But I'm going to a party in Kinsale. Leo, who's going to do the makeup for the movie, has invited me. It's going to be in a pub and his cousins are hosting it. I don't know any of them but he asked so nicely so I said yes. Thought it would be fun. I'm staying at a B&B there overnight.'

'That sounds great,' Rose said. She winked. 'Take lots of selfies with any hot men you meet and post them on your Insta page. Just to make us all jealous.'

'That's a good idea,' Lily agreed. 'And maybe,' she drawled with a mischievous look. 'You-know-who might see them...'

Vi couldn't help laughing. 'You two are so devious. I don't think I'll meet any hot men in Kinsale. They'll all be in Aran jumpers and jeans drinking pints and spilling beer on people while singing silly songs. It'll be fun, but not in any way glamorous.'

'You'll have a ball,' Lily said. 'Just what you need right now. It will take your mind off, well... you know.'

'Yes, maybe,' Vi said, knowing Lily was right. She needed to turn her mind away from Jack. Who better to do that with than a sweet, fun man like Leo?

As soon as Vi got home, she looked up *The Irish Times* online and found the photo Rose had mentioned after a bit of scrolling. She stared at a shot of Jack with a blonde woman, her heart sinking. It was quite obvious the couple, sitting in a car, were more than friends. They were locked in an embrace and seemed oblivious of the fact that they were being photographed, possibly by someone with a good camera on their phone – or a paparazzi with a telephoto lens. As Vi kept looking at the photo, her eyes full of tears, she realised she knew who the woman was. Liz Wall, the producer of the movie.

22

There were very few 'hot men' at the party in Kinsale, but Vi
enjoyed herself enormously all the same. She had decided to
push all thoughts of Jack and Liz to the back of her mind and do
her best to have a good time. The party was held in the back
room of a quaint little pub near the yacht club. As she had
suspected, most of the people, both men and women, were
dressed casually, in jeans and sweaters or Munster rugby shirts.
The food was delicious and consisted of mostly fish and seafood
served with either white wine or draught Guinness.

Leo was so obviously happy to see her and introduced her to
his cousins and the friends he had made since he arrived just
before Christmas, all jolly Cork people who greeted a girl from
Kerry with great enthusiasm.

'I should have worn the Munster rugby shirt,' she said to
Leo as they were enjoying a plate of scampi and chips by the
fire. 'But red doesn't really go with my hair.'

He looked at her dark green sweater. 'I know what you
mean. And green is so your colour. It brings out your eyes. I
don't really get this Munster thing. I thought you'd be rooting
for Kerry.'

'Cork and Kerry are both in Munster, which is one of the four provinces of Ireland. The other ones are Leinster, which is Dublin, the midlands and surrounding areas, Connacht in the west and then Ulster in the north.'

'Oh I see,' Leo said. 'There's so much to Ireland that I didn't know about.'

'I would have thought your cousins had educated you,' Vi quipped.

'They might think I already knew. And I was afraid to ask in case they thought I was an ignorant British git.'

Vi laughed and drained her glass of Guinness. 'I'm sure they wouldn't. But you can ask me anything and I promise not to tell your cousins.'

'Thanks, I will.' Leo looked gratefully at her. 'One question I'd like to ask is not about Ireland and its geography, but about your research into Kathleen O'Sullivan's life. How is it going?'

'Slowly,' Vi said. 'But I'm beginning to understand her better.' She went on to tell Leo about the letters and what she had found out so far. 'There was some kind of secret that only her husband and this friend knew about. So I'm going to find her and see if I can talk to her. We had a chat over the phone before Christmas but she didn't tell me much then.'

'Where's the nursing home?' Leo asked.

'Somewhere in Dublin. I'm going there before I go back to London for the rehearsals and costume fittings.'

'I'll go with you,' Leo offered.

'You will?' Vi stared at him, forgetting her plate of scampi. 'That's very kind of you. Are you sure?'

'Yeah.' Leo dipped a chip into his tartar sauce. 'I can just as well go to London from there. Never been to Dublin so I'd like to take a look around the city.'

Vi nodded. 'Great. I'm going up on the train from Tralee on Tuesday, then I'll be catching the morning flight to London on

Thursday. I'm staying in my mum's flat in Stillorgan. There's a bus to the airport from there.'

'I'll look for a B&B in the centre,' Leo suggested. 'I'd like to see all the famous sights. The Book of Kells in the Trinity library and that Guinness place and the pubs in Temple Bar. We could meet up somewhere if you can get away. I'm sure you'll want to spend time with your mother, though.'

'She won't be there,' Vi explained. 'She lives in Donegal. She only uses the flat as a base when she's in Dublin occasionally. She says she'd go mad without a little retail therapy from time to time. It's tiny, just one bedroom and a sofa bed in the living room. We all have a key and can stay there whenever we need a place to crash for a night or two. I might pop into town on the bus to show you around if you want. In the meantime, I'll find out which nursing home old Fidelma is in and if I can see her. Shouldn't be too hard. The guy at the dance studio was very helpful before.'

'I hope he'll be able to tell you,' Leo said before the music started up and it became impossible to talk. He finished his pint of Guinness and stood up, holding out his hands. 'Dance with me, Vi. It's nearly twelve o'clock. This year will be last year in a little while.'

Vi laughed and joined Leo on the improvised dance floor, dancing with him and everyone else to the loud music. Then the waiters handed around glasses of champagne and they stopped the music while someone opened the window so they could hear all the church bells in Kinsale ring in the New Year.

It was a beautiful moment, and Vi closed her eyes, feeling as if time stood still while the sound of the bells echoed over the still, black water of the bay. She enjoyed the rush of cool sea air against her hot face, and the pounding of the bells in her ears. It had always been a magic moment: when the old year slipped away, along with all the troubles and negativity of the past, and the New Year seemed so fresh and full of hope and promises of good days to come.

'It'll be your best year,' Leo said in her ear and then kissed her long and hard on the mouth while a spectacular fireworks display lit up the sky on the other side of the bay. 'Happy New Year, Violet Fleury.'

'Happy New Year, Leo,' she whispered back, trying to decide how she felt after that kiss. It had just been one of those spur-of-the-moment New Year's Eve things, when everyone kissed everyone else. But Vi saw the sparkle in Leo's blue eyes and knew it meant a lot more to him than that. Then his cousin put his arms around her and kissed her on the cheek, saying, 'Happy New Year,' followed by all the people she had met during the course of the evening and she was caught up in all the hugging and laughing. The music started again and everyone danced and shouted and drank champagne and Vi was lost in the moment and didn't give herself a chance to think about Leo and that kiss or how she felt about it.

But when she walked to the B&B later that night, she finally had a chance to gather her thoughts. Leo's kiss had surprised her – not that he had done it, but the intensity and the look in his eyes as he let her go. Then, when she stopped for a moment and looked up at the stars twinkling in the dark sky, she knew that he could be nothing more than a friend to her. Leo was sweet and kind and fun to be with, but that was all she felt. As she stood there, another man drifted into her mind. A man who she should try not to think about romantically, but she couldn't help herself. She couldn't stop thinking about Jack Montgomery, and for the first time in a long time, Vi knew how it felt to have her heart broken.

As if reading her thoughts, Jack called the next morning. Vi was on her way to the bus that would take her back to Dingle when her phone rang. She stopped, fished it out of her bag and answered without checking who it was.

'Hello? I'm running to the bus, can I call you back in a minute?' she asked.

'Yes, of course. Talk to you then,' Jack said and hung up.

Vi stood there for a second and then, her legs suddenly wobbly, managed to get on the bus, show her ticket to the driver and find a seat by the window. Then she called Jack.

He answered at once. 'Hi, there. Are you on the bus?'

'Yes,' Vi croaked, her throat dry.

'Where are you going?' he asked.

'I'm on my way back to Dingle. I was at a party in Kinsale last night with Leo.'

'Who? Oh, you mean Leo, the makeup guy?'

'Yes.'

'Good party?'

'Great fun, yes,' Vi replied. 'Happy New Year, by the way.'

'Happy New Year, Violet,' Jack said, his voice softer.

'Are you still in New York?'

'Yes. I'm not sure when I'm coming back to London.'

'Why?' Then Vi felt in her gut that there was something wrong. 'Are you not coming to the rehearsal next week?'

'No.' Jack paused. 'That's why I'm calling you. Thought you should know before someone else told you.'

'Told me what?' Vi asked with a feeling of impending doom. He was going to tell her he was in a relationship with Liz. 'What's going on, Jack?' she asked, even though she thought she knew what was coming. But his reply was even more startling.

'I'm pulling out of the movie,' Jack said.

23

Vi froze. 'You're – what?' she stammered.

'I'm quitting the movie,' Jack said. 'I'm not going to be in it. I'll still be producing, but not acting and I won't be on the set much at all.'

'Why?' she asked, her throat tight with shock.

'It's a little complicated.'

'Is it because of your involvement with Liz?' Vi asked, her stomach churning as she remembered the photo she had seen.

'Liz? No, why would it be?' he asked, sounding puzzled. 'Look, I'm sorry. I can't talk about it over the phone. I...' Jack sighed. 'There's a lot of stuff going on, involving the people who have invested in the movie. Nothing to do with you at all, of course. Everything else is going ahead as planned, except with another actor.'

'But...' Vi stammered, 'who is going to play Don now?'

'A very good actor called Peter Black. He's actually from Texas, so a much better choice than me. Not a huge name, but I still think it'll work. Could make his career, actually.'

'I think I know him,' Vi said. 'I've worked with him before. He's a good actor but not like you,' Vi said, wistfully.

She was getting worried; her big break was disappearing before her eyes. She'd been working so hard. Was it all for nothing?

'Nobody is,' Jack said, laughing. 'Nor is he as modest.'

Vi had to smile despite her misery. 'I bet.' She tried not to burst into tears as it all seemed to come together in her mind. Jack and Liz were in a relationship and she had probably told Jack to drop out. The movie would suffer as a result and Vi would end up where she started: having to audition for small parts and then being forced to give up altogether.

'So that's it,' Jack said. 'Now you know.'

'Yes. I can see everything very clearly. But you could have told me earlier,' Vi replied, dismayed.

'What do you mean?' Jack asked, sounding puzzled. 'This happened only yesterday. And now, here I am at five in the morning New York time, calling you so you'd find out as soon as possible.'

'Yes, but you could have told me about you and Liz,' Vi said, her voice barely audible.

'What? Me and...?' Jack muttered. Then he seemed suddenly angry. 'What the hell do you mean?'

'You must know. I saw the photo in the newspaper and it said more than a thousand words.'

'What photo?' Jack asked.

'I'm sure you know. It's out there now, so you don't have to hide it any more. You don't care about me or the movie or anything. It's all very clear to me, so don't bother denying it.' Vi hung up without waiting for an answer. She turned her face to the window while tears rolled down her cheeks all through the journey, until the bus reached Dingle. Then she blew her nose, gathered up her things and got off.

She had completely forgotten that Sylvia was picking her up at the bus stop and walked past the car and up the road in a daze, giving a start as she heard a sudden loud beep. She turned around and saw her grandmother getting out of the car, waving frantically.

'Violet,' Sylvia called. 'What's wrong with you? Did you forget I was meeting you at the bus stop?'

'Oh,' Vi said. 'How stupid of me. I was just a little absent-minded. Late night and a long trip on bumpy roads.' She walked slowly to the car and got into the passenger seat. 'Hi, Granny. Sorry about that.'

Sylvia looked at Vi for a moment. 'You've been crying.'

'No, I think I have a cold or something,' Vi said, turning her face away from her grandmother's gaze.

Sylvia caught Vi's chin and turned her face. 'That's not a cold. Those red eyes are the result of a lot of tears. Is it because of that photo in *The Irish Times*?'

Vi nodded. 'Yes,' she whispered.

'And you immediately jumped to the wrong conclusion. You silly girl.' Sylvia started the car. 'Let's get home and we'll have a cup of tea and then we'll talk.'

'I don't want to talk about it,' Vi protested. All she wanted was to go home and figure out what to do next. With another actor in Jack's place, the film was no longer a guaranteed success. What was she going to do next with her life? She couldn't continue to pretend she was going to make it. She needed to be realistic now. 'Please drive me home.'

'I will not,' Sylvia snapped. 'You're going to come home with me and listen to what I have to say. You have a lot to learn, my girl.'

'About what?' Vi asked defiantly. 'Men?'

'Yes. And life. And what goes on out there in cyberspace. And how not to jump to conclusions and a lot of other things.'

Bewildered, Vi stayed silent until they reached the manor and Sylvia parked the car in the courtyard. Then she got out and followed her grandmother inside and sat down at the kitchen table while Sylvia busied herself making tea and heating up a slice of apple pie. While she waited, she remembered those incidents when Sylvia had tried to make Vi break up with boyfriends she thought 'unsuitable'. Vi had rebelled against it and kept seeing whoever it was, even though she secretly agreed with her grandmother. Vi had had a habit of falling for good-looking young men who weren't either kind or loyal. But that was when she was very young and once she had embarked on her career, she had become a lot less gullible. But this time she had been taken in by Jack's charm and empathy – and his obvious love of Kerry. She realised she had been wrong yet again and now her grandmother would give her another lecture.

When Sylvia had handed Vi a steaming mug and a plate with warm pie topped with cream, she broke her silence. 'So,' she said, sitting down opposite Vi with her own mug. 'Drink your tea and have some pie while I talk.'

Vi nodded and sipped some tea which, with the addition of the smell from the apple pie, made her feel a little better. 'Go on, then. What have I done wrong this time?'

'Nothing, apart from overreacting,' Sylvia said. 'Before we go on, could you look up that photo again?'

'The one with...' Vi started, picking up her phone.

'Liz and Jack, yes.'

'Why?' Vi mumbled as she got to the page she was looking for. 'It'll only make me feel worse.' The photo appeared on her screen and she flinched as she saw it. 'Okay. I have it.'

'What do you see?' Sylvia asked, taking a careful sip of her tea.

'Liz and Jack in a clinch,' Vi mumbled as she peered at the screen. 'Sitting in a car.'

'Take a closer look at Liz. Her hair in particular,' Sylvia instructed.

'Yeah, okay. It's... short.' Vi looked at Sylvia. 'Did she have it cut?'

'No. But that photo is two years old. Taken just before they broke up. Liz let her hair grow out and now it's all the way down her back, isn't it?'

'Yes, that's right. It was the last time I saw her.' Vi looked at the photo again and saw what her grandmother meant. Liz's hair was cut in a pixie style and Jack also looked different. His hair was very short. 'He must have had that style done for the thriller he was in at that time,' Vi said.

'Exactly.'

'Oh.' Vi took another sip of tea to steady her nerves, then dug into her pie. 'How do you know all this?' she asked when she had swallowed her first bite.

Sylvia put her mug in the table. 'Jack called me just after he had spoken to you. He said you had hung up before he had a chance to ask why you were so curt with him and then you didn't answer when he tried to call you back.'

'He called *you*?' Vi stared at her grandmother incredulously, her spoon with pie frozen in mid-air. 'Are you serious?'

Sylvia looked slightly awkward, brushing fluff off her cardigan. 'Yes, we've had a few chats over the phone from time to time in the past weeks.'

'Chats? About what?' Vi couldn't believe her ears.

Sylvia waved her hand. 'Oh, you know, life, love, men, women, relationships, family...' She sighed and shook her head. 'He hasn't had a very happy childhood or youth. He left and went to drama school to get away from it all. And then he found he was good at it and began to love acting. He worked so hard in the early years. And then all that fame... It didn't sit well with the folks back home.'

'He told me some of that,' Vi said. 'But you... I can't believe that you've been talking to Jack all this time and never told me.'

Sylvia took Vi's empty plate and got up to get another piece. 'Well, I think he didn't want anyone to know. But then, I thought it would be best to tell you. And to make you understand what was going on, after what happened with that old photo and his past history with Liz. You needed to know the truth. And to learn an important lesson.'

'What lesson?' Vi asked angrily.

Sylvia cut a piece of pie and put it in front of Vi. 'Not to believe what you see on social media. Isn't that what you've said to your sisters?'

'Yes. Oh, okay, I know what you're saying. And now I feel stupid.' She picked up her spoon.

Sylvia patted Vi's hand. 'You overreacted because you're in love.'

'I'm not sure about that,' Vi protested. 'We have only met a few times. It's not possible to fall in love that fast.'

'Of course it is. I met Liam, your grandfather, on a train,' Sylvia said. 'We chatted for hours and by the time I got off at my station, I knew I loved him. We were married two months after that.'

'Yes, but that's unusual,' Vi argued as she absentmindedly started eating. She'd heard the story many times. 'I mean, people normally have to know each other a long time before they know how they feel.'

'How do you know?' Sylvia asked, sitting down again opposite Vi. 'I don't think you've ever been really in love, have you?'

'No,' Vi confessed. 'Well, I've had boyfriends but I was never serious about any of them.'

'You've been too busy building your career,' Sylvia said.

'I didn't want anything to distract me from my work,' Vi tried to explain. 'And I was right. Look what's happened now that I'm... attracted to someone. He's decided to quit the film. Everything is ruined. The movie will bomb and I'll be back to square one.'

'I'm not so sure.' Sylvia looked thoughtful. 'He told me something...' She paused. 'Well, maybe I shouldn't say anything and let you work it out yourselves.'

'Please tell me,' Vi urged. 'I need to know what else he said.'

'He said he had very strong feelings for you.'

Vi felt her heart flip. It was exactly what she had been wanting to hear all winter, but now everything had changed. What did it mean? 'Did he tell you why he's dropped out of the movie, then?' she asked, digging into the apple pie, feeling she needed some comfort food to settle her stomach.

'Not in so many words. I'm guessing it's about a lot of things. I know he has another project he thought wouldn't happen but now it has. He wants to produce rather than act in future as well. But I'll leave it up to him to tell you.' Sylvia drew breath and drank her tea. 'So there you are. You know everything now.'

Vi nodded, scraping her plate for the last bits of the apple pie. 'Yes. I'm sure he'll never want to talk to me after the way I behaved. I bet no woman ever hung up on him like that.'

'I'd say not,' Sylvia agreed, looking amused.

'What am I going to do?' Vi asked. 'Call him and say sorry?'

Sylvia shook her head. 'No. I'd leave him alone for now. Let it settle. Work on your lines, prepare for the movie.'

'What did you say to Jack? About me, I mean?' Vi asked, unable to leave the subject alone.

'Just that I love you dearly and that you're a lovely, kind, sweet girl with a bit of a temper. And that I'd explain everything to you about him and Liz.'

'Oh.' Vi nodded. 'I see.' She thought for a moment. 'But you know what? I think there is still something between him and Liz. I could tell that they're very close during that interview I did with the whole production team.'

'He said they'd had a bit of a fling a few years ago, but it's been over for a long time. You have to trust him, Violetta. Concentrate on the movie and working with that other actor. Jack will get in touch. If he has truly broken off with Liz, he'll want to see you and talk to you.'

'And if not?' Vi asked.

'Then you still have to move on and try to get over it,' Sylvia said. 'You're a strong girl behind it all. You wouldn't be where you are if you were weak.'

'I suppose,' Vi said miserably, wondering how she was ever going to get over Jack. But she had to try and not feel sorry for herself. 'Maybe I should stick to my original plan and keep avoiding men,' she suggested.

'You can't do that forever, Vi. It would be such a shame. To share your life with someone is a wonderful thing.' Sylvia patted Vi on the cheek. 'Feeling better?'

Vi finished her tea. 'Yes, much better, Granny. Tea and pie, that's the best remedy.' She stood up and stretched. 'And now I'm going to go home to take a little nap and then I'll go for a bit of a walk and then back to bed. Tomorrow, as you always say, is another day.'

'It certainly is,' Sylvia said.

Vi stopped on her way to the door. 'Granny, can I ask you something?'

Sylvia nodded. 'Of course. What do you want to ask me?'

'How come you and Jack became so close?'

'Oh.' Sylvia paused for a moment on her way to the sink with the tea things. 'Well, you see, it's funny, but he reminds me so much of Fred.'

'My father?' Vi asked, startled by this news.

'Yes,' Sylvia said, her eyes glistening with tears. 'He does. In so many ways.' She paused for a moment and blinked away the tears. 'It's so strange, but he has the same kind of aura and energy. The same way of looking at you and listening to people.' She shook her head. 'Lots of other things, too, that I can't really explain.'

'I see,' Vi said. 'That makes him special to me too. Even if we can never be more than friends.'

'That's a good start,' Sylvia agreed.

24

How odd, Vi thought as she walked to the gatehouse, *that Jack reminds Granny of my father, who I never knew. There must be more to it than she told me. Is it his sense of humour, his love of the ocean, or simply the way he speaks and moves? Or that my father was the same age as Jack when he died?* Or was it just a meeting of minds – perhaps Sylvia and Jack were somehow kindred spirits despite the age gap? It wasn't the physical appearance, as Fred had had reddish hair and green eyes and Jack had dark hair and eyes. It had to be in their similar personalities, which intrigued Vi and made her feel a little sad that she couldn't figure it out because she hadn't known her father at all. To Sylvia, losing her only son would have been the worse tragedy. Maybe making friends with Jack gave her some little bit of comfort. This made Vi's feelings for Jack even stronger and the fear of losing him a lot worse. She knew Sylvia was right and that she should let things settle down a bit before they met again. Otherwise there was a danger that she would overreact again and push him away. For good.

Lost in thought, Vi gave a start as her phone rang. She

pulled it out of her pocket and peered at the caller ID and saw that it was Leo.

'Hi, Leo,' Vi said. 'How are you?'

'Only slightly hung-over and a little tired. But it was a great party, don't you think?'

'Oh yes, a lot of fun,' Vi said. 'Thank you for inviting me. I really enjoyed it.'

'You survived the trip back on the bus, then?'

'It was a little rough,' Vi replied, remembering how she had wept nearly all the way. 'But I'm fine now. I'm going to have a little nap in a moment, though.'

'Good idea. I haven't even got out of bed, actually,' Leo confessed. 'I've been lying here watching an old Kathleen O'Sullivan movie on my iPad. Just to get the feel of her hair and makeup and all that nineteen fifties stuff.'

'She was great, wasn't she?' Vi said.

'Fabulous,' Leo replied. 'But hey, I called you to find out if you're going to Dublin on Tuesday? We were supposed to go to the nursing home, remember? Is that still on?'

'Yes, of course,' Vi said, pulling herself back to the present. 'I'm going to call the dance studio tomorrow to see if that guy, Finbarr, can put me in touch with Filomena's family, so I can find out which nursing home she's in. I'm catching the morning train from Tralee on Tuesday morning. And then we'll go and see her before we catch the flight to London on Thursday.'

'Sounds like a good plan,' Leo said. 'I'm actually getting a lift with one of my cousin's friends who's driving up to Dublin tomorrow. And he offered me a bed in his place, so I'm sorted for a place to stay. It's in an area called Donnybrook, near the centre, he said.'

'Not too far from where I'm staying,' Vi said.

'So give me a call when I arrive and we can go for a pint somewhere.'

'That would be nice. I'll get in touch when I've found out

where Fidelma is.' Vi said goodbye and pocketed her phone. She thought about what her grandmother had said about her romantic life. Even if things didn't work out with Jack, Sylvia was right that Vi had spent too long avoiding love. She wanted a partner: someone to spend long evenings walking on the beach with, someone to go over lines with her and plan a family with. She thought of her nieces and nephews. Perhaps that was at the heart of her comments about Rose and Lily last year. Was she jealous of the wonderful families they'd built?

Leo was a wonderful man, but even with Jack out of the picture, she knew he wasn't for her. She thought of the kiss they shared on New Year's Eve. Perhaps she should make sure he understood how she felt about him next time they met.

Jack's beautiful bright eyes came to Vi's mind. Love can't be planned. It has no rhyme or reason and it can strike like a bolt of lightning and then you either accept it and let it sweep you away, or try to move on and forget it had ever happened. *Either way, it breaks your heart in the end*, Vi thought as she walked down the path, the breeze from the sea soothing her frayed nerves.

Two days later, Vi and Leo stood outside a Victorian redbrick house in a leafy suburb of Dublin. It was surrounded by a garden that would be lovely in the spring and summer, but now seemed a little drab in the early January light. Drops from the bare tree branches fell onto their hair and shoulders and the air smelled of damp earth. Vi shivered, anxious to get inside before the next shower. It hadn't been difficult to find the home as Finbarr at the dance studio had managed to get the name of it from Fidelma's daughter.

Vi turned to Leo before she pressed the button on the intercom. 'So, here we go,' she said. 'Wish me luck.'

'Good luck,' Leo said, patting her shoulder. 'Are you sure you don't want me to go with you to visit the old lady?'

'Yes, I am,' Vi replied. 'I was told Fidelma is a little frail and gets confused if there are too many people visiting at the same time. She knows I'm coming and sounded happy to see me, a member of staff told me when I phoned. There is a cafeteria on the ground floor, they said, where you can wait for me.'

Leo nodded. 'Okay. That seems like a good plan.'

'I'm glad you came with me, though,' Vi said to reassure him. She'd also been glad that he'd given friendship vibes ever since he arrived. There didn't seem to be anything romantic between them any more. 'It's good to know you're nearby and that I can share whatever I learn straight away with someone I trust.'

'Whatever it is will stay between us,' Leo said.

'I know. But we'd better go in.' Vi pressed the button, said her name and who she was visiting when prompted by a tinny voice and then the entrance door opened. They stepped inside and Leo disappeared through a door marked CAFETERIA. Then Vi walked to the desk in the reception area and rang the bell.

A nurse appeared within seconds, smiling at Vi. 'Hello, can I help you?'

'My name is Violet Fleury and I'm here to visit Fidelma Sheridan,' Vi said.

'Oh yes, of course,' the nurse said. 'She's expecting you.' She pointed at a door. 'It's through there and down the corridor. Then the second door on the right. Her name is on it.'

Vi felt increasingly nervous as she walked down the corridor. Here was the moment she had been waiting for since before Christmas. What was Kathleen's real identity? Did Fidelma know? *Is it right for me to dig into this?* Vi asked herself as she reached the door with Fidelma's name on it. *Would it be better to leave well enough alone and just follow the script? No,* she answered herself, *the truth has to come out, or at least be found so that I can play the real Kathleen and not some glossy image of who the public thought her to be: the feisty Irish colleen.* In any case, it would be nice to meet the woman who had known Kathleen when they were both young and hopeful.

Vi took a deep breath and knocked on the door. After several minutes, a soft, melodious voice called: 'Come in.'

Vi slowly opened the door and peered in. A tiny woman with a shock of white curly hair sat on an armchair by the window. She smiled at Vi. 'Hello, are you Violet?'

'Yes,' Vi said and walked into the room that was bright and welcoming with walls covered in framed prints of flowers and beautiful landscapes. The room smelled faintly of lavender. 'Hello, Fidelma. Thank you for agreeing to see me.'

'Why wouldn't I?' Fidelma asked. 'I like having visitors as long as they speak softly and have happy faces.' She looked at Vi for a moment. 'Yes. You have a happy face, even if your eyes are a little sad. But you also look very like Kathleen, the way I remember her. The red hair, the green eyes, the freckles... Very similar, as if you were sisters. Except...' Fidelma paused and leaned forward, staring at Vi. 'You don't dye your hair, do you?'

Vi flicked her hair back from her face. 'Not, this is my real colour.'

Fidelma sat back. 'Thought so.' She gestured at a chair beside her. 'But please sit down so we can chat properly. Do you want a cup of tea? I could ring the bell and ask someone to get you whatever you want.'

'I'm fine, thank you,' Vi said, smiling at Fidelma's ladylike manners. 'Unless you want some tea yourself?'

Fidelma shook her head. 'No, dear. I don't want anything right now. I just had lunch and it was delicious. Thank goodness my daughters got me into this home which is expensive but well worth the money. They sold my house in order to pay the fees, but I really didn't mind. I was a little homesick at first, but now I'm content to stay here, where there are people to look after me. Things were getting difficult in my big house, you see. Dusty and draughty and full of leaking pipes and a roof that needed repairs. Who wants that in their old age? Not me, that's for sure. I don't miss that old pile one little bit.' She smiled mischievously as Vi sat down on the chair. 'But don't tell my daughters how happy I am. I like to make them feel just a tiny bit guilty. Keeps them on their toes and gets them to visit me often.'

'I won't tell,' Vi promised, trying not to giggle. Fidelma was so endearing with that glint of humour in her pale blue eyes.

Fidelma nodded and patted Vi's knee. 'Good girl.' She sat back and looked at Vi for a moment. 'So,' she continued. 'You have come here to talk about Kathleen?'

'Yes,' Vi said. 'I'd like to know as much about her as you can tell me. Whatever you remember.'

'No problem,' Fidelma said. 'I remember things that happened a long time ago better than what I had for dinner last night. And my year at the dance school was probably the most wonderful time in my life. Except for getting married and having my daughters, of course. But that had to do with my adult life. When I was young...' She paused for a moment, her eyes wistful. 'I was so excited to start lessons at the school. I had been practising ballet at a little dance school in our neighbourhood and had just started on pointe shoes. The dance studio was very well known and only for students who showed promise. My parents had scraped together enough money for a year's tuition. They hoped I'd become a ballerina like Anna Pavlova.' She laughed. 'My mother had these dreams for me, you see. And then I ruined them by getting married and becoming a housewife. I don't think she ever really forgave me.'

'I'm sure she did,' Vi remarked, getting impatient. She wished Fidelma would get back to her memories of Kathleen without any more distractions. 'So you met Kathleen at the dance school?' she asked, hoping to get Fidelma back on track.

Fidelma smiled. 'Oh yes. We met the very first day. Kathleen was in the more advanced class then, I was in the junior class. But we started to chat in the changing room that first day. She was so kind to me. Made me feel more confident. She said she was envious of my slim frame. Kathleen was quite statuesque and not really built for classical ballet. But she was very good at it all the same. I used to love watching her practise. She was so graceful.'

Vi nodded. 'Yes. I've seen her movies and that lovely gracefulness was part of her beauty.'

'Exactly,' Fidelma agreed. 'But she was also very kind and very ambitious. I do remember that Christmas show where the talent scout noticed her. It changed her whole life, really. She had wanted to go on the stage, maybe get a part in a play at the Abbey Theatre in Dublin. That's what she was working towards. But then Hollywood came calling and she was whisked away to a life she wasn't really prepared for.'

'I can imagine,' Vi said, trying to envisage what it had been like to get an offer like that when Kathleen was still so young.

'She was only nineteen,' Fidelma said as if reading Vi's thoughts. 'It was in nineteen forty-eight, just after the war. I was a little younger and I thought it was like a fairy tale. But when she left, I missed her terribly. We had become close friends during my first year at the school.'

'How lovely,' Vi said, shifting on her chair feeling more and more impatient. How could she get Fidelma to reveal what Vi really wanted to know? 'So then,' she started, 'when she left, you must have been upset.'

Fidelma nodded. 'Yes. I missed her terribly. And of course, she missed me. She said I was her only true friend in whom she could confide her deepest thoughts and secrets.'

'What kind of secrets?' Vi asked, feeling she was getting closer to the point.

'Who she really was,' Fidelma said. 'You see, she wasn't... Oh I don't know how to explain it.' Fidelma stopped, looking emotional. 'I haven't spoken to anyone about this,' she said. 'It feels like a betrayal in a way.'

Vi touched Fidelma's hand. 'Well, you know, I'm going to play Kathleen in a movie about her life and it's going to be especially about the love story between her and Don. But I've been feeling off about it from the very beginning. I've read the letters she wrote to you; she was independent, full of ambition, and depth. Her story is much more than just a romance. I want to show who she really was.'

Fidelma nodded. 'I see what you mean.'

Vi continued. 'I'm sure she protected herself because the truth would affect her career. But that's not at risk now. If she was battling with something, if she had this amazing career despite some incredible hardships, I think that's a part of her story we should tell. She wasn't just a beautiful woman. There was much more to her than that.'

'You're right. She was so much more than Don and their love story. And I appreciate that you don't want her to be like a cardboard cut-out. That's understandable. It means you're a real actress, not just a pretty face either.'

'I hope so,' Vi said softly.

Fidelma sat up. Vi's heart was beginning to beat faster while she waited with bated breath to learn the secret Kathleen had hidden from the world.

As Fidelma began to speak, Vi's eyes widened and her breath caught in her throat. This was incredible and more startling than she had expected. She knew then that the movie would have to be a lot more than a mere account of a love story. It had to depict a woman carrying a secret she was terrified to reveal. If it didn't, Vi couldn't play the part.

25

When Vi joined Leo in the cafeteria half an hour later, she felt so shaken she had to sit down to catch her breath for a moment before she could speak.

Leo looked at her with concern. 'You're as white as a sheet. What happened?'

Vi met his gaze, knowing she should tell him what she had just learned, but no words came out. Then it felt wrong to tell him; he shouldn't be the one who heard the news first. 'I can't tell you yet,' she said. 'I have to talk to Jack first. And the rest of the production team. The story, the script has to be changed. If they agree to do that, this movie will be so much better, the plot more dramatic and the whole story a lot deeper and more true to the real Kathleen and her relationship with Don.' She drew breath and put her hand on Leo's arm. 'Please don't be upset, it has nothing to do with you.'

'Only with the fact that I'm just the makeup artist,' he said with a touch of bitterness. 'I get it.'

'It's not like that,' Vi protested. 'I really appreciate our friendship and that you came with me. But this is about the movie and how to handle what I've just found out. It has to be dealt with sympathetically and be a big part of the love story in the movie. Then that "happily ever after" ending will be even more touching than what's in the script right now. It will be *real* instead of some cheesy Hollywood ending.' Vi stopped, feeling exhausted. 'I'm sorry if I upset you.'

Leo smiled. 'It's okay. I'm not insulted. I understand that it's important to you and that you can't talk about it until you've spoken to the producers. And I'm glad if I could help in any way.' He got up and held out his hand. 'Come on. Let's get out of this mausoleum and grab a bite to eat and a pint of the black stuff. On me.'

Vi took his hand, grateful that he was so supportive and not too hurt by the fact that she hadn't told him what she had found out. He seemed to understand that it had to be kept under wraps until she could speak to the producers of the movie.

They walked out of the nursing home and down the street until they found a small, cosy pub where they had a cheese sandwich and a pint of Guinness. Vi decided to contact Jack later that evening, when she was back in the flat and could talk to him in private. After an hour in the pub, they parted company, Leo to go into town and Vi to catch the bus back to Stillorgan. She hugged Leo goodbye and promised to call the next day so they could meet up for lunch before they both took the bus to the airport and got on the flight to London.

'Thanks a million again,' she said as she pulled away. 'You've been such a brick.'

'Glad to have helped,' he said, his deep blue eyes warm and empathic. 'I know it took it out of you. Feeling better?'

'Yes, much better,' Vi said, smiling. 'Thanks for the sandwich and the pint. That helped a lot too.'

'Nothing more cheering than some Guinness,' Leo remarked. 'But I see the bus coming down the street. You'd better get going or you'll miss it.'

Vi turned and started to run towards the bus stop. 'See you

tomorrow,' she shouted over her shoulder before she jumped onto the bus. She waved at him through the grimy window before she sat down. She saw that he waved back. Good old Leo. What a friend in need he had turned out to be. It felt good to know he'd be there all through the filming, like a solid wall to lean on.

Then Vi's thoughts turned to Jack and what she was going to tell him. How would he react when he learned the truth? She hoped he wouldn't let what had happened between them cloud his judgement and that he would see that the script had to be changed and that it would make the movie into something more than just a clichéd love story. She would have to call him as soon as possible and set up a meeting with him – and Liz. Not a prospect she liked but it was necessary. Jack and Liz... were they still in some kind of relationship? That photo was an old one but the attraction between them had been obvious. If they had been in love then, there had to be something still there, whatever it was. If Liz didn't agree to change the script, there would be a real problem if Jack took sides with her.

Vi knew she was going to have to fight for what she wanted to achieve but it would be worth it. It might seem unfair to Kathleen's memory, but Vi believed it would show her to have been a strong woman who'd had to hide who she really was in order to make it in the world of show business in the 1950s. It might seem crass to have lived this lie, but Vi felt in her bones that it had been necessary in order for Kathleen to succeed. If only Jack would understand and agree to make this movie what it should be – a woman's struggle to survive.

Just as Vi let herself into the little apartment, her phone rang. She fished it out of her pocket, her mind so full of thoughts of Jack she imagined for an instant it was him. But it was her mother, calling from Donegal.

'Hello,' Patricia Fleury said. 'How are you managing in the flat? Everything okay? Is the heating working and did you find the clean sheets and a warm duvet?'

'Yes, Mum,' Vi replied. 'Everything is fine and working. Don't worry about me. And I'll turn off the water before I leave and put the sheets in the linen basket and switch off all the lights and lock up properly.'

Patricia laughed. 'Sorry. I'm such a control freak. I wish I could be there with you. It would be fun to have an evening together. But I couldn't get away. I have to organise the sale of the farm before I can think of doing anything else.'

'I know. It must be hard.' Vi felt a dart of pity for her mother, who had to cope with the sale of the farm and everything to do with her old life with her late husband before she could move on and think of herself. 'It's been two years,' she said. 'And you're still trying to sort out all the probate stuff.'

'Yes, and I'm an accountant,' her mother remarked. 'Imagine what it must be like for people who're not trained to deal with this kind of stuff. But never mind me. How are you getting on with the preparations for the movie?'

'Fine,' Vi said. 'I'm going to London for rehearsals and costume fittings and then I'll get back to Kerry and we'll start shooting in March.'

'Sounds exciting,' Patricia said. 'How do you like the flat?'

'It's very nice.' Vi looked around the small but cosy living room. 'Great to have a crash pad in Dublin.'

'Yes, that's what I thought. Handy for us all. Anyway,' Patricia said, sounding tired, 'I just called to see if all was well with you. I'll pop down to Kerry when you're back there. I want to see the grandkids. They must have grown since the last time I saw them.'

'Oh yes, they're all growing and thriving.' Vi smiled as she thought of her nieces and little nephew. 'It's very busy down there now. I hope you can sort everything and leave all the sorrow behind soon, Mum. It's been a tough time for you.'

'It has indeed,' Patricia agreed. 'Can't wait to start living again. Good luck with everything. I'll see you soon.'

'Bye, Mum.' Vi hung up, happy that her mother seemed a little brighter. She had been very distant while her husband was ill and then, after his death, all the financial affairs had to be sorted out. Lily and Rose had been too busy with their children to help their mother, so Vi had stepped in and tried her best to be supportive. But then lately, with the movie and everything else associated with it, she had forgotten to call as often as she used to.

Oh the movie, she thought, the memory of what Fidelma had told her flooding back into her mind. *I have to call Jack.* Vi picked up her phone again and dialled Jack's number. He answered straight away.

'Violet?'

'Yes. It's me. Look, I'm sorry if I was rude to you the other day. I know what happened and I'm—'

'Please stop,' Jack said. 'Let's not go into all that. Sylvia explained it all and said she'd talk to you, which I assume she did. So let's move forward.'

'Okay,' Vi said, slightly taken aback by his brisk tone. Apparently his feelings for her had cooled too. 'I didn't call to talk about the photo of you and Liz. That's none of my business, really.'

'No, it isn't,' Jack said drily. 'You jumped to the obvious conclusions, I assume.'

'Maybe,' Vi said, feeling a lump in her throat as he hadn't denied that there was some truth in the rumours. 'But there is something else I need to discuss with you. It's about the movie and the script and Kathleen...' She stopped, trying to pull her thoughts together. She hadn't planned what she was going to say and now his deep voice confused her. 'I have just found out something about Kathleen,' she started. 'Something that has to be included in the script. In fact, it could change the whole plot and make it much more dramatic.'

'Really? That sounds interesting.' Jack sounded intrigued. 'Could this insert even more spice into the mix?'

'Absolutely,' Vi agreed. 'But I can't talk about it over the phone like this. If you're in London, maybe we could meet? I'll be there tomorrow evening.'

'Yes, that would be great. Can you come straight to our office? I'll get Liz to come too. I'll contact the script writers and see if they can join by video link from LA. This sounds serious.'

'It is,' Vi said, feeling a jolt of disappointment that she wouldn't be seeing Jack in private. But this wasn't about them and their feelings for each other, it was about Kathleen and the movie depicting the most important part of her life. 'I could have kept this to myself,' she added. 'But I felt that the script needed more than just your ordinary love story.'

'It certainly does,' Jack agreed. 'I'm really grateful to you for taking the trouble to find out whatever it is. I'm looking forward to hearing it. And...' He stopped.

'Yes?' Vi asked, her throat suddenly dry.

'I'd like to have a chat with you on our own too. We could have dinner after the meeting. Would that be okay?'

'Yes,' she said again, nervously. Why would he want to do that?

'Great. I'll text you about the meeting with the team. Bye for now, Violet.'

'Bye, Jack,' she whispered, although he had already hung up.

Vi sat on the chair, holding the phone to her chest, going over the conversation. He had seemed anxious to hear what she had found out. He also seemed open to rewriting the script in order to improve the plotline. But not only that, he wanted to see her in private, and it made her heart sing.

26

The following evening, Vi arrived at the office building straight from the airport. She paid the driver of the taxi, took her bag and went inside, feeling only a little bit apprehensive about what she was about to do. It seemed enormous that she would be able to ask to change the plot of such a high-profile movie, but at the same time inevitable. She was driven by a strange loyalty to Kathleen, a woman she now knew so well, despite the fact that she had been dead for over thirty years.

Vi knew where to go, as Jack had texted her with the details of where the meeting would take place. She found the room on the second floor without any problems. Standing outside, she didn't know if she should knock, but then simply pushed the door open and went inside, finding a small room with a round table where Liz, Jack and David, the director, were already sitting, deep in conversation. There was a screen behind them, for the video link, Vi assumed.

Jack looked up and smiled as Vi came in. 'Hi, Violet. Thank you for coming here straight from the airport. I hope you had a good trip.'

'It was fine.' Vi sat down on the chair Jack had pulled out for her. 'The usual Heathrow hell before I found a taxi. But I'm here now, so all is well.'

'We're all dying to hear your news,' Liz said. She poured some coffee from a large thermos on the table into a mug and pushed it across the table. 'Here. Coffee. Help yourself to a bun.'

Vi smiled and took the mug. 'Brilliant. Just what I needed. Thanks, Liz.' She took a small cupcake from a plate and ate a large bite, washing it down with coffee. 'That's better.' She looked at everyone. 'So do we wait for the writers to come online before I start?'

'Yes,' David replied. 'We'll be connected in a few minutes.' Just as he spoke, the screen lit up and the faces of a man and a woman appeared.

'Hi,' the woman said. 'I'm Monica and this is Rick. We're ready to hear your story.'

Jack nodded at Vi. 'So are we. You can start now, if you're ready.'

'Okay.' Vi clasped her hands in her lap, cleared her throat and started to speak. 'As you know, I went to Ireland to get a grasp of Kathleen's character, and in doing so I managed to find an old lady who knew her as a young woman: from her days at a dance school to the height of her fame. Fidelma was the only person who knew the *real* Kathleen and her true story, which is very different from her official image: the Irish colleen from the Emerald Isle with the red hair and Kerry accent.'

'So that was not true?' Liz asked, looking intently at Vi.

'No.' Vi paused and took a deep breath. 'Kathleen O'Sullivan was not Irish. She was from Poland. She came to Ireland in nineteen forty-one, when she was twelve.'

There was a stunned silence while they all tried to take it in.

'Wow,' Jack said under his breath. 'That's quite a revelation. But how did she... I mean...'

'Go on,' David said. 'Why did she come to Ireland?'

'To escape the Nazis,' Vi replied. 'Her father had been in the Resistance in Poland. When he was killed, her mother realised she had to leave in order to save herself and her daughter. They managed to get to London, where they met a man called Brendan O'Sullivan who helped them to get to Ireland. He was from Kerry and he brought Kathleen and her mother to his farm near Castleisland. Brendan then married Kathleen's mother in order to help her become an Irish citizen. Not difficult in those days. Actually, Kathleen's mother was very beautiful and she and Brendan were very happy together. But that's another story.'

'Could make a great movie,' Monica said from the screen.

'Maybe,' Jack said. 'But go on, Vi. I can imagine the rest of it, but I'd prefer to hear it from you.'

Vi nodded. 'Okay. Well, Kathleen's real name was Katarzyna, which is the Polish version of Katherine. She changed her name to Kathleen when she started school in Kerry in order to blend in and not appear to be different. It might also have been because her mother was afraid that they'd be found by Nazi agents or something. I'm just guessing, but it could be true. Katarzyna also took her stepfather's surname and became Kathleen O'Sullivan. She soon learned to speak English fluently with a Kerry accent, and seemed to truly feel Irish after a year or two at school.'

'So she adopted a persona that she believed in herself?' Liz asked.

'That's what Fidelma said,' Vi replied. 'And Kathleen built on that when she went to acting school. She dyed her hair that fiery red colour we all know so well and took Gaelic lessons so she could get parts in all those very Irish plays.'

'And then she was discovered by a Hollywood agent who was looking for the typical Irish colleen,' Liz filled in. 'Which she really wasn't. So that was the big secret she was harbouring all her life?'

'Yes,' Vi said. 'She always felt she was a bit of a fraud. Having to hide her Polish roots and pretending to be Irish was weighing on her mind. She felt she was living a lie and the strain of that wore her down. The only two people who knew were Fidelma and Don, her husband and the love of her life. And he was apparently very understanding when she finally told him just before their wedding.' Vi turned to the two scriptwriters. 'So I thought we could use that story and write some scenes in that aren't in the script now.'

'Oh, yes,' Rick said, looking excited. 'It would become a whole different story. A better story with more depth and drama.'

'That's right,' Vi agreed. 'I also need to tell you that Don and Kathleen often had heated rows and fell out with each other from time to time. I think that needs to be in the script too.'

'Fabulous,' Monica said.

'But it would demand a lot more from the actress playing Kathleen,' Liz remarked, looking at Vi with a critical expression. 'I mean... Maybe we'll have to rethink the cast?' She glanced at Jack. 'Could we get another actress maybe?'

Vi's heart dropped. This might be the end of her part in the movie.

Jack raised an eyebrow as he stared coldly at Liz. 'And break Violet's contract? I've seen some of the movies Violet's been in. She is a hell of an actress and can certainly play the part and make Kathleen come to life much more realistically than with the old script.' He looked at the screen. 'Guys, we have to move fast on the rewrites. I want to see the new material at the end of next week. It has to be strong, dramatic and deep. I know it's a tall order and it means you working overtime, but...'

'We're on it,' Monica said on the screen. 'Right, Rick?'

'Absolutely,' Rick said. 'It's worth it. We'll rewrite some of the scenes and add two or three and maybe scrap some that won't work now that we're making this into a lot more than a romance. It'll mean some all-nighters but hey, an Oscar or two is worth the slog.'

'We'll get going straight away and do an outline and send it to you tonight,' Monica suggested. 'It'll be the middle of the night for you, so you'll have to be on the ball, too, guys.'

'If we agree to all this,' Liz cut in.

'Why wouldn't we?' Jack asked.

'Because I don't believe a word of this story,' Liz replied.

27

'What do you mean?' Jack asked, glaring at Liz.

'What I just said,' Liz replied and pointed at Vi. 'She comes in here with this story she heard from some old dear, she tells us. But it could just as well be some ploy by Violet to make her part more dramatic so she can flex her acting muscles. You haven't been happy with the script from the start, I thought so during your audition.'

'You mean you think I made it up?' Vi asked, feeling close to tears.

'It's possible,' Liz said.

'That's a little unfair,' Jack said, frowning.

'Maybe,' Liz said. 'But if she didn't, how do we know this story is true? How do we know that this old woman is not making it up? You know, the way old people get confused and make up stuff they think they remember but it was a dream or something. We have to check all those facts before we can go ahead. There will be records.'

Vi looked around, shocked. Jack had put his head down, studying his notes. Wasn't he going to stick up for her?

'I'm not going to agree to anything before we have some

proof,' Liz continued. 'Let's discuss this in more detail in private. If you don't mind, Violet?' she said, gesturing for Violet to leave. Violet was speechless, as was everyone else. She grabbed the handle of her suitcase and started to roll it to the door. She had expected Jack to stick up for her, for someone to say something, but she only heard the wheels of her case against the laminate as she left. She couldn't believe what had happened.

And then she heard footsteps behind her. It was Jack.

'What about dinner?' he asked as he shut the door to the room behind him.

'I'm not really hungry,' Vi replied. 'I just want to get to my flat and go to bed.'

'You're not going to take the Tube?' Jack asked incredulously.

'No, I'll call an Uber,' Vi said and pulled her phone out of her handbag. She knew it would be expensive, but she just wanted to get home so she could crawl under the duvet and cry. Her eyes were already stinging with tears and she wanted to get out of there, away from their probing looks as fast as she could. 'Let me know what you decide about the movie and everything.' She started to walk to the door, but as a thought hit her, she stopped and turned around. 'You know what? I could do what you did and pull out of the movie altogether.'

'How can you do that without breaking the contract?' Jack asked.

'I can if there's a health issue. It's in my contract, so you can tell Liz I'm feeling quite sick right now.'

'What's up with you?' he asked, putting a hand out to stop the door closing. 'Liz's comments were extreme, but she does have a bit of a point... we need to verify this.'

'I'm just a bit tired of everything,' Vi said. 'I tried so hard to find out what Kathleen's secret was and then, when I finally did, you don't believe me.'

'I do,' he said. 'But we have to be careful. Someone could expose us if we tell a story that isn't true,' Jack argued. 'It would be bad for the reputation of our company. Liz and I started this together and we have worked so hard to produce good movies.'

Vi nodded, wondering if that meant he couldn't stick up for her? 'Okay. I understand where your priorities are.'

'Not only that, but there is an issue you might not have considered.' He paused. 'Look, we need to talk. How about that dinner? Or a drink? Or I could get my car and drive you home. Then we can chat during the trip to... where did you say you live again?'

'Croydon,' Vi said. 'I'm sure you've never been there or anywhere near it. And it's a long way from your comfort zone.'

'Why are you so angry?' Jack asked, looking both puzzled and irritated.

Vi felt tears of frustration well up. 'I don't know,' she whispered, now so tired she could hardly stand up. She knew he had stood up for her but then he had agreed with what Liz said and that, to Vi, was a sure sign there was still something between them.

Jack took his hand away from the door of the lift and stepped inside, pulling Vi with him. 'You're exhausted, overwrought and sad. I'm going to call my driver now and then we'll chat in the car on the way to Croydon. I do know where it is, by the way.' He pressed the button for the ground floor and took his phone from his pocket. 'Hi, Tom,' he said. 'I'll need you to take me and my friend to Croydon. We'll be waiting outside the office. Thanks.' He pocketed the phone and looked at Vi. 'All sorted.'

'Thanks,' Vi mumbled, unable to argue. In any case she was, as Jack had said, both physically and mentally exhausted.

They went outside into the cold, wet evening and when the car arrived a few minutes later, Vi was grateful to get into the warm, comfortable interior, letting Tom the driver take care of her suitcase. Then the car swept them away, zigzagging through the heavy evening traffic.

Jack looked at Vi in the dim light. 'You want to talk?'

'What about?' Vi asked. 'I think I know where you're coming from. You need proof and you need to agree with Liz on everything. You're business partners and maybe partners in private as well – how do I know?'

'We have nothing going on in private,' Jack protested. 'We're friends, but nothing more. Yes, we had a little flirt going once but it wasn't serious. I'm fond of Liz as a friend and I like working with her, but that's all. That photo you saw was years old.'

'I know. Granny told me.' Vi leaned her head against the headrest. 'No need to dig that up again. But I thought... I had a feeling you were still together. You seem so in tune somehow. She's very attractive and smart and a lot of things I could never be.'

'Yes, she is. But you are a lot of things that *she* could never be if she tried for the rest of her life. But could we concentrate on the movie and Kathleen now?' Jack took Vi's hand. 'You're frozen,' he said, rubbing it between his own warm hands.

'What was that other thing we have to take into consideration?' Vi asked, secretly enjoying the touch of his hands. The issue of his relationship with Liz still burned in her mind but this was not the right time to discuss it.

'About Kathleen? Well,' Jack started, 'if she's a kind of legend in Ireland, would it be kind to her memory to expose her like this? She was, after all, a lovely Irish girl as far as everyone knows. Someone to be proud of, like the flag and the harp and the music.'

'I see what you mean.' Vi sat up and pulled her hand out of Jack's grip. 'I didn't think of that angle. But... I have a feeling it would be good for the image of modern Ireland and all the people who have come from all kinds of countries to start a new life. Maybe these days, they would see the story as a contrast to the world we live in today. It was during the war and everyone was suspicious of strangers. If the writers take that angle and don't expose her as a fake, but as a woman's way to survive in the harsh climate of the times she lived in, I think it would work. Nobody has to hide who they are today, but she had to in order to succeed in her acting career.' Vi drew breath and leaned back again. 'Fidelma and I discussed the idea that this is more true to Kathleen's legacy.'

'I see,' Jack said. 'That's a great idea, actually. I didn't think of it that way. So if we manage to get that message across, we'll have an even stronger story than before. Subtle but very poignant. All we need now is proof of the story and I'm sure Liz will agree. Unless you want to go on sick leave, of course,' he added with a touch of laughter in his voice.

Vi managed a smile. 'I'll think about it.'

They were quiet while the car neared Croydon. Tom asked for Vi's address and she repeated the street and the number and told him it was quite close. Then the car pulled up outside the building and Vi started to get out.

Jack put a hand on her arm. 'Hold on. I'll help you with your suitcase.'

'Okay.' Vi got out while Jack took her suitcase from the boot and went with her through the entrance door to the lift. She pressed the button and while she waited for the lift to arrive, turned to him. 'How long do you think the delay will be?'

'I'd say we'll have to wait a couple of weeks and then we'll be back on track. Liz will come around, don't worry. She just likes to have all details lined up and shipshape. That's the way she is.'

'You want that, too, I bet,' Vi countered. 'But I don't think it will be hard to get confirmation of Fidelma's story. There'll be records from Castleisland, the town where Kathleen grew up, and where her mother married her stepfather. The church records are a good way to start. The school she went to will also have records of her attendance there.'

'I'd say Liz is already on the case,' Jack said.

'Well, you know her better than I do,' Vi remarked. 'Here's the lift now. Thanks for driving me home.'

'You're very welcome.' He leaned forward and touched her cheek with his lips for a second. 'I'll be in touch.'

The kiss had been as light as a feather but it burned her skin like a thousand flames all the same. Flustered, Vi took her suitcase and went into the lift, still feeling the light touch of his lips on her cheek all the way up to her floor.

She opened the door to the flat, her mind full of what had happened during the past few hours: the meeting at the office, Liz's accusations, the argument with Jack and then him kissing her cheek. It was a kaleidoscope of impressions and conversations which, despite her exhaustion, kept her awake until the early hours of the morning. Then she finally fell into a dreamless sleep and woke up just before noon, wondering if she had dreamed it all.

The flat seemed dull and dreary in the grey winter light and Vi knew she couldn't stay there. It was too depressing. There was only one place she wanted to be: Kerry and Magnolia Manor and the gatehouse she had come to love. As the movie was now being delayed by several weeks, why stay in London when she could go home and wait there for everything to start up again? Jack would send her the new script by email but she didn't need to be in London for that. And it seemed to Vi that it would be better not to hang around and look needy while Jack and Liz might be trying to sort out their relationship – business and personal. It made her heart ache to think of the two of them together, but if they still had feelings for each other, there was no hope for Vi. She booked a flight to Cork the following morning, where she would take the bus to Dingle and then Granny would collect her when she arrived. That felt like a very good decision. No better place to be right now than Magnolia Manor where the garden and the ocean and the sound of the waves would soothe her frazzled nerves. And her broken heart.

28

The text from Leo – which came as Vi was at the departure gate – asking her out for a drink in his favourite pub in Soho made her feel a little guilty. She texted back to say she was on her way home. He called about a minute after she had sent the text.

'Why?' he asked. 'I thought you'd be rehearsing here in London with the cast.'

'There's been a delay,' Vi explained. 'Liz kicked up a fuss when I told them about Kathleen's past and said she needed to check the facts.'

'What was the big secret, anyway?' Leo asked. 'Can you tell me now that everyone else knows?'

Vi looked around the departure area to see if there was anyone nearby who might be eavesdropping. But everyone else was either on the phone or arguing with someone beside them or busy with their hand luggage. 'Okay, I can tell you briefly. I'll fill in the details next time we meet. But here's the gist of it,' she whispered into her phone. 'You see, Kathleen wasn't really who she claimed to be – she was a Polish refugee who arrived in Ireland when she was twelve. And her real name wasn't Kathleen.'

'Wow,' Leo said, sounding shocked. 'That's some story.'

'I know. Anyway, there's more but I can't tell you right now.'

'I see. So the delay is because of the script having to be rewritten?'

'Partly. And the facts having to be checked. So now we're waiting for the go-ahead and the rewrites of the script. I thought I'd wait at home rather than hang around London. I feel better there.'

'I see.' Leo paused. 'And I was going to take you on a tour of my favourite London hangouts. Maybe next time, eh?'

Vi could sense the disappointment in his voice and tried to think of a way to cheer him up. Then she remembered how he had kissed her on New Year's Eve, and realised again that he might be feeling more than friendship for her. How could she soothe his bruised ego without giving false hope? 'That would be fun,' she said. 'I'll give you a shout when I get back to London. I like to see where my friends hang out. Maybe we could make it a group event with some of the cast and crew?'

'Maybe,' he said. 'That would be a different evening to what I had in mind. But why not? Let's talk when you get back. Have a nice time in Kerry.'

'Thanks, I will. Bye for now, Leo.' Vi hung up, feeling bad for him, but what could she do? She had been there before, killing a possible romance before it could happen, sometimes with a heavy heart, but mostly feeling relieved. *What's wrong with me? Am I so cold and unfeeling?* she asked herself. *Or do I stop myself falling in love to protect myself, to be independent and free to make my own choices? Or maybe to pursue my career without distractions or complications?* But she had fallen in love with Jack and that was something she had not been able to stop. It was making her miserable and she couldn't shake herself out of it. Her grandmother had hinted that Jack had feelings for her but the last time they met he had been quite matter-of-fact and cool. Except for that little kiss on the cheek when they said goodbye. *But that was just him being polite,* she told herself sternly.

The flight was boarding and Vi hurried to join the queue, feeling happy to leave London and all the problems with the movie behind for a while. She knew she needed a break from everything and she longed to get home and get the rest and distractions that being at Magnolia Manor would provide.

Vi had been right. Only hours after arriving back in the gatehouse, she began to feel better. After saying goodbye to her grandmother, who dropped her off, she put her bags in the hall and went for a long walk. As always in early February, spring was in the air with a mild salt-laden sea breeze, the sound of birdsong and warm sunshine. Vi noticed that the magnolia tree in front of the manor had big buds and she remembered that the annual Magnolia party would be held as usual in a few weeks. This year, the party would be held in the orangery to take the pressure off the ballroom, where the movie people would be busy preparing for filming the first scenes of the film. Vi wondered idly if it would ever be made. It felt so distant and unreal right now. Would Liz ever get the facts she was looking for and give the go-ahead for the rewrites of the script? Vi had initially planned to do her own research but right now she was tired of the whole thing and felt like letting go of everything. The walk in the mild sunshine with the distant sound of the waves in her ears made her forget all her worries, and even her heartache eased a little. This was where she was meant to be and she wanted to stay here forever.

She laughed at herself, knowing she was just tired and would probably be raring to go and be every bit as driven as before after a good night's sleep – and some apple pie and tea

with her granny. Still, this day and the walk in the winter
sunshine was just what she needed.

Then a few days later, Jack emailed the script to Vi with a
message that said:

> This is just a draft and not the final script. We still need to get
> proof of the full story. But I think you'll love the rewrites. The
> writers have done a great job, don't you think? We've found
> a little bit of proof already, so I'm certain Liz will come
> around. I might hint that I'll resign if she makes too much of a
> fuss.
>
> I'd like to see you so we can discuss the new material. How
> about dinner tomorrow? Please let me know and we'll decide
> on a time and place.
>
> Best wishes,
>
> Jack.

The message made Vi glow with new hope. He was
prepared to fight with Liz for the new script. And he wanted to
have dinner with her. That must mean something. But he
seemed to think she was still in London, so dinner wasn't possible. She sent back a reply to say thank you for the script.

I can't wait to read it, she wrote. *I'd love to discuss it over
dinner but I'm afraid it's not possible as I'm in Kerry. I thought it
better to stay here during the delay. I'll come back as soon as I'm
needed. In the meantime, I'll learn my lines.*

All the best, Violet

He didn't reply until the following day with a short message that said he understood and hoped to hear from her soon. The message was short and Vi felt confused, wondering what he meant by it all. First, he wanted to have dinner with her and they seemed to be getting closer, but then he sent her a rather curt message that felt cold and distant. She decided not to read anything at all into either message and to try to gauge Jack's feelings when they met again. She was starting to feel relieved that she wouldn't have to work with him – that would have been too difficult. Peter Black, who had been cast instead, would be easy to deal with. He was nice and friendly and there had been no vibes between them when they had worked together on a TV series a few years ago.

Putting all those thoughts to the back of her mind, Vi opened the attachment and started to read the new script. When she got to the rewritten scenes, she sat up and stared at the computer screen. The new dialogue was truly wonderful: dramatic and deeply moving. The writers had really understood what Kathleen had been going through which delighted Vi. She couldn't wait to start acting out these feelings which would demand a lot from her as an actress but might also be the watershed moment she had been waiting for. She read on for another hour, then decided to print out the whole text to be able to practise her lines and read them over and over again. She only wished she had someone to rehearse with and hoped she'd get the go-ahead to go back to London to rehearse with the rest of the cast soon.

Excited by this new challenge, she sent a short email to Jack, telling him how much she loved the new script. She felt he should know what she thought of it. He was, after all, one of the producers.

Vi used the printer in the office of Magnolia Manor and once she had the printout, started to read the script several times over the next few days. There had been no reply from

Jack and she hoped Liz would find the proof she needed soon and get the movie back on track. In the meantime, she spent her free time taking long walks, spending time with Lily and Rose and their families, especially enjoying playing with her little nieces and nephew. She tried her best to push all her worries away, even if the long wait was difficult.

29

The following week was a calm time during which Vi felt all her energy return, despite still waiting to hear if Liz had finally approved the changes. The shooting would start when and if she agreed to it, so there was no need for Vi to come to London. While they waited, Dave the director and Jack had arranged for them to rehearse at Magnolia Manor, while the scenery was being prepared. This way, they would be ready to start shooting as soon as they got the go-ahead and make up for lost time, he said. Vi had a niggling worry that Jack's gung-ho attitude to quit the company if Liz didn't come around had fizzled out. He was probably not prepared to burn all his bridges for her. Understandable, but disappointing all the same.

A few days later, the first scene of the movie was finally being rehearsed. It was the scene where Kathleen met Don for the first time at the country house in Ireland, a house very similar to Magnolia Manor, but without the backdrop of the sea. That was a minor detail and the difference in location would not be noticed by the majority of the audience, Liz had explained. Vi was prepared to swallow her protest and 'stop the nit-picking', as Liz had put it, and do her job. It was a small price to pay if she had achieved what she wanted – the real, true story of Kathleen O'Sullivan. In any case, the new screenplay was wonderful and Vi fell into her role as if Kathleen herself was directing her. She felt Kathleen's presence very strongly as she said her lines and had no problem rehearsing the love scenes with Peter Black, who also loved the script and the dialogue that now seemed more realistic than before, especially with a lot of drama and arguments between the main characters. It was fun and challenging and very stimulating at the same time.

Leo was a wonderful help. He had a gentle touch when he practised applying her makeup and even helped her remove everything, giving her a lovely little face massage at the end of the day. They were now close friends and all the tensions between them were gone. It was as if that New Year's Eve kiss had never happened.

Vi hadn't heard from Jack after her last email to him and that upset her. But preparing for the movie helped her turn her mind away from her heartache and she supposed she would, in time, accept that he wasn't as interested in her as she had thought.

There was a long break after the rehearsals, as they all seemed to be holding their breaths while they waited for the final go-ahead. Everyone was happy to have some time off before the hard work began, however. Everyone except Vi, who now had plenty of free time to think about her feelings for Jack.

Vi did everything to distract herself during the break, feeling restless and nervous as she waited for the decision to start filming – or not. She even volunteered to babysit one evening when Lily and Dominic went to an Irish music event in Killarney where Dominic's band, The Fiddler's Elbow, was performing. They were staying the night in a hotel and, as their au pair had the night off, needed someone to mind Naomi and Liam.

'Are you sure?' Lily asked when they were having tea with Sylvia one wet and windy Thursday afternoon. 'They can be a bit of a handful, especially Liam.'

'Oh, I can manage,' Vi assured her. 'They know me well by now. Naomi is a great help. The best big sister.'

'She can act up too,' Sylvia cut in as she served them another slice of apple pie at the kitchen table. 'Don't let her get the upper hand, Violet.'

'I won't,' Vi said, smiling. 'I'll be a step ahead all the time. I know the rules and Naomi knows I know.'

'So there'll be no "Mummy always lets me eat sweets before bedtime",' Sylvia quipped. 'She tried that with me but I didn't fall for it.'

'But you did fall for "Mummy always lets me watch TV until ten o'clock",' Lily remarked.

'Well, yes, but that was because we both wanted to watch *Mrs Doubtfire*,' Sylvia said. 'I knew she was having me on, but I went along with it. Why would I want to sit there alone and watch it? We had fun. Sorry, Lily.'

Lily laughed. 'She has you wrapped around her little finger, Granny. But she loves you as much as we do.'

'And that's all I want,' Sylvia stated, taking a bite of her apple pie. 'This is a delicious pie. Must tell Nora it's especially good. Must be because the Bramley apples last year were so abundant.' She looked at Vi. 'So how are you getting on with everything, Violet? The movie and that handsome rascal and everything?'

'It's coming along,' Vi replied. 'All we need now is for the weather to improve so we can shoot the outdoor scenes in the garden.'

'Jack told me...' Sylvia started but stopped, putting her hand to her mouth. 'Oops. I wasn't supposed to say anything.'

'Come on, Granny,' Vi urged. 'You have to spill the beans now that you've started.'

Sylvia sighed. 'Oh, what does it matter? It's just that Jack told me what you had found out about Kathleen. Which I sort of knew already, of course.'

'Sort of?' Vi said, lifting an eyebrow.

'What are you talking about?' Lily asked. 'What's this stuff about Kathleen O'Sullivan?'

Vi put more whipped cream on her piece of apple pie. 'It's a secret that will be revealed when the movie comes out. But I'll tell you now anyway if you promise to keep quiet.'

'Your secret is safe with me,' Lily said, leaning forward. 'So come on, let's hear it.'

Vi told Lily what she had found out from Fidelma.

Lily's eyes widened. 'Oh wow? Really? She wasn't Irish at all?' She turned to look at Sylvia, who was making another pot of tea by the sink. 'And you knew this all the time and never said anything?'

Sylvia shrugged. 'I didn't know if it was true. It was a rumour that started to circulate when Kathleen became very famous over in Hollywood. Then it died down when we all wanted to claim this famous actress as our own. She did a lot for Ireland in her day. So everyone stopped saying anything about the fact that she might not really be Irish, because that's what we wanted her to be. Our very own fresh-faced nice Irish colleen from the Emerald Isle.'

Lily smiled and nodded. 'I see what you mean. Well, that'll be quite a story on the screen, won't it? Something that will resonate with people who came here from abroad and then became Irish. They don't have to hide their origins, but she did.'

'Well, she didn't *have* to,' Sylvia argued. 'She did it because she wanted to fit in. Then she kept her new identity and didn't reveal the truth when that talent scout found her. Why would she? It was the ticket to Hollywood for her. And then, of course, she had to keep it up.'

'I know, but people who have emigrated will identify with her,' Lily countered. 'A bridge across the generations and nationalities, so to speak.'

'That's true,' Sylvia agreed. 'So then the story has become something else, something deeper and more meaningful, all thanks to Violet.'

'Well done, Vi,' Lily said.

'Thanks.' Vi smiled at Lily. 'Now all we have to do is to get to shoot that darn movie. I've had enough of delays and complications.' She got up from the table. 'I'm going home to do some more reading. I need to practise my lines a little more. And I'm going to email Liz with what you just told me, Granny. If it was widely known, even if not talked about, that might convince her.'

'I don't see why not,' Sylvia agreed. 'I can talk to her myself if you want.'

'That would be a great help.' Vi beamed a grateful smile at her grandmother. 'I'll let you know what happens.'

'I'll have to get going too.' Lily rose from her chair. 'I'll help Granny tidy up and then I have to head home. Gretel will have picked up the kids from school and preschool. See you Saturday, Vi.'

Vi kissed Lily on the cheek. 'See you. Looking forward to minding the kids.'

'You might regret you said that,' Lily warned with a wink.

Only an hour into her babysitting evening, Vi did indeed start to regret her hasty offer to mind two small, very tired children. She had waved goodbye to Dominic and Lily, laughing at their concerns, saying she would cope very well and they were to go off and enjoy the break and not worry. 'And please don't phone every half hour,' she ordered. 'I'll call if there is an emergency. But there won't be, so you two have a ball and dance the night away.'

They had taken off laughing and waving. Vi went inside to make the evening meal for the children, planning what she would watch on TV once they were asleep. Which they would have to be soon, after a day of playing on the beach with some of their friends during a very active playdate. She was also going to read the script yet again so she would be word perfect once they started shooting. She had emailed Liz with what she had learned from Sylvia earlier and hoped to get a reply soon.

The trouble started at the kitchen table when Vi served up chicken meatballs, mashed potatoes and peas, which Lily had declared was their favourite. Not so, Naomi said.

'We want Coco Pops for dinner,' she declared. 'We always have that.'

'No, you don't,' Vi argued. 'This is what Mummy said you wanted. And Coco Pops are bad for you. Full of sugar. You know the rules, Naomi.'

'Yeah, but tonight is Saturday,' Naomi tried. 'That's when we're allowed treats.'

'You can have treats when you've eaten your dinner all up,' Vi said. 'Then I'll give you Coco Pops for dessert.'

Liam banged his spoon on the plate. Then he threw the spoon on the floor and started to eat with his fingers. Vi decided to let him. It was easier than arguing with a two-year-old. Larry, the big white dog, sniffed the floor waiting for any crumbs that might drop down. Liam threw one of the meatballs on the floor, which Larry wolfed down in seconds.

'Liam is rude,' Naomi said, pointing at him with her spoon. 'He's feeding meatballs to Larry. And he's messy. Look – he's taking the ketchup and getting it in his hair, ha ha!'

Vi looked at Liam and discovered that Naomi was right. He

had taken the bottle of ketchup when she wasn't looking and squirted it all over his nearly clean T-shirt and his face and now he was smearing it into his hair. 'I eat ketchup,' he said, laughing. Then he dug into his meatballs again and ate most of what was on his plate, stuffing his mouth full and grinning.

Vi sighed. 'I'll just let him finish and then I'll give him a bath.'

Naomi nodded. 'Yes, that's what you should do. Look, I'm eating my dinner all up with my spoon and not spilling.'

'You're the best girl.' Vi kissed Naomi on the top of her head.

Naomi nodded. 'Yes I am. So I can watch TV with you when Liam is asleep.'

'We'll see,' Vi said, not wanting to start another argument. Then she saw that Liam had finished and scooped him up in her arms, not caring that she was getting ketchup and mashed potato all over her shirt. 'You can watch the cartoons now while I give Liam a bath and get him into his pyjamas.'

'And then I can have Coco Pops?' Naomi asked, looking hopeful.

Vi nodded. 'Yes, because I said you could.'

'Me too,' Liam shouted. 'I want Coca Pops too!'

'Okay,' Vi agreed. 'When you're in your pyjamas. And then you'll both have to brush your teeth and get into bed.'

'Then you have to read us a story or we won't be able to sleep,' Naomi stated, sliding off her chair.

'Of course,' Vi said, mentally waving her peaceful evening goodbye. She lugged the little boy up the stairs and started to run the bath, then she sat on a stool and peeled off his dirty clothes. 'You are a mess, Liam.'

Liam laughed as she put him into the warm water and started to splash, soaking Vi. She smiled at him and looked down at her wet T-shirt dotted with ketchup stains. 'I'm a mess too.'

She had just finished washing Liam and was drying him with a towel hanging on the radiator when the doorbell rang, making Larry bark furiously. 'That's all I need,' Vi groaned. 'Open the door, Naomi, but don't let in any strangers,' she called as she walked towards the stairs carrying Liam wrapped in a towel. She could hear Naomi opening the door. 'Who is it?' Vi called.

'A man,' Naomi replied. 'But he's not a stranger. And Larry likes him.'

'Is it Martin?' Vi called, remembering that he had said he might drop in to see if she needed anything.

'No,' Naomi called back.

Vi arrived downstairs and went into the hall to see who was at the door. She stopped in her tracks and stared at the person on the doorstep smiling at her and holding out a bunch of flowers. 'What are *you* doing here?'

30

'It's a long story,' Jack said, patting Larry on the head. 'But I'm here now. Are you going to let me in?'

Vi backed away from the door. 'Okay. Come in.'

'Are you giving the flowers to Auntie Vi?' Naomi asked. 'I can put them in water for you, if you like.'

'Thank you very much, young lady,' Jack said and gave Naomi the flowers. 'And yes, they are for Auntie Vi. Because I want to say sorry for not replying to her emails and to celebrate a few things.' He looked at Vi for a moment with a fond smile. 'You look lovely.'

Vi was suddenly aware of her wet and dirty shirt and the soap suds in her hair. 'I'll just go and get Liam into his pyjamas and tidy up a bit. Naomi, show Jack into the living room. I'll be back in a minute.' She carried Liam back up the stairs, dried him off and put his pyjamas on. Then she left him in his room to play with his teddy for a moment while she quickly went into Lily and Dom's bedroom and found a blue cotton sweater in Lily's wardrobe and changed into it before she brought Liam back downstairs.

'Coca Pops,' Liam said when she arrived at the bottom of the stairs.

'Okay. Just a sec,' Vi said, and put him on the floor. She ran into the kitchen where Naomi was taking a crystal vase out of one of the lower cupboards. 'Thanks, sweetheart,' she said and took the vase from Naomi. Vi filled it with water and put the flowers – a lovely bouquet of red and pink roses and white daisies – into it and set it down on the kitchen table. 'They're lovely flowers, Jack. Thank you.'

Liam pulled at the legs of Vi's jeans. 'Coca Pops, Auntie Vi. Now.'

'Say "please",' Naomi ordered.

'Pleeease,' Liam repeated.

Vi lifted Liam onto his chair and glanced at Jack, who was standing in the middle of the floor, looking at them with an amused smile. 'I'll just sort the Coco Pops,' she said. 'Then I'll put them to bed and...'

'It's okay,' Jack said. 'I have plenty of time. Is there anything I can do to help?'

'Thanks, but I'm on it.' Vi busied herself cleaning up the ketchup stains and then got out the Coco Pops and milk and filled two bowls. As soon as the children had finished, she told them to go upstairs. 'Just a quick story, and then I'll be back,' she said to Jack.

'I want a long story,' Naomi protested.

'Hey, I'll tell you a story,' Jack offered. 'It's a true story too. Very exciting. Do you want to hear it?'

Naomi nodded. 'Tell it to me now.'

'Not until you have your pyjamas on,' Jack said. 'I'll wait here and when you're ready I'll come upstairs and tell you the story.'

Naomi seemed to consider this option. 'Okay,' she finally said and started towards the stairs. 'I'll give you a shout when I'm ready.'

'Me too,' Liam shouted and started to run after Naomi. 'I'm in my jammies already.'

Vi laughed and ran after them, making sure Liam didn't fall down the stairs. She glanced over her shoulder at Jack, who had started tidying the dishes on the kitchen table. 'You don't have to do that.'

'I know but I want to be useful. I'll be up in a minute.'

When Naomi and Liam were tucked up in Naomi's bed, Jack sat on the edge and looked at them. 'So,' he started, 'I'm going to tell you about a lamb that was born on our farm in England when I was a little boy.'

'What was its name?' Naomi asked.

'Lucy,' Jack replied and then went on to tell them the story about his pet lamb and what happened on the farm. His voice was low and monotonous and it didn't take long for both children to nod off.

Vi carefully picked Liam up and put him to bed in his room, switched off the light and tiptoed back to Naomi. She tucked her in and closed the door as gently as she could. Then she followed Jack down the stairs and into the living room. 'Thank you,' she said to him. 'You're a genius. Sit down on the sofa and I'll get you something to eat. I was going to heat up a pizza and you can share it with me if that's okay? It's all I have, I'm afraid.'

'Perfect,' Jack said and sat down on the sofa, staring out through the window across Ventry Bay where the reflection of the moonlight glittered in the dark water. 'This must be wonderful in daylight.'

'It's amazing.' Vi found the pizza in the freezer and turned on the oven. 'I loved the story of the pet lamb. What happened to her in the end? Lambchops?'

'No.' Jack shook his head and grinned. 'I made it all up. I never had a pet lamb.'

Vi let out a giggle. 'You'd better not tell Naomi. She

believed every word.' She put the pizza on a tray and pushed it into the oven. 'I had no idea you were so good with kids.'

'Neither did I,' Jack said. 'I just improvised. I don't know much about children, to be honest.'

'Then it's even more impressive. Do you want a glass of wine? Dom left a bottle of chianti out for me. Said I'd need a drink after dealing with the kids. I realise now he was right.'

'Just a glass for me,' Jack replied. 'I'm driving and I don't want to risk being caught by the Irish Guards. They look friendly but I'm sure they can be pretty tough if you misbehave.'

'That's true.' Vi wiped the table and put out two placemats followed by wine glasses and cutlery. Then she opened the wine. 'The pizza should be ready in a minute.'

Jack got up and wandered over to the table. 'Great. And we do need to talk.' He sat down and poured wine into both glasses.

Once the pizza was ready, Vi cut it up into slices and put it on a platter that she placed on the table. 'Help yourself. And then tell me what on earth you're doing here.'

'Okay.' Jack took a bite of pizza and a sip of wine and then looked at Vi across the table. 'I came because I wanted to see you. For so many reasons. And Sylvia told me where you were and said I had to come here and give you a hand.'

Vi rolled her eyes. 'Of course she did. So go on, what is so important that you had to tell me in person?'

Jack put down his wedge of pizza. 'First of all, Liz has finally agreed to the changes to the script.'

'Really? That's fabulous news,' Vi exclaimed. 'What a relief.' She looked at him for a moment. 'So you pulled out all the stops and said you'll resign?' she asked, even though she suspected what had happened.

He looked a little sheepish as he met her gaze. 'No, I chickened out in the end. It was actually her own research that did it. We should be able to start filming just before the Magnolia party that Sylvia has invited me to.'

'I hope so.' Vi nodded, her mouth full. 'Are you going?'

'I'm not sure I can.' Jack paused. 'You see, there is something else I want to tell you. I'm going to be in an Ibsen play in the West End in April and we start rehearsing very soon.'

'What?' Vi stared at Jack. 'When did this happen?'

'Only a few weeks ago. I always wanted to do theatre and especially Ibsen. It's been my dream for a long time. And now, this theatre producer got in touch with my agent and asked if I could do it – I jumped at the chance. That's why I pulled out of the movie but I couldn't tell you. It was all under wraps until now. It will be in the papers tomorrow.'

'Oh.' Vi looked at Jack, unable to think of anything to say. She understood that he wanted to realise his dream but at the same time felt miffed both that he hadn't told her and that he had pulled out of the movie just like that. 'Well, that's... I mean...'

'And I did have a bit of a change of heart before that. I started to think that the film would be a lot better without me,' Jack said. 'With you in it...' He suddenly reached out across the table and took her hand. 'It would be complicated.'

'Complicated? Because...?' Vi stared at Jack, holding her breath.

'There is something between us,' he said in a low voice. 'Something I know you feel too.'

'Something?' Vi whispered, forgetting her pizza. 'Like what?'

'Like attraction and chemistry and perhaps, in time – love?' Jack looked suddenly shy.

Vi kept gazing into his eyes without replying. Was this true? Did he really feel the same connection between them that she had felt since the beginning? She met his eyes and saw, not the glamorous film star, but the man behind the glitzy façade. A man who had been through a difficult childhood and youth, had a complicated relationship with his family and had somehow lost his roots. 'Something like that,' she said. 'I didn't know how you felt, but yes, it was there all the time. Especially after your first visit and I saw how affected you were by everything here. And how you kind of melted into the family and connected with Granny.'

'That's only part of it.' Jack kept holding on to her hand while he spoke, his eyes gleaming with emotion. 'It's all part of *you*, my darling Violet. What makes you so special and unique. You're smart and strong and beautiful and funny as well. And as stubborn as hell. I've never met a woman like you – or your sisters or your grandmother and even your little niece.'

'You're in love with them too?' Vi asked, smiling.

'Not as much as I'm in love with you,' Jack declared, leaning over the table and placing a light kiss on her mouth. Then he sat back and smiled at her. 'There. I said it. What do we do now?'

Vi got up and went to his side. 'Kiss me again, maybe?'

Jack shot up from his chair. He put his arms around her and their lips met in a long kiss. In his arms, Vi felt a sense of security that she had never felt with any man before. All her fears and hesitations disappeared as he pulled away for a moment and looked deep into her eyes with an expression she knew was not pretence or acting, but came from real feelings. Then he kissed her again, and this time she kissed him back, her heart full of happiness and gratitude to have found love at last.

EPILOGUE

The Dublin premiere of *The Irish Girl's Secret*, the Kathleen O'Sullivan movie, was a glittering event. The red carpet was rolled out on the pavement outside the Savoy cinema and all the glamorous people of Dublin were photographed against a back-drop of shamrocks and tiny silver harps. Hundreds of people were lined up outside the barriers and there was a roar of excitement through the crowd as Jack Montgomery, in black tie, stepped out of a limousine and held out his hand to help his date for the evening get out. Then there was complete silence as the woman, in a red dress with a fur-trimmed cape around her shoulders, stood beside Jack smiling at everyone.

'Who is this amazing-looking woman?' a reporter asked, holding a mic.

'It's Sylvia Fleury,' Jack said into the mic. 'The lady of the manor where the movie was filmed. But the spotlight should not be on me, but the stars who I see arriving now,' he said as another car drew up in front of the cinema, and Vi and Peter Black got out. Vi was dressed in a green full-length gown with the Fleury emeralds around her neck. Jack stood between her and Peter, telling the reporters how proud he was to have produced this amazing story and how moving the performance of the actors was.

Vi blinked in the glare of the flashes from many cameras and did her best to smile and do a twirl to show off her dress. Then Liz and Dave and more stars of stage and screen arrived and the spotlight was off her for a while. Rose and Lily came to her side and the three of them posed for the cameras as Jack introduced them as 'the Fleury bouquet from Kerry'.

'That's a lovely dress, Violet,' a female reporter remarked. 'Who is it by?'

'I have no idea,' Vi said. 'I found it in a charity shop for ten euros.'

'That's amazing,' the reporter said, looking at Vi with respect.

'So what *was* the Irish girl's secret?' another reporter asked.

'You'll find out when you see the movie,' Vi replied with a broad smile.

Jack came to Vi's side and put his arm around her waist. 'And that is all we're going to say. Now, please come into the cinema and watch the story with us. I'm sure you'll be just as amazed as we were when we found out.' He gently pushed Vi forward. 'Come on, enough questions,' he mumbled into her ear. 'It's freezing and you'll catch your death standing here.'

Vi pulled back. 'Just a minute. I thought my mum would be here by now. She was supposed to come early but there is no sign of her.'

Jack looked across the crowded street. 'I don't see anyone. Oh wait, there's a taxi coming this way. Could it be her?'

Vi looked on as the taxi came closer and then pulled up just past the barrier. Then she brightened as someone opened the door and got out. A tall blonde woman in a black padded coat with a hood. 'That's her.' She started to wave frantically. 'Mum, over here!'

The woman hurried towards them and Jack nodded at a

security guard to let her through the barrier. Then he beamed a smile at her, holding out his hand. 'Hello there, you must be Patricia. I'm Jack.'

Patricia looked at Jack and then at Vi and smiled, still breathless. 'Yes, I am. Hello, Jack. Please call me Tricia. All my friends do.' She kissed Vi on the cheek. 'Hello, sweetheart. Sorry I'm late but I couldn't get a taxi. The weather, the traffic...'

Vi hugged her mother. 'But you're here now and I'm so happy. Rose and Lily have just gone in with Granny. You're sitting with us.'

'Wonderful.' Patricia started to walk towards the entrance while she eased off her coat.

Jack rushed to her side and helped her. 'Let me. I'll get someone to take care of it while we watch the movie.'

'Thank you,' Patricia said and handed her coat to Jack. She was wearing a simple white wool dress and pearl earrings: an outfit that was elegant in all its simplicity.

'Mum, you look amazing,' Vi whispered into her mother's ear.

Patricia took her daughter's arm. 'So do you, my darling. I'm so proud of you.'

'So am I,' Jack said quietly as he escorted the two ladies into the cinema where they quickly found their seats. Patricia kissed both Rose and Lily and nodded at Sylvia. Then they sat down while the lights dimmed and the movie started.

Patricia took Vi's hand as the credits rolled. 'I'm so excited to see your name at the top,' she whispered.

'I can't believe it's happening,' Vi said, looking at her name on the screen. Despite the long months of preparation and then the many weeks of acting – of *being* Kathleen – it still felt unreal to see herself up there. She hadn't seen the rushes, knowing it would make her feel too self-conscious. But here it was, the finished product, the story of Kathleen, revealing who she really was.

There was silence in the cinema as the movie continued, with an odd gasp here and there during the scene where Kathleen reveals her true identity to Don. It had been a difficult scene full of emotion and sadness. Vi had truly felt Kathleen's fear that she would lose the only man she had ever loved and had acted out those emotions as if they were her own. In a way they were, as she kept thinking about her feelings for Jack. It had been a little strange to say those lines to Peter Black instead of Jack, but in the end she felt it was better to not mix up her private life with her acting career, even if her experiences played a big part in her work.

As Vi watched she suddenly felt as if Kathleen herself was on the screen and wondered if this was the way it had actually happened. She felt tears well up at Kathleen's despair when Don left her without a word to consider what he had just learned. She had felt sad when she was acting it out but on the screen all the feelings seemed so much stronger and more intense.

'Spooky,' Jack whispered beside Vi and took her hand. 'It's you and her rolled into one. How did you do it?'

'I don't know,' Vi whispered back. 'I just used all my senses.'

'Amazing.'

Vi didn't reply as the movie ended with Kathleen and Don united at last and everyone in the audience applauded and congratulated the actors, producers and directors. There was a buzz in the cinema as Vi, Peter, Jack and Liz were mobbed by well-wishers who hugged and kissed and shook hands with them all, praising the movie, the scriptwriters, the actors, and Leo, who had done an amazing job with hair, makeup and some of the costumes. It was a true success story and the after-party in the five-star Gresham Hotel lasted until the early hours of the following morning when the morning papers with the reviews were brought in and read out by Jack and Liz in turn.

'Nothing but rave reviews,' Jack said as he and Vi managed a quiet moment together in the bar. 'Congratulations, sweetheart. You're on the way to bigger things.'

'What could be bigger or better than this?' Vi asked. 'The movie was a huge success and everyone is happy. You were a huge hit in the play in London. And then... there's – us.'

Jack looked at her and kissed her hand. 'That's the best part, isn't it? Us. When do you think we should tell them?'

'Not yet,' Vi protested. 'Not here, anyway. Can we wait until we're in Kerry for the weekend? Isn't that what we agreed? I want to have all the family around us when we tell them our plans.'

Jack squeezed Vi's hand and nodded. 'Yes, I think you're right. Your family must hear the news first.'

'They will be your family too,' Vi countered.

'That thought makes me very happy. It doesn't matter if we don't have a plan of how we're going to manage our life together.'

'Not a bit,' Vi assured him. 'If there's a will there's a way, as the saying goes. We'll work it out.'

Then they were interrupted by some of the cast who wanted to take selfies with them and the party continued. Vi managed to sneak away with her mother and get into a taxi before anyone noticed. Sylvia, Lily and Rose had already left and were staying in a nearby hotel before they'd catch the early morning train to Tralee. Vi and Patricia, who were staying in the flat, would follow later on, and they would all be together at last. It would be wonderful to have a break at Magnolia after all the excitement. 'No better place to recharge one's batteries,' Patricia said before they went to bed.

. . .

It was truly wonderful to get back to Kerry and Magnolia Manor for the weekend. The weather had improved and the skies cleared after a few days of storms and heavy rain. When Jack arrived in his rented car, the sun shone from a cloudless sky and the light breeze brought with it that lovely salty tang of sand and seaweed that he had loved ever since the first time he came. Vi rushed into his arms as he stepped out of the car and wrapped her arms around his neck. 'Granny has invited us for dinner. Just you and me and the rest of the family. We can tell them we intend to live together then.'

Jack laughed and hugged her tight. 'I hope they won't be too shocked.'

'I think they know already,' Vi said. 'Granny put champagne in the fridge and Nora baked a chocolate cake, which she always does for special occasions. It's to celebrate the movie, but also that we're together at last.'

'And that we plan to get engaged a little later on and then...'

'Yes, I know,' Vi said. 'But let's not rush into anything. We have only been dating for a short while after all.'

'I know,' he replied. 'But I also know this is for real.'

'Of course it is.' She took his hand and pulled him towards the garden. 'Come on. Let's go for a walk in the garden. I have something to tell you. A plan of sorts.'

'A plan?' he asked, looking intrigued. 'But I need to park the car and get my bag out. Did you say I could stay here with you?'

'Yes, you can. Mum and I made up the spare room for you. Not five-star accommodation,' she warned. 'Only one bathroom with pipes that rattle if the water gets too hot.'

He grinned. 'It'll be just like home.'

'Thought so. But come on. You can unpack later.'

Jack smiled and let Vi lead him up the path, tucking her hand under his arm. 'Why the rush?'

'I feel I can explain things better in the fresh air,' she said.

'What things?'

'About where we're going to live. I know we'll have to travel for work and things, but we need a home that's more than a base.' Vi stopped and looked at Jack. 'I want to buy the gate-house from Granny. She often says she wants to sell it as she doesn't want to keep paying for repairs and stuff. So I thought...' Vi stopped and stared at him. 'You look funny. Do you think it's a terrible idea?'

Jack shook his head. 'No, my sweet Violet. It's the best idea I ever heard. Of course we should keep the gatehouse as our home, our haven, our bolthole. I just want us to buy it together. Would that be possible?'

Vi nodded, nearly speechless with joy. 'Very possible, my darling Jack.'

'You don't know how happy that makes me. I get to own a little bit of this amazing, heavenly place. And I get you, and your family.'

'A family made up of mostly difficult women,' Vi remarked. 'Are you sure you can cope with us?'

'I'm not sure of anything,' Jack said with a laugh. 'Only that I won't be bored.'

'That I can certainly promise,' Vi declared.

A LETTER FROM SUSANNE

I want to say a huge thank you for choosing to read *The Girl with the Irish Secret*. If you did enjoy it, and want to keep up to date with all my latest releases, just sign up at the following link. Your email address will never be shared and you can unsubscribe at any time.

www.bookouture.com/susanne-oleary

I hope you loved *The Girl with the Irish Secret* and if you did I would be very grateful if you could write a review. I'd love to hear what you think, and it makes such a difference helping new readers to discover one of my books for the first time. This new series, that I called the Magnolia Manor series, is set on the Dingle peninsula, where we are lucky enough to spend most of our summers, enjoying the beautiful scenery. I also love to spend any nice day on one of the gorgeous beaches, wandering along the shore and swimming in the crystal-clear water of the Atlantic. All this, and the warm welcome from neighbours and friends in Kerry, inspire me to write my stories. I hope I manage to bring my readers to these stunning places in their imagination.

I love hearing from my readers – you can get in touch through my social media or my website.

Thanks, Susanne

KEEP IN TOUCH WITH SUSANNE

www.susanne-oleary.co.uk

 facebook.com/authoroleary

 x.com/susl

goodreads.com/susanneol

ACKNOWLEDGEMENTS

As always, huge thanks to my brilliant editor, Jennifer Hunt, and everyone at Bookouture, who work so hard to turn every one of my books into a polished product for readers to enjoy. They are a real dream team to work with. Also my family, especially my husband, who cheer me on and give me space and time to write, which is hugely appreciated. Friends near and far also deserve a big thank you. And last but by no means least I want to thank my readers for their enthusiasm and support which has meant so much to me.

PUBLISHING TEAM

Turning a manuscript into a book requires the efforts of many people. The publishing team at Bookouture would like to acknowledge everyone who contributed to this publication.

Commercial
Lauren Morrissette
Hannah Richmond
Imogen Allport

Cover design
Debbie Clement

Data and analysis
Mark Alder
Mohamed Bussuri

Editorial
Jennifer Hunt
Charlotte Hegley

Copyeditor
Jon Appleton

Proofreader
Becca Allen

Marketing
Alex Crow
Melanie Price
Occy Carr
Cíara Rosney
Martyna Młynarska

Operations and distribution
Marina Valles
Stephanie Straub
Joe Morris

Production
Hannah Snetsinger
Mandy Kullar
Jen Shannon
Ria Clare

Publicity
Kim Nash
Noelle Holten
Jess Readett
Sarah Hardy

Rights and contracts
Peta Nightingale
Richard King
Saidah Graham

Milton Keynes UK
Ingram Content Group UK Ltd.
UKHW020601281124
3195UKWH00041B/73